JADED

JADED

A Novel

Kevin E. Taylor

iUniverse, Inc.
New York Lincoln Shanghai

JADED

iUniverse books may be ordered through booksellers or by contacting:

iUniverse
2021 Pine Lake Road, Suite 100
Lincoln, NE 68512
www.iuniverse.com
1-800-Authors (1-800-288-4677)

Cover Design by Kevin E. Taylor
Photo by Dreamstime.Com

ISBN-13: 978-0-595-40787-3 (pbk)
ISBN-13: 978-0-595-85151-5 (ebk)
ISBN-10: 0-595-40787-0 (pbk)
ISBN-10: 0-595-85151-7 (ebk)

Printed in the United States of America

To everyone who ever believed in love…

hopefully, prayerfully, sincerely,

may this book give you one more

day's hope, to hold on.

And to my son

Ga'Vel Qwame

because everyday you give me a reason to keep on keepin' on!
(LOVE, DAD!)

ACKNOWLEDGEMENTS

THE JADED JURY: Ms. Millicent Alexis AKA Minister Miche, Stephen Lewis Spaulding, Kia High, Gina Cushenberry, O. David Jackson, my brother David Taylor, Samarra!, and especially the brilliantly gifted author LM Ross and the equally talented scribe L. Michael Gipson, for your feedback, notes and input. I really cannot tell each of you how much your words really helped to push me forward.

Rod 2.0 aka ROD McCULLOM for always being such a strong supporter and such a dear friend.

Thanks to everyone who encouraged me to write, write and WRITE. Be careful what you ask for.

FLYING COW MARKETING & MEDIA

CHAPTER 1:
THE CELEBRATION

KNIGHT

IN SHINING ARMOR

PRESENT:
Joshua Knight
Tasha Holloway (Exec. Asst.)
Paula Williams (VP of Marketing)
Sal Schwartzman, Coca-Cola
Kenneth Milner, Coca-Cola
The Knights in Shining Armor
Specialty Team

The room erupted with applause and Joshua Knight simply smiles. He has every right to do so. He's been working on this day, this moment for almost a month and the culmination is sweet. His hard work, and the little touches—video commissioned by director Bille Woodruff, mock-ups of the campaigns for various outlets and even the new slogan—showed that Joshua had sealed this project in his mind from the word go. He looks over at his associates and they are beaming at another job well done. But this one is The Mothership. With this new Coca-Cola contract, Joshua is poised to bring several million dollars in new revenue into his company and to be able to solidify his place in the New York arena. As the chief executives of Coke shake hands with Joshua and his key staff, his assistant is already calling the caterers and preparing for the party that many had always hoped would come, but didn't sit around waiting for, not wanting to get hopes up, only to have to rocket love them back down to earth. But now, it's ON!

⌘

The celebration is in full-blown party mode. The offices are lit up with laughter and everyone is celebrating for the bonuses that they just know are soon to come. Everyone is jubilant. Anyone would be.

Everyone, that is, except Joshua Knight himself.

It's not that Joshua isn't happy, for himself, his investors and his employees. It's just that he's not beaming. He hasn't beamed in a while. It's hard for people to believe that there isn't some special joy on the inside for Joshua Knight. He's got an amazing business. He's the best boss in the world, according to his entire staff. He's a great son to his mother and a great brother to his siblings. He's the best friend in the world, according to Carlton, who is in Paris at this every moment, because of a trip given to him by his best friend, not for a birthday or any reason other than love and appreciation. The recent loss of his mother had Carlton losing focus and disconnected, so Joshua sent him the one place he had been talking about wanting to go for 3 years now. Joshua is a great friend.

He is also quite a man to look at, and there is something about him that makes you look. Standing about six foot one, he's a caramel/honey brown that seems well, lickable, edible, truly kissed by Sun and Moon. He's bald by Gene, not by genes, as he spends every Saturday at Level's keeping his dome chromed. He finds it authoritative and disarming, but somehow warm. Joshua considers everything. He has a smile that makes you nervous if you are blessed enough to be standing nearby when he unleashes it. Something in his smile is unnerving and something in his eyes dances when he shows his Pearlies. He's about average in build, not too thick and definitely not slim. He's the kind of man that you would refer to instantly as husband material. Not some man you want to bed at first thought, but rather a man you see yourself standing beside at the right gathering of friends, or laughing with and telling about your day. He's the man who is always assumed to be with someone special and whose style only makes him appear all the more taken. The more you gaze upon Joshua Arrington Knight, the sexier he becomes—not finer, not more handsome…sexier. Everything about him comes together and you just find yourself drawn to him. It's not physical. Not really. It's more sensual than sexual. He's seems to radiate confidence. He seems to beam. He is definitely husband material; the man you want after you get that naked tall sexy thug at the club and you have finally decided to come to your senses and settle in and settle down. Somehow, you just know that this man will be there, working hard, and waiting for you, to settle down and settle into a sweet life together.

But this particular gentleman is not in the mood or the mode for such frivolities. He's got bigger fish to fry and they don't include oysters. No need for the aphrodisiac of the sea. Joshua's not swimming those waters anymore. Something died in Joshua a long time ago, and he's built a brilliant façade to protect the rest of him, his inner self, from ever being hurt again.

Five years since that civilized, but stunning breakup and Joshua still keeps his heart in a vault.

There, love can't hurt him again and he won't have to ever relive a day like the day he came home and found Greg in bed with the man he had sworn was only a friend.

Their bed.

Their love.

Their sheets that they picked out that sweet Saturday afternoon at Macy's. Their apartment, in which they swore, when they were curled up together and laughing at a stupid episode of "Good Times," (the one where JJ had to paint the gangster's girlfriend and she says "that ain't hardly me!") that they would move out of soon and buy a house, *"because it really is time for the next level and to fully and finally invest in us."*

They danced out of bed and starting singing the theme song, at the TOP OF THEIR LUNGS…buck naked and giggling…AIN'T WE LUCKY WE GOT 'EM…GOOD TIIIMES, YEEEAH!

"LYING JUDAS! I HATE HIM!"

Suffice it to say, Joshua hasn't dated much since then. OK, he hasn't dated at all. Unlike many friends who swear that all he need is to get some and get over Greg, Joshua is just way too much of a romantic to lay down with someone at night that he's not trying to spend time with in the morning. So, knowingly and maybe unconsciously, he transported all of that love and affection and intensity to building this then-fledgling firm into the Power Player it is now poised to become.

Joshua Knight wasn't expecting the arrival of any knights in shining armor in his own life, so he simply became that to businesses, usually small and mid-sized, until the buzz about him reached Coca-Cola and epic proportions. Joshua Knight is adept at problem-solving and image restructuring. He's the guy you go to when your first impression wasn't that impressive and you need to do it again, quickly and right. Joshua was a fixer and he liked that about himself. It bode well in business and he was just fine with that being his focus. Joshua was beyond content, he was happy. The lack of someone at home was not as aching as it used to be.

"Joshua, please tell me that you are not going to spend all evening in this office!"

Tasha was part sister, part friend and always professional. She had stuck her head in the door to let Josh know it was time to celebrate. They had built a real working relationship where she knew all of the details of his life without crossing the line of employee/boss reverence. But she could still talk to him like a man. She respected as her boss, yes, but she cared about his as a person. She was dolled up, knowing that this was going to be a major day. Her newly sable-brown colored hair, pinned up in an elegant French roll, looked so flawless against her warm brown skin. Her light-brown eyes sparkled and were framed with copper and grey shades of makeup surrounding her eyes and lips. She smiled because she knew that Joshua had inspected her outfit—a tailored-to-impress navy and white suit and navy pumps, with a simple pearl necklace—and approved. Tasha was such a beautiful woman that Joshua sometimes didn't understand how, with all she had going for her, she was simply his assistant. But he was thankful that she was.

"The food out here is amazing, thank you very much, and it's like Christmas for everyone but you. Don't make me start calling you Scrooge, Ebenezer."

Tasha came all the way into Joshua's immaculate office—with its chrome and steel and sleek coolness that he hopes reads successful and not elitist, clean and open, not distant—and hugs him from behind as he sits at his mahogany and cherry-wood desk.

"I knew that you would do it but that video put things over the top. That was dazzling. I could see and feel your vision all in it. Now come and enjoy the festivities. Take a moment to say 'thank you' to the staff and receive some 'you're welcomes' in return."

Tasha always knew how to snap Joshua out of his workaholism and make him at least have moments. She was a lifesaver with her moments.

There was the moment she remembered his 30th birthday by having a friend at Columbia Records have Nancy Wilson record a special birthday greeting that played in the staff meeting instead of Joshua's mock-up of the "Carol's Daughter" campaign that he was pitching. Resplendent in a silver pantsuit and shot in some moody jazz club, Ms. Wilson sang "How Glad I Am" like she was in Carnegie Hall. Joshua, for the first time in years, was so overwhelmed that he almost cried. Almost. But the shock of the doors opening and individual deliverymen bringing in every single Nancy Wilson album that she had ever recorded was just too much. Joshua shut the offices down and gave everyone the day off. For his birthday. That's just who he is.

Or the moment when she looked into his eyes, The Morning After, and without saying a word, she let him know that she knew, was devastated, he would survive, I'm here for you, call me if you need me, and I will never leave you, all in one squeeze of the hand, as the staff gathered for their weekly pow-wow completely unaware. Joshua was going to be fine, as long as he focused on business, and had Tasha by his side.

Joshua was going to be fine.

It's not that he has denounced love and will never be open to it again. It's not that at all. It's that he swore, deep down, that Gregory Stephen Marshall was the one and he didn't know what to do now. How do you get up from Heaven?

Greg tearfully swore, "It just happened." Joshua couldn't help reliving it all over again. He always did that when his life got really good. He remembered the ways he had failed. Joshua thought too much:

> *Sure, he just happened to be there, again. You just happened to spend time laughing and carousing. He just happened to smile while you both just happened to be drinking. You both just happened to get aroused. You both just happened to forget that this was our home. You just happened to forget that you love me, long enough to just happen to get naked. He just happened to find that spot on your neck that I am sure just happened to help remove your pants and your commitment to me. You just happened to find the bedroom, where you both just happened to get naked, erect and sweaty, all the while forgetting that I would be home at some point. You just happened to not hear me when I walked into the house and made noise in the kitchen, as I was preparing to prepare dinner. You just happened to not hear me as I called out your name before I opened the door to our bedroom. It just happened that I couldn't breathe while I watched you kiss and grope and paw over another man and a man whom I had welcomed into our home because he was your friend and I never, ever wanted to be that Man, who suspected that every gay male friend was his man's ex-man or his next man, so we talked about it and you made me feel safe in getting to know Kevin, separately, as my man's good friend and confidante. It all just happened so quickly, so methodically, so deceitfully that I just happened to lose my footing and my breath and my mind all in one felled swoop.*

"I am not one to scream and break things or grab weaponry, but this wasn't just one of those things. What do you do when your heart cracks at the same time that your face does? What do you do when your past and everything you've ever shared with someone comes up and brings your lunch with it? What do you do when you face the Rise And Fall Of Paradise?"

Joshua fainted.

"Dammit," he said to himself as Greg and Kevin tried to avoid the obvious absence of clothes, discretion and respect, and ask him if he can hear them, as they rushed to his side.

Joshua simply opened his eyes and stood to his feet. With a tact that must have required more grace than most people can fathom or call upon in times like these, Joshua simply gathered a suit from the closet, a pair of shoes and accompanying socks, underwear, tie and cufflinks. He then gathered his bag of toiletries from the bathroom and left. As Greg ran behind him, gathering his decorum and the drawstring to his lounge pants, Joshua remained calm, not sure if he could stop himself from losing it and hurting somebody. He wasn't ever a violent man, but this wouldn't be an act of violence, as much as a reaction to it. He had been violated.

"Sweetheart, please, listen to me. PLEASE!"

Greg was beside himself. He thought that Josh, a name that very few used, would at least listen to him.

"It wasn't what you think. He didn't have sex."

"But you were about to Greg," snapped Joshua. "Just because I walked in and rained on your parade doesn't mean that you were not fully prepared to screw that…man and take him to the same Heaven that I thought was reserved for me."

Greg's eyes dropped and so did the tears from them. Joshua was right. The condom on the nightstand, the smell of sex in the air, the tension that he tried to avoid with Kevin, that always seemed to surface when they were alone, but trying to respect other's relationships, all told Greg that he had nothing else to say to Joshua Arrington Knight but goodbye. That fact broke his heart.

Greg's guilt instantly consumed him. "How could I destroy the relationship I prayed for? How could I lose the very man who made me feel like I could do anything and encouraged me? How could I have been so stupid? How will I explain this to myself in the morning, when the thrill is gone and so is Josh?"

Greg grabbed Joshua's shoulder and turned him to face him, for what they both knew was the last time.

"I never didn't love you. I dreamed dreams of being with you while I was with you. I have no idea how or why I let this happen, but," as tears roared from his eyes and hurt told the truth all over his face. "I am sorry. I will be out by the morning."

With that, Greg turned back to the bedroom and Kevin and away from the only man who knew in this world wanted the best for him.

Joshua stopped, garment bag in hand, taking up the space where his heart once was when he offered it to Greg, and he sighed. "My God, what a dignified breakup," he thought. "Somebody's supposed to be throwing something or screaming something or losing something up in here."

Joshua didn't lunge at Greg or even Kevin. Joshua didn't seek to destroy property or even to slap faces. He just didn't do that.

When Joshua left DC and came to NYU for his Master's, he came with a new sense being as well. He wasn't angry. Just maybe a little jaded. He thought DC had changed that.

⌘

During his time at Georgetown, he found Inner Light and he found God, all by himself and all for himself. He had always gone to church with his parents and he had always had a rapport with God, but not a relationship. So when he came to DC, he went looking, for a place where he could worship, but where he could also be free. It was identified as "The Gay Church" to many in DC, but it was so much more than that. Gay men were there with their partners, but some were there with their mothers and friends and some were there alone. But the presence of so many people, different people—obvious lesbians and she-can't-be lesbians, couples, older folks, churched folks in regal clothes, young folks in jeans and fitteds, and mischurched folks with sad, recovering faces, people who were looking around like they had never been to church folks—all made Joshua feel like he could be here. But it was Bishop Cheeks' sermon that made him join that faithful Sunday. He had been attending for a few months, but this Sunday and this sermon spoke to his heart.

"I APOLOGIZE" was the title. The Bishop talked about pain and hurt and how we can hold onto it. He came from Psalms 23 and really broke it down. When he talked about how "forgive our debts as we forgive our debtors" is really a plea to the Lord to forgive me at the same level I forgive others, Joshua sat up in his seat.

> "Most people walk around mad at the world, mad at past relationships, mad at jobs passed over. We get so mad that we snap at people in the morning, at coworkers and old ladies on the bus. But you are really mad at you,"

The good Bishop said, as he moved away from the lectern, fully exposing his beautiful Kente clothed robe.

> "When you can forgive yourself, for every stupid relationship you stayed in for too long, for every job you were afraid to apply for, for every time you let fear stop you from moving forward, you will be free. Go home tonight and write a Letter of Apology to yourself. You cannot move forward until you go back and get that You that you hurt and apologize. Apologize for not listening when You told you that this wasn't the one. Apologize for not hearing when You said 'go for it' and you didn't apply to that college because you were scared at the time to be Black and Gay and Out on that campus, and now You wonder what you missed. Apologize for not seeing it the first time, when she told You who she was and you didn't want to know, so she had to show You and she betrayed you and finally convinced you that she really wasn't ready to be this happy with You or anyone. Say it. 'I APOLOGIZE' and let not your heart be troubled. Say it. 'I APOLOGIZE' and forgive yourself for being who you were then, because that's all you had to work with and now is now. Say it. 'I APOLOGIZE' and then hug yourself and redeem yourself and lift yourself up to where you belong. You weren't wrong to think what you thought but now, with new information, it's time to change your mind."

With that he opened the doors of the church for new members to come and receive Christ. Joshua was already baptized. His parents did that at 11. But this felt like the first time that Joshua had taken the privilege of taking

EVERYTHING to God in prayer. Finally, he understood that 'where two or more are gathered in my name, thereto shall I be," because this was the first time that Joshua felt like he had brought all of the parts of himself together in the same place. He was normally so compartmentalized, so that he could be all things for all people.

Joshua surprised even himself when he broke down at the altar. It wasn't sad or angry, scared or confused. It was a purging. As the Bishop held him and prayed with him, Joshua let go of all of the things that he was holding against himself—the tentativeness, the responsibility of being Mr. Perfect, the Good one, the Smart One, the Unworthy One—and he let his heart open up to full capacity that day.

"BOMP BOMP BOMP BOMP BOOOOMP!"

The big booming band sound of the song brought Joshua back to the present and his office and the fact that no one was around. He heard her, or at least he thought it was a her, but he didn't hear the lyrics. Joshua was surprised because he could feel the song. It had gotten into him and said something. It swelled and sang and tickled his soul. He heard strings and horns, harps and happiness. He wasn't paying attention, so he had no idea what or where this happiness had landed, but he felt it in the music. That's it. Joshua came back, from his daydreaming because he had felt something, in the air.

Tasha had brought him a plate and it remained untouched on his desk. The video was on repeat on the monitor visible from his office and a tear had made its way to his cheek.

Joshua remembered Greg and the good times.

He remembered meeting Carlton and how they thought that they might be perfect for each other and actually had the conversation about it in Carlton's dorm room, before they got naked, and realized that they were destined best friends who happened to share the same sexual orientation. They laughed and still held each other that night, without conflict or struggle. The Hunt for the Perfect Best Friend wasn't as emotional as The Hunt for the Perfect Man, but the discovery was every bit as sweet.

Joshua remembered singing in the choir at Inner Light, and then graduating to the Board of Trustees before he decided that he was going to move to NYC and finally do what God had placed in his heart.

Joshua remembered that he had lived a pretty great life in his 33 years. Between few fights with his brothers about being gay (and oddly, the fights were about the men he picked more than that they were men in the first place), and the cool offices that he had found on a lark in SoHo and the great assistant and good health and enough money in the bank to send his friend on a trip and then some, Joshua realized that he couldn't complain.

He finally got up and made his way into the main offices, only to find that he was alone, sans the cleaning staff. He looked for Tasha, but she was gone and so was everyone else.

"Who was that singing?" Josh had asked the question aloud. That song really did shake something up in him. "Hmmm," Josh said as he looked around the office to see if any stragglers were still about.

"Excuse me, Mr. Knight," said that sweet woman of all of 5' 3" and upswept church-lady hair. "Do you want me to put all of this leftover food in your refrigerator or,"...she said as she dropped her head, thinking 'Please don't be so uppity that you are going to throw it away'..."do you want me to just get rid of it?"

"Miss Evelyn..."

Joshua addressed her with the reverence that she deserved, even though some of his friends always thought it funny that he spoke to older black people with Miss or Mr., but he was raised that way.

"I know you don't want to hear this, but I am going to say it anyway. Please take this food home for yourself. You know that if it goes into my refrigerator, it's going to just sit in my refrigerator. I don't want it to go to waste and I know that wonderful family of yours would appreciate it and you get to not cook this weekend. Please."

She smiled and she hugged him and Joshua was home again, in the arms of a Black mother's love.

Miss Evelyn always steps into my office when she finds me working my way through an evening that's best spent, according to her, at home, and offers the same sage words of advice.

"Mr. Knight, don't let Mr. Morning find you still sitting at that desk not living Mr. Life."

It would always make me close down my workday. It's my alarm clock of assurance. It was time to go home. But what was that? Where was home?

CHAPTER 2: THE REVELATION

What A Difference A Day Makes

My Saturdays were generally routine.

Carlton and I would normally have brunch and spend a few hours being best friends, before I leave to get dry cleaning and then some groceries. I would make my way home from the Farmer's Market at Union Square and get home, unpack and just enjoy my home. I had made my space my Sanctuary. The colors, the couches, the furniture and the feeling all supported me in my need to be able to be home and be still.

After Greg and our old place, I almost swore I could never be at ease at home again. He said he would be the one to leave, but I was. He could live with himself and what he had done in our home, but I couldn't. I tried to go back there to get my things, but I almost lost it again when I felt my knees buckle, so Carlton handled the move. So dramatic of me, I know, but it's real.

But this Saturday seems different. No Carlton, first of all, but I hear from him every night and it really seems that Paris agrees with him. He told me that he went to the River Seine and poured out some Evian for his mother, as he spoke her name. I think he must have cried because I could hear his voice crack. Carlton had gone with me a few times to Inner Light, where the Bishop would pour Libation for the Ancestors. He said that he wasn't sure he believed in all this church stuff, but he loved the fellowship. But he did like church enough to come with me for big events and some socials like the Annual Fish Fry. I was warmed to see that he had picked up that ritual and put it to use when he needed it. Mother Bridges, I know you heard him.

No Carlton around, so my rhythm was already off, but in a good way. That song would creep into my thoughts, but without words, I could only feel it. I would feel it when I noticed more people looking at me, noticing. I could feel it when I saw a brother or 6 smiling my way and trying to gain my attention. But this afternoon, this time, was and will remain, mine. I like the walking and the wondering of Saturday afternoon. I like the sense of discovery that I was feeling. I felt like I was going to find a priceless heirloom at the junk store or maybe see a young and brilliant new artist hawking their wares on the street. I could feel something in the air. Then that song would come to me again. So I found myself in the Virgin megastore. I figured I might as well try to find it. I may as well try to do something with my time before I find myself back in Sanctuary and not in-joying the day. I read somewhere that if you don't do a thing IN JOY, then you shouldn't be doing it. So I am in-joying the day and I'm going to just see if I can find this blessed song. Why won't it leave me alone?

So I walked into the store and asked the young worker who approached me with vigor where I could find the jazz section. I figured I would thumb through some cds and discover this Black Woman Goddess on my own. It was a woman, right? I remember Nancy Wilson saying once that she was influenced by Little Jimmy Scott, so maybe it was him or some other brother with a unique style.

Little did I know when I got off of the escalator, that the jazz section would be The Jazz Section and take up an entire floor?

"My God," I said to myself, and everyone in earshot, "this place is humungous. How could anyone find anything in here?" As I tentatively stepped forward, yet another young clerk approached. She was young, equally perky and seemed eager to please.

"Hi, can I help you find something?"

I had no idea where to start, so I said "How would you suggest I find a record if I don't know the artist or the title?"

"Well, we have computers right there, there and there," said the young lady with a permanent smile. "You can search by genre and maybe you'll come across something."

"Ahh, sure," I said, as I approached the machine, not sure what information to feed it. What do you ask a computer when you don't know the question?

For about 15 minutes, I walked around The Jazz Section and saw box sets for every icon you could imagine. I grabbed a wonderful collection of Lena Horne's Best for Granddad, just because. That would make him happy and give us some more material for our next sit-around. I even purchased an Ella Fitzgerald collection for myself. I know that they called her the "First Lady of Song" at the Grammys one year and it's about time that I discover why.

I left The Megastore and though I had some Ella and some Lena, I had no song.

Later, I gathered a few dozen roses in some colors that were just spectacular. I still don't understand how these markets can sell 2-dozen roses for 8 DOLLARS!!! But, as a person who loves fresh flowers in my house, I am not complaining.

Anyway, I got sidetracked again. This time, it was all the way up to Broadway's center. I thought, as I wandered around, that maybe Colony Records, up in the 50s or late 40s—streets, not eras—would be of some help. The staff there is always so knowledgeable, sometimes overly so. I remember going there looking for the soundtrack of Diahann Carroll in "No Strings" and the older gay man behind the counter ended up talking to me for 40 minutes, about Diahann and Divas, Patti—Labelle and LuPone—and he really was a blast. But this time, I was on a mission. But I still didn't have any more information.

When I entered the store, I was elated to be reminded that not all record stores had become conglomeration of cds and coffee, multiplexes and magazines. This was just a simple, though overwhelming for its own reasons, record store. Colony Records is legendary, for its sheet music and its posters, for its vintage collections and for its “we can find anything” attitude. I approached the counter and the same man was there to greet me.

“Oh, hello. I remember you. You’re Diahann Carroll,” he laughed.

“Yes, indeed I am,” I retorted, without a missed moment. “Thank you again for helping me find that and for turning me on to that live ‘Dreamgirls’ recording. It was amazing. Maybe you can help me again.”

I went on to explain the song, or what I could. I really explained the sentiment of it, the feeling of it and he asked something I didn’t expect.

“Are you sure it was a Black woman?” He meant that thing. He searched my eyes and was really waiting for a response. “It could have been some white woman or even a latina, like Celia Cruz. Oh but she doesn’t sing in English. Are you sure you heard English? Anyway, you would be surprised to hear Anita O’Day or Kay Starr or some of the voices from that era and realize that they were not Black women. Peggy Lee, Julie London, the list would surprise you. Especially if you are looking for a big band era type of song, you have quite a search on your hands. Those girls were all trying to out-chanteuse each other. But, anyway, let’s go a-listening.”

We studied some of everything. The musical smorgasbord was almost too much. A little Merman, a little McRae. A little O’Day, a little Lady Day. A little Peggy Lee, a little ol’ Ree Ree (I had no idea that Aretha Franklin started out singing jazz!). Before I knew it, it was after 4pm and I still hadn’t visited the market way down in Union Square. With new music in hand, but still not my song, I got out of there. Granddad and I would have enough listening materials for the rest of the year. He would surely be able to school me about what I am sure he will suggest I should have already known. God knows that man forgets I’m 33 and not 63 sometimes. He thinks I hear Nancy and Lena on the radio everyday. But I love him and our time together is always a hoot.

I’m traveling pretty light, all things considered. Just a few bags with of cds, not a heavy load, and a shopping bag from the market, but I’m on my way home. I thought I would walk through the Village, just to take the edge off of rushing. If I was going to in-joy my Saturday afternoon, I should treat myself. I thought that

I might find a little café where I could have a sandwich and a pause. I had to stop myself from looking in windows and through sales racks. I just wanted to breathe and stop and relax and take in this day.

"God, what a perfect day you made," I said out loud and meant indeed. It was about 64 degrees, breezy, and just the right kind of day. With a fresh haircut, from my stop on the way home last night at Level's, and the right light jacket on, you couldn't tell me that I didn't have some God-pull, because this was the kind of day that made me happy. I studied African artifacts in this window and jewelry and boots in that one. I saw chaps and India, shoes and Singapore, all on the same 2-block stretch. I knew that I wasn't in danger of buying anything else, because this stuff was too eclectic for my taste.

But I always in-joy strolling through the Village. It's so New York City. It's so why you are glad to be alive and grown. It's so Whatever-The-Day-Brings. It's perfect for running into friends and having a good conversation on the street that turns into 'let's take this to the Pink Tea Cup.' I know people think that that little spot is just *too little*, but I love the service when I go and I really love the food. If I wanted soul food and ambiance, I would have gotten on the train and taken myself to Delta's in New Brunswick. This guy I was dating lived there and took me to dinner at this space and I loved it. Anytime I want to treat myself, I go there. Hmmm, I wonder if he ever got married. He was definitely the marrying kind. Sometimes, I wonder. Anyway.

I was sure that I remembered this really cool café around here somewhere. I think it was on the corner of Bleeker and Christopher or Perry and Bleeker, no that's Pink Tea Cup. It's not Manatus, but it is near there, but on the other side of 7th Avenue. I was lost, but not really. If I didn't find it, I would be fine. I would just grab something or maybe just have a seat anywhere and take in the view and a cup of tea. Maybe, I will just make my way home and take my time making dinner. It's only 5:30 or so, and I am in no rush. I definitely have to learn to stop and smell the….

"Wow," Joshua said, as he spotted the little storefront record shop from across the street. "Maybe they can help. If that's not an Ad Slogan, nothing is!"

Joshua prepared to enter the shop and, just maybe, find some remedy to the musical ailment that wouldn't leave him alone.

CHAPTER 3: THE SIGHTING

ROADHOUSE RECORDS

"WE SPECIALIZE IN THE BEST AND THE REST"

I saw him.

The second I walked in, I saw him over there in the corner. Okay, let me be real. I felt him over there before I ever saw his face. I wasn't in the mood to do anything but come in, find this record that was driving me crazy and get home. But I must say that I did take him in, I had to acknowledge his presence.

It was the combination of him that did it. He was about 6' 3" with locs, which seemed to be the thing these days; his were very neatly done and adorned his head like a crown of glory. The goatee was tight but not overly so and he had on glasses. The cream sweater he wore looked handmade and coupled with the jeans that hugged his thighs and the palomino cowboy boots; his style was so New York. Topped off with a tattered leather blazer and an eye-catching amber ring, he was something simple and put together all at the same time. He was the kind of handsome that was visible from every angle and that flourished and bloomed the more you considered it. With a chocolate leather saddlebag thrown over his shoulder, he was rummaging through the records like he was on a mission.

I wasn't in the mood or mode for consideration.

He was looking at the albums like they held some truth that he alone could discover and the intensity of his work ethic said leave him alone. Not fast, but furious.

"That's fine with me," I said under my breath, and then laughing at my own rebuke, I pressed on. I, too, was on a mission.

I approached the clerk to see if I could get some help and then be on my way. I hoped that this place could finally solve this mystery for me. I was pissed at myself by now.

"How could I get this caught up in a song?" I said, bewitched, bothered and bewildered all at once.

I made my way to the counter and an old black man, who reeked of age and travel, said "How can I help you, son?"

"Am I in New York?" I thought to myself as he stood to give me his full attention. I smiled because his manner made me feel like my Granddad was hiding out, living a fantasy and running a record store.

"Sir, I am looking for a song and I don't have much to go by."

"Okay, son, tell me what you know. Singer? Male or Female?" His face looked at me and lit up, as though I had come to him with a treasure and a promise.

"Definitely female…I think, but very husky, kind of Sarah Vaughn-ish, but maybe heavier, moodier," I offered, trying to not seem a complete music novice.

While many of my friends love to say that I was trapped in another time, I like what I like and I like the records my Granddad used to play when we sat down in his basement and just hang out. He would listen to Nancy and Lena, Dinah and Sarah like they were some exclusive club that no other singer could enter. So if it wasn't one of them or a rare other few, I really was lost. These voices got me through college—exams, fears, homesickness, relationships; happiness, heartache and hopelessness—and probably most other life experiences that we love to set to music. I could find a song to get me through it. But now, I was clueless. It sounded like something from the same era, but I was vexed to figure out who the lady with the song was and how I could take this record home and finish the purge that began in my office.

Anyway, the questions continued from the master who seemed to be studying my face while he was going through the computer of his memory to put my dilemma together.

"So was the song slow and moody? Fast and boppy? Son was it a big record, with lots of instruments or simple and clean? Help me help you help yourself."

He spoke with such lyricism that I had to laugh. He was definitely a musician.

"It was a big moody song and the ending was like this woman was rambling and the music was lots of strings and something else…all I really heard was the ending, kind of."

"Alright son, we are gettin' somewhere."

As he pondered, he signaled me to follow him and we found ourselves among Hadda Brooks, Betty Carter and Carmen McRae, whom I had heard of but never heard, and all the female vocalists in between. They didn't close until midnight and it was 5:42pm, so I was going to be there for a while. This riddle would be resolved tonight.

But after searching through Shirley Horn, Eartha Kitt, Gloria Lynne and even Jessye Norman, I was worn out and just ready to give up.

"Damn it! It's a record. A simple song. Why don't I just call it a day and maybe I will figure it out someday." I had given up and couldn't believe that I was still here and still searching, for a dumb record. What has gotten into me?!

"Oh come on son. You can't give up. It can't be that simple. If it was just a song, it wouldn't have stayed with you. If it was just a song, you wouldn't have been to the 3 or 4 stores you went to before this one."

"Wait, how did you know that?" I said, mouth wide open.

"If it was just a song," he continued while he looked me like it was 8:33pm and I hadn't just spent a Saturday night in a record store, searching through stacks and stacks and listening and learning, but still not satisfied.

"If it was just a song, you would have given up on it. This was more than just a song. Whatever this was, whoever this was, they woke something up in you and that's not something you can just ignore."

"Okay Willie Wiseman, you got me there," I said, ready to commit to midnight if I had to, as he said, "It's Claude, not Willie, Claude Henderson to be exact."

"I really do appreciate your patience and your expertise, Mr. Henderson."

All the while, Mr. New York Style was intermittently catching the corner of my eye and skillfully building a fortress of albums at the counter and showing no signs of departure. He had laid down his saddlebag and clearly his burdens, because he had gotten so comfortable that he was singing various tunes from his iPOD. Not just any songs, but classics from Marvin and Memphis, Aretha and Atlantic Records. He definitely had an ear that was intriguing, because just when I thought he was some old school aficionado, he would break into something contemporary that I had I heard on the radio in the main lobby, but never really stopped to inhale.

"Wow, he looks like he's going to buy the joint out," I said, having to finally own out loud that I saw him.

"Oh, he's a regular. A real collector. I think he's a singer or a producer or a disk jockey or something."

"A disk jockey?"

Who says that anymore? Who ever did? We pressed on, though I was ready to call it a day and maybe come back some other time. I was tired and weary. I was sad, because this song had indeed awakened something in me, but maybe it was just for a moment. Maybe after all of the time I had spent convincing myself that I was over Greg and over men and over relationships, I was just numb inside. I wanted to believe that this song had burrowed its way through my pain and my anger, through my tears and my truth and got me square in the heart. I wanted to believe that this song had caused those tears because something in me still believed. But maybe, after "Stormy Weather" (Thank You Miss Lena Horne, Granddad's all time favorite), I was just finished or just not ready. Maybe I would have to just let the moment be what it was or I'll grill Tasha about the music and the source on Monday. It was either the radio or something from the party that was playing. I didn't make the damned record up!

So I was preparing myself to convince myself that *we* didn't care—me, myself and I—and maybe buy a few albums and discover some new musical resources, something I could share with Granddad to let him know that I was listening and learning. So I was just going to grab some Carmen and some Betty and make my way home.

And then it happened.

I hate corny moments and I swear to God in Heaven, if I could have stopped this moment from happening to me, I would have. I would have stopped him from singing. I would have stopped the words from piercing my ears and taking me right to where I was this time yesterday. I would have stopped the ache in my heart from coming back to life and I would have stopped my mind from considering again. But, I couldn't, because it happened and I wasn't The Wiz or a wizard, and I had no powers of magic or persuasion. It just happened and I was frozen and freed in one moment.

At exactly 9:49pm, with a mint condition copy of Ms. McRae's "Great American Songbook" in my left hand and Betty Carter's "Tight" in my right, with Mr. Claude Henderson suggesting that I investigate the works of Miss Joyce Bryant, it happened.

Mr. New York Style, long ago lost in his own world, stopped bopping and bouncing and he smiled. But don't get it twisted; the smile had no effect whatsoever. It was what prompted the smile that transported me. He looked up, as though acknowledging an old friend who had gone to Heaven and walked into the room at the same time. He blew a kiss up to the ceiling of the Roadhouse Records building and he began to sing:

Birds Flying High
You Know How I Feel
Sun In The Sky
You Know How I Feel
Breeze Drifting On By
You Know How I Feel
It's A New Dawn
It's A New Day
It's A New Life For Me, yeah
It's A New Dawn
It's A New Day
It's A New Life For Me,
And I'm Feeling Good…

(Anthony Newley/Leslie Bricusse)

And then he made these big rousing drum sounds with his mouth, and he continued his search. But mine was complete, because he was singing the song that I was looking for all evening.

"I'm Feeling Good, why couldn't I remember that?"

I almost grunted it under my breath and I realized that I couldn't remember it because I hadn't known it in a long time, not really, not like this song sang it. I couldn't recall it because I couldn't recall the last time I felt good.

The look on my face must have alerted Mr. Henderson, because he touched my shoulder and said "Son, that's it isn't it? You got your heart fixed by Nina Simone."

I didn't hear him.

All I know is that Mr. Intriguing was killing me softly with his song and I needed to approach him. I couldn't even hear what Mr. Henderson was saying, as I walked away from him and made my way, heart, soul and body in tow, to this stranger with the impeccable style and the warm tenor, who had just rectified my mind.

With his demeanor, and a history with New York brothers under my belt, I was prepared to deal with his swagger just long enough to find out the name of the song and leave him to his Journey Through Music. I didn't want him to think that I was trying to push up on him and I definitely didn't want him to think that I was trying to pick him up. I just wanted him to release the name of the song that he had captured in his words and I would give him his solitude back.

"Excuse me, I don't mean to bother you, but…"

I made my approach cleanly and very matter-of-factly. I put on my 'at work' face and extended my hand with assurance and abruptness. No better way to let someone know that you only mean business than to put on "The Voice." But with the earplugs in and a song in his heart, he couldn't hear me. He looked up just as I walked up and he stepped up, like he was expecting me and didn't mind the company. He removed the plugs, extended his hand in kind.

"Oh, I'm sorry brotha. I couldn't hear you. What can I do you for?"

I think I almost laughed. I was ready for Brooklyn Bounce in his words, and when he spoke Mississippi and molasses dripped from his lips. Warm. Thick. Sweet. Patient. I was confused and convicted. I was beyond intrigued. I was at ease. This man, with his dazzling disposition, was something out of a novel and today, Lord, I was going to make time to read a new book.

It's time that I let myself meet someone new, other than the new delivery guy from The Hunan Garden. It's time that I let myself recoup and recover and rediscover just being. Damn, it's time for me to just exercise some social graces again. It's just a hello, Joshua. Jesus! Breathe and say hello! Nothing else. Just hello.

"Hello," I said as I offered my nervous hand. "Who are you?"

Did I just say that? Am I prepared, at any level, to find out?!

CHAPTER 4: THE INTRODUCTION

LET'S TAKE A LONG WALK

"Elijah Monroe. My friends call me Eli, but I guess that comes later. And who are you, Mr. Searching?"

"Mr. Searching? Where did you conclude that?" I asked, thinking he could see hunger or desperation in my eyes and it was really just inquisition. I mean it was really just information. I mean it was really just befuddlement, but damn, please don't let THAT be visible.

"I'm in here once a month, at least, and I can spend a few good hours up in here looking for classics and hard-to-finds. I have never seen anyone on a hunt for a record like you seemed to be. You put old Mr. Henderson to work today, but he loves it. He generally just sits behind that counter while I do my thing. But on to more important matters, like the name your Momma gave you, which isn't, I'm sure, Mr. Searching."

Joshua lit up. He couldn't help it. It wasn't so much a drawl in Elijah's voice, but the tone. It was lilting, but strong; slow and inviting. It dripped of welcome and be still. It was a voice that you wouldn't mind hearing on phone calls throughout the day or on your cell when you turn it back on to invite the world back into your space. It was morning and warm tea and a crackling fire and sexy and easy, like Sunday Morning. It was....

"Are you just gonna let my hand fall off?" Elijah said, as a playful way to break the trance that Joshua seemed to be in, and as a play on Billy Dee in "Lady Sings the Blues." It worked.

"Huh? I am so sorry. Just a little taken....I mean tired. Been a long time since I spent this much time in a record store. I'm Joshua, Joshua Knight. It's very nice to meet you Elijah Monroe. Now, I came over because, if you can believe it or not, the song that I have been digging and hunting for all day just came out of your mouth. That's crazy but after all this time, you just started singing it. I had to come and find out who that is and end this torturous expedition. Who is that?"

"Oh, Man. That's the legendary Miss Nina Simone, God rest her soul. 'The High Priestess of Soul' she will always be! She's one of my favorites. That song wakes me up every morning. "Feeling Good." I heard it in a movie called "Point of No Return," with Bridget Fonda playing a double agent for the government. It was a tight movie, but the soundtrack took me away. I was in Tower Records RIGHT after the flick ended, searching for that soundtrack and for more Nina Simone. I left 3 hours and 15 cds later. The most expensive movie date I have ever been on, and I was flying solo that night."

Elijah laughs to himself, but the music of it reaches Joshua's ears and makes him smile. **MY GOD WHO IS THIS MAN AND WHY AM I STANDING HERE CHEESING LIKE THE NERD AND THE CAPTAIN OF THE FOOTBALL TEAM?!**

"Wow," Joshua finally says, "I hope that I don't get sprung on her like that. But that song really did grab me. Never had that happen before with a song."

"I understand," Elijah smiles. "I remember when I first heard 'La Costa' by Natalie Cole. She did this joint in like 1977 and it had seagulls and wind and waves in the music, which had this pure piano intro. Man, I went somewhere else listening to that record the first time. Luckily, I know music a little, so I recognized her voice, but she was pure R&B at the time and this was a jazz joint that was so crazy tight. I was walking on a beach; the day wasn't as long or irritating. I found paradise in that song. I came to THIS SPOT after I first moved here a few years back and heard it on WBLS. I've been coming back here every month since, just buying the place out and keeping Mr. Henderson in business. Anyway, I understand, man. Believe me. Music is my sanctuary."

"Wow, I never thought of it like that, but it did feel like I was transported to another place and time. So, let me go tell Mr. Henderson and put his mind at ease, and spend some money so his day wasn't a complete waste with me."

Joshua prepared to turn from Elijah, who seemed to whisper, "I'm sure that that's not possible." Did I hear him right? Did he say that?

"I'm sorry. Did you say something?" Joshua asked, just trying to make sure he wasn't hearing or creating things in his head.

"I simply said that spending an entire day with you could never be a waste, I'm sure."

Elijah stood there, so beautiful, so erect in his stature and so assured in his skin. It was shocking to Joshua. He never felt so invited, without feeling invaded. Hmmm, what does that mean? Is he hitting on me? Am I interested? If so, in what? God, I need to stop. The brother is being nice and a gentleman and I'm ready to go into The Faggish Inquisition of grilling the brother's potentially good intentions. Joshua caught himself.

"Let me go and find this record and make my purchases. I'll be right back."

I'LL BE RIGHT BACK?! Who said that? Did he say he wanted you to come back? Did he say he was interested? Well, yes, he did and he's still looking at me, I can tell. Stop it Gloria! Joshua says to himself as he looks back a la Loretta Devine in Waiting to Exhale, to find Elijah back in the groove of his iPOD but definitely still looking and he waves, even.

"Can you believe that Mr. Henderson? That's the song. He was singing the song. It's called...."

Mr. Henderson stops him by placing "THE BEST OF NINA SIMONE" on the counter, along with his Carmen and Betty acquisitions and says "That will be $37.16 and a lifetime of thank yous."

"Pardon me?" Joshua says, not getting the last part and oblivious to the fact that Mr. Henderson had already determined the song, the artist and clearly the outcome of the hello.

"You heard me, young man. That song is going to bring you something a lot more joyful than just an afternoon of music. He's a nice fella. Always polite and well mannered. From Louisiana, I believe. Came up this way to produce some music with some rappers from down that way and he stayed after they went back home with their millions. He's a producer, I think. I say that 'cuz every once in a while, he will sing up in here on a Saturday afternoon and I think he's on the wrong side of the microphone. Sounds like Sam Cooke and Brooke Benton, but you wouldn't know nothin' about them. Anyway, he's a good man. Gone, go and finish what Nina started."

Joshua was flabbergasted. *Mr. Henderson had peeped the entire conversation and I guess in watching the gesturing saw something more than just a hello. This wise old man has peeped my hold card and didn't mind saying so. Hmm, I wonder what his life was before this record store. I wonder if he's gay or just some old dude who has just watched people and change long enough to know. I wonder if he goes home to music and spends all night with her and some memories. Or maybe he plays up in the Village Underground on odd nights of the month. Maybe Mrs. Henderson is home up late, waiting for him to get home. Mr. Henderson. Nice man.* Joshua heads back to Elijah, who's still busy digging through records, this time with a mint condition copy of Stevie Wonder's TALKING BOOK in his hand. As Joshua gets closer, he looks around for Mr. Henderson, who has discreetly disappeared. Joshua shakes his head and, yes and once again, smiles.

"Thank you again for…singing. If you hadn't opened your mouth and sung that song, my entire day would have gone wasted and I know me. I would have given up after that. So thank you Mr. Elijah Monroe. You have a really nice voice. Are you a singer? Do you perform somewhere regularly?" Joshua thought that would be a nice, unobtrusive way of seeing Elijah in his element, and again.

"I'm more of a producer. Haven't really decided to get my feet wet in the NY music scene. Seems a bit more than I can handle. Dianne Reeves one night here. Carlos Santana over there the next night. Now, that's competition that I don't think I'm up for," Elijah laughs. "I even went to the Village Underground one night to just see singers doing their thing. Well man, it was supposed to just be regular singers, regular Broadway or background cats, I thought. Man, Ashford and Simpson was there. Mariah Carey was in the house, cheering on this chick that used to blow with her. Trey Lorenz, Lisa Fischer, man I couldn't find the voice to get up in from of all of those heavyweights, so I didn't. But maybe one day. Maybe one day soon. I love to sing and I usually do it a lot, but that was before New York. But, I'm getting ready. It's about to go down sooner than later."

Joshua was mesmerized.

"I am so glad to see that brothers still dream big dreams. Maybe one day indeed, because your voice is amazing. You sang that song without any fear or worry and you sang it from your soul. Nice to see that passion is still alive and singing songs."

"Those are nice," Elijah said, looking down at Joshua's feet, which were adorned with a nice pair of Prada sandals. Even though the weather had started to change and it was a bit crisp outside, Joshua still liked to give his feet some air. He was in corporate lace-ups all week and though he didn't mind, he appreciated the break. He was in denim and a sweater because the days of fall were upon us, but he liked the sandals and he still couldn't believe that he let Carlton talk him into buying these expensive things, but he was right. You only live once and they are nice.

"Thanks man. I wouldn't normally have bought something so extravagant but my best friend talked me into them at a moment of weakness. But glad you noticed. A brother has good taste in shoes too, huh?"

"Shoes?" Elijah smiles and his eyes sparkle like someone whipped out a spotlight. "I was talking about your feet. Not all brothers have nice feet and I noticed yours. Sorry, it's a quirk of mine. Hope that wasn't too...personal."

Now, Joshua is blushing and a bit shaken. A fetish? Did he just tell me about his fetish? Does that mean he wants to suck my toes or something? Is he already getting sexual on me and he doesn't even know if I have a partner or a boyfriend or anything? Joshua could feel himself tighten up, so he breathes and smiles and….

"It was a first, that's for sure," Joshua says and takes in Mr. Elijah Monroe again, noting his good taste and direct eye contact. "But thank you for the compliment. Never had someone start off with my feet, but I guess that means that the only way to go now is up," Joshua said, trying to make light of the comment and change the tone of the conversation.

"Or we could go down," Elijah adds, with a wit and slyness that could be off-putting. Joshua's eyebrows raise and he is preparing his righteous indignation and his response, when Elijah finishes "to this little café that I really like and have proper conversation, if you are interested, Mr. Joshua Knight."

Joshua thinks he heard a swoon come from his mouth, but prays that "that would be nice Mr. Monroe," is all that escaped.

Elijah takes his latest collection of new rare finds, that includes that Stevie, Natalie Cole's 1978 Live album, Sparkle by Aretha, some Charles Mingus, some Miles Davis, some Miriam Makeba and some more Nina Simone, as he makes his way to Mr. Henderson, who is magically back behind the counter, as if he never vanished. They clearly have a solid rapport, as Mr. Henderson approvingly peruses Elijah's selections and rings them up, taking care to wrap them his own special way.

Elijah says "'Night Papa Henderson. I'll see you next month, unless you call me to tell me that that Dionne and Isaac duets album gets found. Take care."

Elijah returns to Joshua and smiles, adding "Shall we?" as he extends his arm towards the door, in a gesture that's part doorman, all gentleman. As they take Manhattan and come back down to earth, they walk. The restaurant is only a few blocks away and as they stroll, they don't say much, awaiting a nice table and quieter surroundings. But what they don't say is connecting them all the more. They make their way to the same windows to look at odd things and rare finds. They both seem to stop and inhale a sweet fall breeze that warbles over the night. As they turn the corner, the café seems quiet and intimate, though not empty. It's the perfect place for conversation and acquaintance. Elijah really picked a nice spot, Joshua thought, wondering if this is where he brought all of his pick-ups and then hates himself for the cynicism. *Anyway, Josh, it's just a conversation. It's not even a date. Breathe.*

Elijah opens the door and awaits Joshua's entry before him.

"Is he assuming I'm a bottom?"
"Is he taking the lead?"
"Nice to see someone do that."
"Hope he doesn't think I'm a punk"

All those thoughts ran through Joshua's head ALL THE TIME. Every potential date. Every inviting smile. Every simple gesture. Scrutiny. They were each and all greeted with scrutiny—unnecessary, unwarranted, but surely not unprecedented. Joshua had opened his heart before and been hurt and now he was watching, for signs. But he was still trying to be available, accessible, present in the moment, so he says "Thank You" for the kindness of the gesture and took the lead to ask for "seating for 2, near a window please." As they approached their table, Joshua let Elijah walk in front of him this time and he shocked himself by taking in the view.

Elijah was a tall, thick, country-bred brother, who could be called nothing if not strapping. His legs were pressing against the jeans he wore and his walk was this swaggerish kind of stroll that took its time while you took it in. Joshua had to catch himself as the music started in his head and the unexpected tone shifted in his pants and in his libido. Just a conversation. Breathe.

"So can I get you two handsome gentlemen something to drink?" The waiter was a sultry, olive-skinned foreigner who was comfortable with his customers. He could have been gay, but foreigners have been doing metrosexual long before the Men of America got the concept. He was well groomed, stylish and tanned, but he was flirting.

"I'm your waiter, Guisseppe and I will be servicing you…I mean serving you tonight."

Both Joshua and Elijah caught the "slip" and had to laugh.

"I'll have some hot tea, if you have something herbal," Joshua says, looking at Elijah to see what he orders.

"I will some hot cocoa if you got it."

"As you like," says the saucy waiter whose pants are rather tight but his walk is quite loose, answering the question as he saunters away.

"That was funny," Elijah says. "Dudes here can be so forward, especially with black guys in the Village. A little too much sometimes, but hey, it's the Village."

Joshua remembers the time a guy at Pride just grabbed his crotch, and he could only agree with Eli's point with a smirk.

"So, Mr. Elijah Monroe, that accent is so nice. Where is it from? I'm thinking Alabama, because of drawl in it."

"You are close," Elijah smiles, "but it's Louisianan, a little town called Lake Charles, as a matter of fact. Probably never heard of it."

"You're right, I haven't. But that's a nice name. Sounds inviting."

"And what about you Mr. Knight? Okay, enough of this. How about you Josh…I mean Joshua? Didn't mean to be too familiar. How about you Joshua? Where are you from and what made you on such a hunt for Nina Simone?"

After Joshua told him the story, as best he could without sounding silly or feeling like an idiot, Elijah smiled. As a producer, he loved music and was not surprised to see it affect someone else like that.

"But I never heard of a story like that. Why didn't you just wait till you got to work on Monday and found the cd that was playing? Okay, stupid question, because I know what it feels like when a song gets in your head. True confession time," Elijah smiled and lowered his head in mock shame, "but I once spent 8 hours in that same shop, looking for a Dionne Warwick and Isaac Hayes duets album. We went through the attic and into and through almost every box. I helped Mr. Henderson restock the store that day, all because he was so sure that he had a copy of it in there, somewhere. By the time I left, I had 27 albums under my arm and I've been hanging out with Papa Henderson once a month."

Joshua thought that his commitment was sweet, but he was all over the place. He was lost in the way Elijah's eyes danced while he told the story and the way his brow curled while he 'searched' and the way he paused for a moment and got embarrassed that he was telling the tale in the first place, to some guy he had just met and he so imperviously brushed it off, figuring he was too deep to turn around and try to clean it up now.

"You are something Elijah. That kind of passion is so rare these days," Joshua said, genuinely touched by Elijah's need, real, tangible need, for that album. They talked. They shared. They laughed. They connected.

It was 12:14 AM.

Time and tension got away from them as they got to know each other and time was well spent. Somebody once sang it but Natalie said it sweetest—"What A Lovely Way To Spend An Evening."

But then Joshua got up to go to the bathroom and finally, time met him at the door. "Oh my God! It's almost 12:30AM," he said as he sat back down with Elijah and came back down to earth. "I haven't been home all day. This has been the most adventurous day I've had in a long time."

Elijah replied, proudly, "Well, I'm glad to have played a small role in it, kind sir." Joshua looked at him like he wasn't real. What a sweet way to say that. Who are you, Elijah Monroe? How do I find out without getting my heart broken or my feelings hurt? Day-by-Day, I guess.

"So where do you live, Elijah?" Joshua offered, trying to bring close to the Lovely Day that Bill Withers sang about so fortuitously.

"I'm actually in walking distance. I'm right down on 14th and Grace, not far from here. What about you, Josh? Where do you stay? And when are you gonna just say Eli? Say it. Eli. Come on. EE-LIE."

Joshua was taken with the fact that Eli had noticed that he was still purposely using the more formal Elijah and sometimes tacked on the Monroe. But it wasn't that he was being contrary. He was Joshua. Josh to a rare few and he didn't know if he was okay with this man, whom he just met, taking up the JOSH banner and walking around with it so flippantly. But he was so good to it that Josh had to submit, at least on this simple point.

"Okay, Eli. Sorry, I wasn't being formal, just respectful. We just met and I didn't want to come off too formal, too soon….he says 4 hours later."

Joshua couldn't believe that he shared his wit aloud, right in front of Eli. I didn't go unnoticed.

"Well, actually, its 12:27am, now and so that makes it officially 6 hours, 55 minutes and 8…9…10 seconds since our eyes since met, but who's counting?" Elijah said as he lifted his eyes angelically to the sky, and smiled.

"So what do we do now, Mr. Time Traveler?," Joshua asked, quite nonchalantly.

Whatever happened now would be just fine. Joshua knew that he wasn't going to slip up and wake up naked and unaware, because they had only gotten drunk on conversation and connection. Since he wasn't a "first time, third base" kind of guy, he didn't even think he had to worry about going almost too far.

But he knew he didn't really want the evening to end but it had to and so he was a bit shocked at himself when he suggested, "Why don't I walk you home and I can grab a cab to Brooklyn from there?"

Eli didn't want to end the night either, but knew that he wasn't about to suggest a nightcap at his place, because well, he didn't drink and they had consumed enough coffee, tea and water to send them both to the bathroom for some release. So, begrudgingly, he obliged. At least they could take a nice long walk, and feel the vibe.

One of the first things that you get used to in New York City is walking. You find that your feet move much faster than the traffic most time and on a nice night, you just don't mind it at all. Joshua and Elijah barely spoke on the long walk, but they said a lot. They said, "I in-joyed your company" by the way they paced their stroll to an almost crawl. They spoke "I'd like to see you again" by the coyness with which they looked and then looked away. They articulated their understanding of each other's needs by the way Elijah took Joshua bags and didn't take his manhood in the gesture and in the way that Elijah let Joshua look both ways for them both as they crossed busy streets. Something was happening for them both, but all they really cared about, in this moment, was this moment and they took that long walk step by step.

Then they arrived.

Elijah's building could blur into every other big city apartment building USA. They stood there not knowing what to do next, either of them. Numbers didn't have to be passed. They did that in the restaurant. Plans didn't have to be made. They said that they would get together for dinner sometime next week. So now all they had was right now and it was awkward and sincere and new and still just a bit uneasy. What do we do now?

Too new for a kiss and too grown for a giggle, they simply said "Thank you for an amazing evening," at the exact same time. The exact same words. That did it. That broke enough ice to send them on their respective ways comfortably. Joshua wasn't sure what was happening as Elijah leaned in for a hug. Some 3 inches taller than him, Elijah's scent, some mixture of African oils and something in his hair, descended upon Joshua and it was almost intoxicating. Eli said something in his ear that was completely inaudible since he was still sniffing and still whirling within Elijah's arms, not fondling or fidgeting. Just holding him, a measure too long, a gesture too right. This "Good Night" could take forever and Joshua would be fine, indeed.

But it didn't as Elijah broke free from him and said "Let me go before I get myself in trouble."

He smiled at Joshua and said, "Now it's my turn," as he extended his hand towards the empty yellow cab with his available light on.

G726.

Eli and his odd memory. He knew that he would remember that number forever.

As he placed Joshua Knight into Yellow Cab G726, he said to the driver, as he handed him a $20, "Be careful. You are carrying priceless cargo."

Elijah looked in the backseat, at Joshua, who was looking at him but trying to not stare, and said "Good Night Joshua Knight. I look forward to our next long walk."

Elijah turned to ascend the stairway to his apartment, but looked back just in time to catch Joshua turning around in the cab. Their eyes locked. They both smiled and put their heads down, in a giddy glee that made one man's heart race in delight and the other's palpitate in an almost fear.

"Who is this man?" Joshua thought to himself and wondered to himself if he was ready to find out.

"Maybe I have just met a really good friend," he thought to himself as he considered that Elijah barely touched him, didn't invite him in and never talked about whether he was partnered.

"Maybe he's just a really dynamic man, who shares the same love of good conversation."

Joshua thought it but it felt ridiculous to consider, because he was always dismissing men who found him attractive. But he also didn't just want to instantly sexualize the brotha. But he is phyne. Joshua liked Elijah and Elijah was so inviting and so warm. Plus, Joshua always had a problem taking compliments. Surely, he realized, he might have a problem realizing a first date when he saw it. But whatever it is, he was glad to have spent such a wonderful day with this man, Elijah Monroe.

Eli.

Joshua had the cab stop about 5 blocks from his house. He wanted to take the rest of journey home as a walk. He got out of the cab. A cool breeze washed over him. A smile made its way to his face. He was taking in the night—the trees, the smells, the air, and the peace of it. He was opening himself up and letting the breeze rustle old feathers that had been dormant and still. He let himself feel the jubilation in the moment. He let himself wonder and consider.

His cell phone rang.

CHAPTER 5: THE UNSETTLING

BROOKLYN DAILY NEWS

JOSHUA KNIGHT Gets Blindsided!

Joshua panicked.

His phone never rang past a certain hour, unless Carlton was bored or his parents had an emergency. Well, sometimes it was Tasha, but with Friday going off without a hitch, it was not likely her. He looked at his phone. He didn't recognize the number, even the area code. Was it Carlton, hurt in Paris? Was something wrong?

Joshua stopped at his front stoop in Brooklyn, somehow believing that if he didn't take the bad news into his house, it wouldn't be as bad. He looked up at the house that he worked so hard to purchase and the sadness of wanting to share it with Gregory washed over him.

Oh My God! Is this Greg, after all this time, calling me to say he was sorry? Can he come back? Or was he only calling because he was hurt and something told him to reach out while he still had the chance?

Joshua needed to breathe.

He realized that he hadn't breathed since the phone rang. He was so caught up that he barely caught the call before the next ring would exile it to voice mail and he would have to endure the process of calling into the vacuum of technology to retrieve whatever sadness or tragedy was visiting him at 1 o'clock in the morning.

Joshua took a breath and answered.

"Hello, this is Joshua Knight."

"I'm glad about that, Mr. Knight. I think that you are about to walk into your door. I was hoping that my timing was perfect and I would catch you just as you got home," the voice said with a sexy drawl that could only be....

"Who is this?" Joshua asked, already so panicked that he could barely think, so hearing was not an option.

"Wow. Less than 30 minutes and already forgotten? A brotha definitely thought he had more staying power than that," Elijah laughed.

"Oh, Elijah. Hi. I'm sorry, my phone never rings this late and my mind was just somewhere else. Is everything okay?" Joshua tried to regain his composure and was a bit taken aback that Elijah Monroe was on his phone less than 30 minutes after leaving him.

"Sure it is," Elijah said through a smile. "I'm just a brotha who was raised a certain way, and I'm not comfortable with the fact that I couldn't see you to your door. So, I thought to myself and decided to do the next best thing—walk you to your door by phone. I hope you don't mind, might be a little corny, but I will sleep better knowing that you are safe and settled at home."

Safe? Joshua thought as he unlocked the door. Sure, I am.

Settled? Hardly!

This man was so unnerving with his sexy Southern drawl and his electric smile and his amazing teeth and his own personal scent and his easy manner and his....

"That's so nice of you, Eli," Joshua said as he finally settled into his skin and realized that he was safe at home, on the phone with a man who cared enough to walk him into the door and tired enough to sleep Sunday through. "I am here. Signed. Sealed. Delivered." Joshua laughed to himself because he knew that the next line of the song was way too personal to say aloud.

But Mr. Music Man Monroe didn't mind.

"I'm yours! I love that song. I sang it once at a high school talent show. Did a pretty good job if I do say so myself." Elijah rips into a quick verse of the song and then catches himself. Joshua was lost in his voice and his easiness with him. He's singing on my phone at 1AM! Doesn't he know that that could drive a man wild?!

"I'm sorry. I got carried away," Elijah offers. "I really did just call to make sure you made it home safe and to offer one final good night. Josh, it was so nice to spend an evening with music and good conversation. If you don't mind, I would love to do it again, soon. I feel like I can be so easy with you. I haven't laughed that much since I moved to NYC. Thank you for that, Mr. Knight. I hope you and your shining armor sleep well. Good night."

Before Joshua could respond, Elijah had pressed the end call button and their conversation had ceased. But the racing in Joshua's heart was just beginning.

"What is this? I'm not about to start dating someone with the biggest campaign in the company's history just opening up." Joshua's conversation with himself was halted when he realized that, without realizing it, Eli had slipped his company's name into his ear, though they never discussed it. It seemed like some subtle sweet sign to stay open. But everything in Joshua wanted to tighten up.

"WHY NOW GOD?! WHY NOW!"

Joshua thought about all the time that a relationship could and would take. He thought about the dating, again. He thought about the phone calls, again. He thought about the choosing restaurants and making plans and getting involved and getting serious and getting hurt, again. Joshua was in a panic.

Joshua was in a pickle, because Elijah Monroe had him asking questions about himself and to himself at 1AM and he didn't like some of the answers.

"What am I doing? I have already dated, married and divorced this brother and we haven't even gone on a real date yet! DAMN! What's wrong with me?"

Joshua just looked at himself in the mirror of his stylish main bathroom and washed his face, with icy liquid. He offered himself a blast of reality in the form of cold water, hoping that the shock of it would snap him out of his lunacy. He was wrong.

He decided to take a shower.

It will cool him down and calm him down, so he can get a great night's sleep. He had a full day and been on his feet for hours, though he's been walking on a cloud for the past few.

He turned on the shower to full blast, so it could steam up the bathroom. Joshua closed the door as he goes into the bedroom to strip before he dipped. He opened his well orchestrated closet and placed his jacket exactly where it belongs. He placed his shirt and jeans in the hamper and looked around and realized that he's done pretty well for himself, but....

He missed the idea of sharing a home with someone but knows that he's got bigger fish to fry. He's not even sure if he would live with someone again. He likes his space, as he convinces himself by walking out of the closet and over to the nightstand naked. But he walked around naked when he lived with Greg. It's not the ability to walk around naked that gives him space. It's the keeping other people at bay, at just enough distance for them not to see the tracks of his tears. He doesn't have to think too much. He doesn't have to get too close. He doesn't have to shift his schedule and he surely doesn't change his plans. He was convinced that KNIGHT IN SHINING ARMOR was all he needed. He was right, until now.

He pushes the play button on the answering machine that he bought to be sure that he checked messages. With voicemail, he would go days without realizing that he hadn't checked it, but with this machine, the blinking light gave him notice.

"Josh! Josh! Where are you Baby Bubba? I am standing in this amazing store just off the Champs d'Elyses. I can't believe I am in Paris. Thank you so much for this trip. Momma would have loved knowing that I came here and that I brought her here with me. I can't believe she got cremated. That was so not like her, but it was her wish. I left her here, right in The River Seine. So I will be back tomorrow. You have all of my flight information, so I'll see you at the airport. And, Josh," Carlton paused and you could hear his rich tenor crack as he sniffled and held back the tears caught in his throat, "thank you for being the best friend I have ever known or had in my life. I will never forget you for this. You are something special. Maybe one day you will let someone else say that to you again. WHOA…guess that's the Romance of Paris speaking again. Have to go. Want to grab a few things before my flight. See Ya Manana!"

Joshua smiled. Carlton always did have this uncanny way of mixing the emotional and the hysterical.

"It will be good to have you home, Brownskin," Joshua said aloud as he exchanged nicknames with Carlton through the air and knew somehow that Carlton heard him. Joshua got into the shower and just let the steam and the heat, the aroma of his favorite wash and the smell of possibility in the air just all have their way.

Thirty minutes later, Joshua emerged from the shower. He was spent. Steam, hot water, baby oil and time had all choreographed a wonderful dance that took his stress down the drain. Man, would he sleep tonight!

Josh climbed into his Heavenly Bed (his treat to himself after staying in a Westin Hotel and sleeping like a baby in Chicago…almost missed his meeting…bought the whole kit and caboodle from their catalogue before he left the hotel) and was asleep in no time.

The sun kissed Joshua's face and God's alarm clock was the only one he ever needed. Joshua didn't like to be jolted out of bed by noise, so he would always tell God what time he needed to be up and like clockwork (no pun intended), he'd open his eyes at or close to that time.

He got up, brushed his teeth and washed his face. He had about 2 hours before he had to hit the traffic to get Carlton from Newark Liberty International Airport. That was a much easier trip from Brooklyn than either of the other two. He went downstairs to the kitchen, made some wheat toast and grabbed an apple and some OJ.

He curled for up for a minute and watched some morning news programs on ABC. He flipped over to BET to catch Ty Tribbett and Greater Anointing on Bobby Jones and made a note to get their cd.

"Wow, these kids are having church up there," he said as he watched them tear up the stage.

Joshua lounged for a little while longer, before grabbing some jeans, a jacket and some sneakers and his car keys. He made his way up the Bell Parkway and onto the Turnpike, right at Exit 13 and then onto the Airport. He got there just in time. His cell rang and it was Carlton.

"Good Morning to you Mr. Man. I pray that you rested well, since you weren't at home when I called. I'z here. Where you at?"

Joshua had to laugh. Carlton is a nut.

"I'z coming. I'z right here," Joshua deadpanned, before shifting back to his post-slavery voice. "I am right about Door #3 at your baggage claim. Come on out, unless I have to circle, but the cops are pretty liberal on Sundays."

Carlton wheeled out his one huge bag and two carry-ons just as Joshua opened the trunk.

"Hey Baby Bubba," Carlton said as he grabbed Joshua's neck. "Man, I didn't miss you at all. That trip was amazing. I didn't expect to see so much diversity in Paris. Americans all over the place, and Africans walking around like royalty. It was so sexy and hoity-toity and so rich in culture. Thank you again for that trip. So what you been up to? Why the glow? Did you have a spa day while I was gone? Looking like you got some from this morning glow on your face, but you and I both know that that's not gonna happen anytime soon, right?"

Joshua froze.

Carlton froze.

"Joshua, wait a minute," Carlton said as his voice dropped from his natural 2nd tenor into the deepest parts of his baritone. "You DID NOT?! Not while I was away?! Who was it?! What's the what up man?! I leave and there's nobody and I come back to The Glow! That's the dealie-o?!"

Joshua felt ridiculous.

Was he glowing over some man he had only known for a few hours? Okay, 7 hours. Joshua tried to turn on the radio? Carlton turned it off. Joshua tried to change the subject. Carlton changed it back. Joshua tried to ignore him. Carlton took the wheel and said "If you don't say something in the next 3 seconds, I am gonna ram this thing right into a guard rail. Now's what's good Baby Bubba? What's this glow about?"

Joshua was flabbergasted. "How do I answer that?" he thought to himself.

"I met a dude in the record store who sang this song and touched my heart and he liked my feet and I thought he was talking about the sandals and then we got something to eat and then we laughed and we talked and then we didn't and it was still nice and he made my smile and he lived nearby and I walked him home and he put me in a cab and said I was priceless cargo and then I got home and the phone rang and I thought it was you or Momma or something wrong or something crazy and it was him, making sure I made it home safe and I was floored and I'm scared and I don't know what to do next and he asked me out again, but I think it's again, because I don't know if that was a date or just us kicking it and I'm freaking out and I hate it and I like it but I don't love it because I don't like feeling this...."

"Okay, Joshua. Breathe! I know how you get when you feel overwhelmed. It's all over your face. Breathe and let's just save this for when we get to the house. I'll just chill there for a few hours. I am in no hurry to get back home to bills and bad milk that I forgot to get rid of before I left."

Joshua was fine with that option. He breathed. He considered what he was going to say when they settled down and settled in. *But this is Carlton, my main man, my best friend, my running partner and my voice. I will just tell him what I'm feeling.*

"Sure you will," the voice inside his head said. "You will never tell him that you are feeling someone like this because you are afraid that he will get jealous. You have always thought that maybe, possibly, perhaps Carlton has a thing for you or more likely, was overly protective of you. You are not going to test that by telling him about Elijah when you don't know who Elijah is to YOU yet!" Damn that rational/irrational voice. Joshua hated it. It was kept his mind racing long after his body had slowed down. UGH!!!

"Maybe I will do something different!" Joshua thought he had said that in his head, until Carlton says "Um, okay then. Do something different!"

They laughed. Carlton knew him too well. Joshua decided then he would just spill it and hope that Carlton's tentativeness about Joshua's former possibilities was just a reflection of the coolness he was showing about them himself. Maybe Carlton was just doing what I was doing—trying to not make a big deal out of them. Does that then mean that this is somehow already a big deal?

BREATHE JOSH…BREATHE!

As they pull up to Josh's lofty manor in Brooklyn, known to his family and friends as Delores Manor, a play on the fact that his Momma loves this house so much that he put her picture and a sign in the main hallway bearing that name, Joshua prepared himself. He knows that as soon as they get in, Carlton is going to bring a bottle of Shiraz from the cabinet, with two glasses and inquisition in tow.

"So, how have you been, Joshua? Tell me all about how the Coca-Cola presentation went."

Joshua was stunned that Carlton had remembered that and that he didn't go right in for the kill.

"It went really well. Milner made a great deal of fuss over my prototype of the commercial and that really sealed the deal."

"I told you," Carlton said. "My boy Bille is the boom. I met him when I had to do a profile on him for this webzine I used to write for, a hundred years ago. We stayed in touch and kicked it when I was in LA and I knew you two would be great together. Excellent. So are we millionaires yet?"

"Not yet, Ivana, but Daddy's on the way!" Joshua laughed, knowing that Carlton was never materialistic and had fought him tooth and nail about the trip to Paris.

Carlton was an independent writer, who had done nicely with 2 books and was running a really popular website now, as well as doing some writing for independent artists and record labels. He lived a good life and didn't like all the trappings of the music industry at large, but loved music. Any big dreams he had, he lived through Joshua. Joshua and he struggled together, building their respective things, and Carlton quickly rebuffed an offer to come and work for him.

"Who's gonna be able to tell you when you are getting too full of yourself if you are my boss, Josh?" Carlton said as he shrugged off the offer. Carlton lived a good NYC life, in his Harlem apartment, with all the luxuries that he needed, which weren't many. Not that his apartment was simple. By no means was it simple. It was adorned with African structures and Indian artifacts and a stylish simplicity that looked like money, but came from selective shopping and good taste. He got that from his Mom.

He was a wreck when his Mom's asthma attack got worse and she slipped away after only a few hours. Carlton was jarred and inconsolable for weeks. It took weeks before he would even let anyone get too close to him physically, but when he accidentally bumped into Joshua one day, as they were passing each other in the kitchen at Carlton's apartment, he couldn't contain himself and he just broke down. Joshua was always on the ready, because he knew how close they were and knew that at some point, Carlton was going to snap. When the floodgates finally opened, Carlton cried for 2 days. Joshua stayed at Carlton for 2 days and just let him cry. His father had long ago left the family—died, not abandoned—so this was it. Carlton was alone. All he had in NYC now was his best friend Joshua. His sister had a life elsewhere and he had Joshua.

"Did that caterer that I recommended to Tasha work out? I had been to their restaurant before, but never seen them cater. Please tell me that they represented. I know with corporate money, you could have gone to Midtown, but I think Harlem can still handle their business," Carlton said, looking like he had his fingers crossed.

"They were excellent," Joshua said, remembering the plate of perfection he consumed on Friday night, when he finally got home. "There is some of it still in the fridge. I only took a plate. I gave the staff the rest. Didn't want to waste it. But it was excellent, man."

"So."

"So?"

"Joshua?"

"Carlton?!"

"Are you going to make me pull it out of you? What's going on man? What's this thing about? What's going on? What's happening?" Carlton said as he went into this crazy funny deadpan of Karen from Will & Grace, hoping to break the tension on Joshua's face but still get at the truth.

"I don't know where to start," Joshua said as he sat down, poured them each a glass and laid back. "I don't know what to say."

Joshua and Gregory had such a storybook relationship that Joshua was now afraid of everything and anything that looked good. Not too good. Just good. He would take a hello to its illogical conclusion. Joshua wasn't narcotic, he thought, just careful. After 5 years away from Gregory and anything that remotely looked like a solid relationship, Joshua was jarred by Eli's style and his sense of courting him. He felt something that he didn't like in Elijah. He felt that kind of style and sense of self that would be cool and well spoken, warm and inviting and it scared him shitless.

How do I just get back out there again, on the horse again, without bringing up old stuff? I deserve to be happy and to be loved, but Gregory broke something in me. Maybe God sent Elijah as my repairman. Joshua told Carlton everything.

The song. The stores. The First Time Ever He Saw His Face, even though it WAS just yesterday. The long walk. The diner. The conversation. The smile. The voice. The laugh. The eyes that looked right into him and said, "I come in peace, but I don't have to go."

Joshua couldn't believe just how much this man, this Elijah Monroe had gotten under his skin.

"Then, Carlton, man, he called me as I was walking in the house last night. At 1AM. I thought something was wrong but it was just him saying 'Good night' and making sure I got home. What kind of…what was that? Does he think that that means I'm gonna just bottom for him? Did he think that I came off like I need a rescuer? He's a nice enough guy…."

Carlton's cutting eyes stopped Joshua from finishing that lie.

"Okay, he's a great guy from what I know, but I don't know much."

"Oh really. His name, his address, his occupation, his background, his roots, his dreams, his likes, his talents. Seems like you know all of those. What don't you know that you need to know in order to go on a DATE? Joshua, don't do it. Don't you sit here and sabotage this thing. I can't believe you are going to give Gregory this much power. You loved him. HE screwed up and now YOU are suffering. Man, he and Kevin have been together since that night and you are still there with them, because you sho' didn't take your heart with you! This may just be a fling. This may be forever, but for God's sake, just BREATHE AND RECEIVE IT!"

Joshua was floored that Carlton was so passionate. He thought that Carlton was happy with his relationship with Donovan, which wasn't exclusive yet, didn't involve keys yet and that was still growing. He had no idea that Carlton was paying that much attention to him. Maybe he was a bit upset that Carlton was so ready to push him off on someone…else.

"I just don't want to be hurt again, Carlton. I don't think I can take it." Joshua lowered his head and opened his heart. "I just don't think I could get through that if something went wrong. I am tired of all of the magnificent starts, but ugly finishes."

"All of what magnificent starts?" Carlton retorted. Before Gregory, you were pretty good at these 6-month things and then just saying that it wasn't The One. No harm, no foul. Then, Greg comes along and you bond and connect and go to the next level. You were amazing together. He cheated. You left. That's it. ONE UGLY FINISH! Now, don't let that determine the rest of your life. Be Joshua, please. Not Joshua-After-Greg-Broke-His-Heart. You don't have any fire in your eyes and all the passion you have in your heart, you use at work. Can you please save some for yourself and this dude who's trying to just be himself with you and see what happens? Sabotage just doesn't look good on you, man. When he calls, just check your sched and if it fits, don't force it. Just chill and see what's what. Cool? It's time for someone else to be your could-be besides me."

Joshua gets up and stands in front of Carlton and pulls him to his feet. "Thank you man. I think you just…." Joshua just hugged Carlton and sighed. "Damn, why does it hurt so bad? Why does it take so long to get up from this?"

"Well, I don't know because I never knew love like this before, so I can't call it. But I do know this. This could be another chance. This could be the chance you have been waiting for your entire life. This could just be another brother, sailing along on life's waters. But you will never find out if you don't let it be. He seems like the kind of dude you dig. He's not stuck on playing The Gay Games (only calling after an allotted amount of time; only meeting in a group so friends can see, et al.). So why don't you remember that you never did that either and just invite him to dinner, tonight?"

"Tonight? Man, I can't do that! I'll look desperate. I can't play myself like that, Brownskin. I will just wait and see."

Carlton moved aggressively towards Joshua and for a moment, he was unnerved. The first thought about Carlton, all stern looks and bohemian/thug attire of denim and mudcloth, wasn't that he was gay, or nice. Joshua had forgotten that Carlton stood as tall as he did, around 6'4", and with his fro all tight and lined up (he found the Black section of Paris and got a cut), his luminous brown skin, the shade of perfect milk chocolate, his shoulders broad and strong, his glasses removed, his thick black brows almost snarling and his steel jaw tight, Carlton looked mad. His strong nostrils flared and his dark eyes, brown and chestnut, cut a hole right into Joshua. Carlton stopped himself and put his head down. Joshua wore him out sometimes. But he loved him so much and he thought that Joshua deserved so much. He was more like his brother now than ever.

"Man, you are NOT gonna become one of those people, are you? Just call the brotha and make plans. Don't overthink it. If he did, you wouldn't be gushing over a 1AM phone call to make sure you got home, cuz he wouldn't have made the call. BUT HE DID!! So chill. Dial the digits and see if the cat has Sunday night dinner plans. If so, make your own for this week. If he doesn't, make plans for tonight. Your Momma taught you how to cook for a reason. Now, I'm gonna get up outta here and make my way home. Donovan knows I'm home by now and I know he's got something planned to surprise me AND I don't need to be one of the brothers who's so married to his friends, he never makes room for his lover. I'll holla before later, but if our plans go right for both of us, it won't be tonight. Peace, Baby Bubba."

With that, Carlton grabbed his bags, and a cab home. Joshua insisted, as his best friend put his bags in the trunk of that cab and hugged him as though he was wishing him well, that he let him take him home.

Carlton sighed, "Make the call, man. Make the call."

⌘

"Hello Mr. Knight. How goes it this sunny afternoon?"

Elijah was so warm and so immediate in his voice that it almost startled Joshua.

"I'm well thanks, Eli. How did you know it was me?" Joshua queried, a bit unprepared.

"Man, I always put numbers into my phone as soon as I get 'em. Otherwise, they never make it. So I program all cards and info into my Sidekick on the weekly. That way no cards to maintain. So I know it was you because 'JOSH KNIGHT' came up on my phone and a smile came to my face. So what's going on with you?"

Joshua stopped. Did he have the balls to extend the invite? What would he say it he didn't? 'Just wanted to say HI?' BREATHE AND…

"I was wondering what you were up to tonight? If you have no plans, I felt like cooking. I got some good stuff at the market yesterday and wanted to return the hospitality you showed me. You up for some baked chicken and roasted potatoes, broccoli and some homemade coconut cake?" Joshua said it with a pride that he knew would entice the Southern gent who was Lost In New York.

"Man, you ain't said nothin' but a word! I would love the company of a good brotha like you and if it comes with some good eats, I'm already there. Just tell me when and where and if you need me to bring anything."

Joshua really didn't expect such an immediate yes, but then again, there is something unpretentious about Eli that can hit you the wrong way if you aren't ready. Joshua wasn't sure if he was ready. Eli seems to be up for whatever the moment brings and you KNOW that's not New York. Give us time to plan and organize and assemble at a later date. But this was cool, too. Breathe.

"Excellent, Eli. Just bring yourself and a hearty appetite." Joshua said, as he gave him the address and directions by train. Unlike Joshua, who did it because his parents lived in Upstate NY now and he wanted to be able to get to them and get away, most people in NY do not own cars. The train is the true mass transportation in New York, since everyone hops it to go everywhere, in ball gowns and baseball caps. So, Elijah already knew the way.

"Brooklyn," he said "is one of my favorite stompin' grounds on Saturday. You aren't far from Courtney Washington's spot, right?"

Joshua was surprised and said, "You got it Mister. So I'm gonna get things going and I will see you at 7pm. Cool?"

"Of course. See you in a li'l bit," Elijah said as he got off the phone and hopped in the shower. Elijah was determined to live his best life now. With the blessings he's also had a fair share of disappointments and heartbreaks, but Elijah C. Monroe was going to be about his and he wasn't going to let a knockdown keep him down. No more surprises. He was going do it on purpose, starting with getting to know Joshua Knight, slowly.

CHAPTER 6: THE REFLECTION

"don't nobody want all that, niggah! I JUST WANT THE DICK!"

Elijah was pumped to hear from Joshua so soon. He knew that they would speak again, because they really seemed to connect. But Elijah had also gotten real used to New York cats who came with heat and then fizzled out real quick. If he wasn't trying to tap that on the first "get-together" (he had to get used to the fact that dating was a dead art in the big cities of USA), he generally got the run-around.

Once or twice, because they were really sexy to him (a smile and a nice butt caught his attention like the next virile young man), he would oblige them. But even in that, dudes knew that Elijah Monroe was a gentleman. Cats who came with "beat it up, Daddy" and "you want this, you love this, don'tcha?" might have gotten to finish the act, but the dance was finished in Elijah's head and he would quickly release so that he could be finished with it. He just wasn't attracted to the porn-style of sex that brothers seemed to be feeling.

"I'm a country boy who still believes in some romance, some kissing and taking my time," he said to one juicy dancer he met while walking through the Village.

"Ain't nobody into all that! Don't nobody want all that, niggah! I just want the dick!" said the flexible chocolate nympho of 5 foot 8 inches of brown tricks and treats. He quickly got undressed and rubbed himself, with the roundest, phattest, most delectable behind that Eli had seen in months, against Eli's tall, solid frame.

Eli wanted to kiss his sweet lips while he palmed that bubble, but the private dancer was already on his knees working with the quickness to get him hard.

"Damn," Eli thought, "is he a professional or just an expert at givin' 'em?" He got lightheaded and brick hard and just let go of any thoughts of romance on this sultry Tuesday night.

That was the last time Elijah had been intimate or sexual with anyone. Tuesday, July 7th of last year. He couldn't believe the crazy drought himself, but he wasn't about to become just another dude who hit it, split it and rolled out. Elijah was crazy enough to believe that he could have a real relationship and even a real love with a quality brotha.

He was opening himself to Latin, Asian, Caribbean and other cultures, too. He even got so open that he dated Kyle Sherman, this amazingly sexy White cat from Boston, with a body that would hurt many and a butt that put a hurting on some Levi's. They had okay conversations, even though Kyle didn't seem to really be passionate about anything. It wasn't black and white differences that stopped them from clicking. It was dreams.

Kyle's only real dream seemed to be to live in NYC, so he was happy. For Elijah, NYC was just the beginning. But they dated for about a month before Elijah finally dealt with the fact that he was attracted to him enough to have sex but not enough to build a life.

That went out the door as soon as they got naked.

Kyle had never said anything racial that made Elijah think he was prejudiced in any way. He was liberal. He was from an urban environment and Elijah wasn't the first Black guy he dated. It wasn't until later that he told Elijah that he ONLY dated Black guys. Had Elijah known that, he would have heard the warning signal going off. But he wasn't told, so he went for it.

He and Kyle were going at it like mad mongrels, hungry for a turkey leg and the castle's bounty. Then, Elijah and Kyle got into a heated 69 that got so twisted that Kyle's legs were wrapped around Elijah's chest while Elijah gave him the rimming of his life. They were on fire. They had about 30 minutes of heated foreplay, when they knew it was time for some penetration. Kyle got the condom from the drawer beside his bed. He rolled it down on Elijah's thick head and down the shaft. He crawled up Elijah's thick thighs and straddled him.

"You want this," Kyle asked, his piercing green eyes staring directly at Elijah.

"Yeah, sit down on it. Let me take my time up in you," Elijah almost surprised himself with that tone, but they had created a fire that could only be squelched one way. They were going at it for a good 10 minutes, with Kyle working his hole just right, with ample gripping and opening…surrendering and controlling. They had a rhythm. Then, Elijah, feeling the heat and knowing that he liked it when he was in it, decided he was going to use his 6 foot 3 frame, which towered over Kyle's 5 foot 10 inches, to his advantage.

That's when it happened.

Elijah flipped Kyle on his back, legs over his shoulders and went so deep that Kyle's breath was audible.

"Oh damn, niggah, that's it. Tear it up you big black mother…!"

"WHAT THE…."

Elijah froze. Did this white boy just say….?

He threw Kyle's legs off of his shoulders and just looked at him.

"What the hell, man," Kyle said, sweating and only part of the way *there*, wondering and completely unaware of why the moment froze and heat went quickly cold.

"I don't get down like that, Kyle. I never would've thought you had some Mandingo fantasy up in your head and I was definitely watching. Been there, ain't gonna do that again. Next time just get a thug. I hear that they like tapping white boy ass and taking out their frustrations on willing holes. That's not my deal. I thought we were....you know. Never mind. I heard you and I'm out. That was pretty foul though. Damn."

Kyle couldn't believe it had come out of his mouth, because Elijah, who he really liked and thought he could build a future with, was always clear about not wanting to be his or anyone's fantasy come true. He wanted to be the man, the partner, they were looking for, not just the thick, tall Black dude who could fill big shoes.

But Kyle had been with brothaz before and most of 'em liked it when he freaked like that. He thought he was just being "down." Kyle tried to call and visit for a few weeks after that. He knew he had messed up. Elijah was done.

But Elijah wasn't done now. He was leaning up against the cold wall in his cold shower, trying to eradicate his problem. He wanted Joshua from the second he walked into that shop and he's not about to mess up getting to know him. So Elijah is in going for relief #2, his insurance that he wouldn't have to worry about another little head/big head conflict.

"Joshua Knight, come here baby. Come here and let me..."

Elijah got quiet, bit his lip and just continued to stroke. As he imagined Joshua's sweet lips kissing his, and palming the butt that he noticed when Josh got up for the bathroom, Elijah let his mind run wild, so that he wouldn't when he got there for dinner. He wanted tonight to really be about getting to know this sweet, sometimes shy, but clearly smart and really warm guy that he met just yesterday.

Oddly enough, Elijah got hotter thinking about their walk and their conversation than he did imagining their sex. The walk was real. The conversation was real. The connection was real and Elijah was definitely going to take his time to get to know this brother and see what they could be before he gets caught up in another man's trip. More than even the white and other ethnic men he had dated, Elijah was most floored by the fantasies that brothas threw at him. With his height and voice and coloring, Elijah got more comments that made his skin crawl from Black men than he ever thought he would.

"Damn, daddy, I bet you could blow my back out."

"You'll love it when I call you Big Poppa!"

"My man and I were watching you and wondered if you would be the top to our bottom. My man is a top but he says he will bottom for you," this beautiful young brotha of about 25 said to him in Chi Chiz that night, as he pointed to his man, a tall, thuggish looking dude who was about the same age, who lifted his beer and gave him The Black Man Nod—chin up, head back real quick—and confirmed the request.

It's not that Elijah wasn't glad to be a top and a real freak when it came to having some good sex. But for him, it had to come with a back-story. He wasn't that cat who would just get horny. He wasn't on the prowl, just trying to break somebody off. He really did want to build something.

That's what he wanted with Reggie.

That's not what he got.

"Come here, Joshua Knight. Come here and let me taste those lips again," Elijah, said out loud as the shower got cold and his desire for Joshua heated up.

Eli was really just trying to push any thoughts of Reggie from his heads. So he continued forward and forward is Joshua Knight.

"Yeah baby. Yeah, that's it," Elijah said and erupted for the second time. He was ready to roll now. He shook and realized that that cold shower had done the trick. He turned on the hot water and rinsed off. He oiled up in the shower and then toweled off, before getting dressed and out the door. Elijah really wasn't in a hurry to get at Joshua, but was excited about getting to know him. He liked the way Joshua looked at him while he told him about his music and his songs and the chance-of-a-lifetime that brought him to NYC with the popular rap group that liked his beats and really put him on. Though they didn't hang out anymore, the royalties for their group and solo projects made him pretty comfortable in the big city.

But Joshua and Elijah didn't talk about that.

They talked about music from Nina Simone and Nancy Wilson. They talked about their first concerts and their best. They talked about places they had traveled—Elijah, just the USA and 3 islands and London; Joshua, not much of America, but London, too, along with most of Italy, some of Japan and Antigua, St. Bart's, Curacao and Brazil.

They laughed when they realized that they were both at the Natalie Cole show at Radio City Music Hall last year. Joshua was there because he loved her new offerings of classic songs that he grew up listening to with his Granddad. Elijah was there because his mom would sit in the kitchen cooking on Saturdays, singing old Natalie R&B at the top of her lungs. Elijah would do his homework at the kitchen table, just so he could hear his Momma singing "I Can't Say No," "I'm Catching Hell" and "Our Love." They made plans to introduce each other to the Natalie that they knew and Elijah remembered that as he grabbed his "Natalie Live" cds, hoping that he had a chance to put it on after dinner.

Elijah put on a bronze T-shirt with "BLACK BOY" in black letters on it that he got from this cool t-shirt company online. He rocked some jeans and a funky pair of boots he got from Eighth Street and he was on his way. He was so excited about seeing Joshua again that it wasn't until the cool air of the evening hit him that he realized that he didn't have on a jacket. He grabbed his leather favorite from the hook inside the front door and headed down the block.

"TWO DOZEN ROSES FOR $8."

Elijah still never understood how they could do that in NYC, but they did. So, he stopped.

"Is it too much?" he asked himself. "I don't want to come off too corny or punked out, but I think Joshua would like them, and the gesture. Better to err on the side of action than thought."

Elijah swallowed his fear about making the wrong step and went with his heart. For $8, he got these apricot and brown hybrids that looked like nothing he'd ever seen before. He hoped that their uniqueness made the move less hokey. He hit the train and was in Brooklyn in no time. Almost too early, as he checked his watch and realized he had some time. He strolled down Fulton Street and stopped in Courtney Washington's shop and then 4West. He loved this block and killed time talking to his favorite vendors in the Collective. He even saw this really cool shirt that he was going to grab, but realized he didn't want to walk into Joshua's with flowers and carrying a bag. But they held it for him. He was a regular and very supportive of the stylish designers who consigned their stuff in the eclectic shop.

Elijah walked back into the evening air and realized he had about 15 minutes to take what would be a 7-minute walk to Joshua's, so he just strolled. He just took in the night air and the surroundings. He looked around and wished he had considered Brooklyn when he went looking for a spot. But he was happy where he was and loved having a neighborhood to come to get away. Ten minutes later, he looked up and he was at Joshua's door.

"Five minutes?", he mumbled. "Should I wait five minutes? Will I look too pressed? Should I do the block one more time?" Elijah was driving himself crazy, so he just took the first step and the next thing he knew, he had climbed all 12 of them. "Just ring the bell and smile," he told himself. So he did. He rang the doorbell.

⌘

Joshua jumped. "Oh my God, he's on time," he said to himself as he checked around and realized that he was about to have a man in his home for the first time, ever. It had been 3 years since he bought this spot and besides Carlton and his partner Donovan, and one of his employees, who came by to take some notes for a presentation. Oh, yes, and that director, who stayed there when they met, because Joshua insisted, and refused to waste 3 rooms and let Bille, who had traveled in from LA, endure the cost and calamity of NY hotels and traffic. Romantically, no man had ever entered this place. Okay, there's the truth.

NO ROMANTIC OR SEXUAL INTERESTS HAVE EVER ENTERED THIS DOOR, he thought.

"Breathe," he said to himself aloud. He turned the stove down to simmer. He wiped his hands on with some sanitizer and then some lotion, so he didn't smell like sanitizer, and then he approached the door.

"Lord, I'm not asking for a lot; just a nice evening, some good conversation and maybe, just maybe, a new friend. That's all."

Joshua opened the door and almost sighed when he saw Eli again. He was more handsome than he remembered. But that smile, have mercy, that smile, almost made Joshua hug him. He extended his hand instead. It was Eli who offered the hug. Joshua sighed as he hugged him with a sincerity that was so familiar, he almost said WELCOME HOME.

Instead, he offered, "Welcome to My Home."

Elijah couldn't believe how good Joshua felt in his arms. He didn't coo or curl into him, but he didn't try to dap him like some dudes do to put you at bay. Joshua leaned into him and reciprocated the gesture, fully. Their embrace seemed like it lasted for an hour, but the hug was short, just sweet. Elijah offered Joshua his "thank you for dinner/corny" roses with a smile and a shrug, that he hoped said what his mouth was afraid to utter—"I am glad to be here, now, with you." Josh took them, smelled them and then noticed the color.

"Wow. I hope you didn't go all out for these. Never seen this color before. Is that brown AND peach? That's pretty wild." Elijah walked into Joshua's brownstone and was floored by the reason Josh had found his flowers so intriguing. Natural woods and shades of brown, orange and yes, apricot, filled the main floor.

"Man, this place is ridiculous. African art and great photos and those album covers displayed like that! I have never seen a place so tight and well put together. This is hot, man."

"Thanks," Joshua said as he showed him around and he was so proud of the wooden, handcrafted frames that he had specially built for his album covers and touched that Elijah noticed them first. "It took me almost a year to get this place together, but it feels like home."

After the tour, Joshua offered, "Can I get you something to drink, Elijah."

Elijah looked at him and smiled wryly, as Joshua corrected himself "I'm sorry, Eli? I have a little of everything. Would you like some water or a glass of something stronger or anything in between?"

Elijah considered and said, "Whatever will go nice with dinner. Surprise me." He realized he had winked and smiled before he could stop himself. Josh looked so cute. He had on this hand painted white shirt that had these cool blue, brown and bronze designs in it and some jeans. "Hmmm, I'm glad he remembered," Elijah said as he noticed that Joshua was wearing a different, but as sexy, pair of sandals on his feet.

"So," as Joshua came back with a glass of red wine, and sat down, Eli said, "cool shirt. Where did you get that? Very funky." My friend hand paints shirts and sell them from his website. I will have to give you the site information. He's actually an author of this really cool book that I bought and we met at a signing and been good friends since." Elijah looked over at a hardback copy of **UNCLUTTER: CLEANSE YOUR SPIRIT AND CLAIM YOUR STUFF** and flipped through some of the pages and inquired, "this is cool. Is it a good book?" Joshua said, "Why don't you take it, read it and tell me what you think. It will give us something else to talk about on a later date....I mean, at a later date....I mean time...."

Joshua couldn't believe his stumble and Elijah had to laugh because he just knew he would do it first.

"It's cool. On another date, at another date, but maybe around the same time. How's that?" Eli reached over and touched Joshua's hand and he could feel him shaking. He didn't know if he should say something, but Joshua's eyes begged him not to, so Eli just held them tighter.

"Something smells crazy good, man. Let me find out you can cook like my Mississippi Momma."

Joshua smiled, "Hey, I wouldn't dare be that bold, but I'm definitely going to put a hurtin' on you tonight," and with that, he got up to check on the food and only halfway, realized the sexual innuendo of his statement. But he had said it and at least with this meal, he meant it. Joshua started to look back but he was afraid he would catch Eli looking at him.

"I shouldn't have worn these jeans. Why did I even let Carlton talk me into buying them? They are just too tight. I wonder if he thinks they are too tight?" Joshua wondered as he turned the corner to enter the kitchen.

"Damn, those jeans are tight, and so is the a.." Elijah shook his head and sipped his wine. "Focus, man!"

Elijah looked around the house and loved Joshua's style. Tasteful and not too showy. Successful, without saying LOOK AT ME! He went to the mantle of the fireplace and found Joshua there with 2 proud peacocks that had to be his parents. They were hugged up on him in a college graduation photo so close that he's almost invisible between them. There he is with (Carlton) his best friend who is identified by the silly "BEST FRIENDS" t-shirts and "rabbit ears" they are making behind each other's heads. There is also a photo of Joshua himself. Must have come from a photo session or something, but Elijah could instantly see why Joshua would keep the photo, even though he's the subject of it. It wasn't vanity. It was the look in his eyes. Joshua is looking outward and is so thoughtful, so at peace, but searching, that the picture just draws you into him, wanting to know what is on his mind. His soul was on display.

"So, you like that photo," Joshua asked as he came into the living room and found Elijah still holding the framed print that would become the cover of NV Magazine's Annual

FORCES TO BE RECKONED!

25 YOUNG BUSINESS OWNERS
ON THE RISE IN AMERICA

that featured

"JOSHUA KNIGHT: SHINING ARMOR, WINNING STYLE"

as the title for the story.

Joshua was very proud of the story, but always searched that photo to see if IT could tell him what he wasn't telling himself: "WHAT IS MISSING IN MY LIFE?"

Looking at the way Elijah looked at him in the picture and then, there, in his own living room, Joshua could tell that he could see it.

"You look like you have a story to tell in this picture. Like you are just waiting for someone to ask you the right question and you could take it from there."

Eli had hit it on the head. Joshua was waiting for someone to ask him the right question. The rest, he surmised, would take care of itself.

"Very observant, Mr. Monroe. Singer, producer and psychic, I see. Odd combo. So I guess that makes you CLEO MAXWELL or some crazy name like that."

"Man, that's crazy that you picked that name, because my middle name is, and PLEASE DON'T LAUGH, Cleophus. I know, it's just country, but that's where I'm from and it's my granddaddy's name. My momma had to carry on his name. I got the privilege."

Joshua didn't laugh. He smiled.

He wore the middle name "Arrington" for the exact same reason. His grandfather. He smiled and shared that fact with Elijah, who wanted to hope that it was a sign, but kept that to himself. They just stared at each other.

Joshua started to turn his head, but Elijah's voice stopped him. "So, Josh. I brought something that I wanted to let you listen to, if we have the time."

"Great," Joshua said, thinking and even hoping that Elijah had brought some of his own music to share and give him more insight into The Man he had come to know very little, yet so much at the same time.

"Now, it's not my stuff. I'm not ready to see what look on your face while you listen to me sing. You know that 'it's cool, but I don't know if it's my thing' look'?"

They laughed because Joshua had always been told that his facial expressions were dangerous if he didn't watch them.

"Then what, My Good Man, have you brought to share with the class?" Joshua asked, trying to lighten up the tension in the room that was part mystery, part memory, part moment and part *"men who are feeling each other, but don't know how or when to say it."*

Elijah reached into his inner jacket pocket and pulled out 2 cds that he had burned for Joshua.

"As promised," Elijah said with a sly smile on his face. "Where is your cd player? Or in this place, your entertainment center or media system or wherever you play music?"

Elijah wasn't wrong. Joshua opened this handmade wooden 7-foot tall cabinet, which included every electronic device you could find for music, movies and probably even for receiving a signal from Deep Space 9.

"Let me help you," Joshua offered, but Elijah took his both hands into him and said, "No sir, let me handle this part. You go check on dinner while I figure out this recording studio you call an entertainment system….Go 'head on…A brotha's got this…"

Eli shooed him away and when Josh didn't go immediately, Eli turned him and SMACK, right to the butt.

"Okay, okay, dag!" Joshua played along, but almost collapsed when that huge hand hit his backside.

"I'm going," he said as he hurried away, just so he could breathe again.

Eli figured it out pretty quickly and realized that he wasn't as obsolete as he had thought.

"LADIES AND GENTLEMEN. LIVE AT THE UNIVERSAL AMPHITHEATRE, NATALIE COLE" the announcer said as the music for Natalie Cole's #1 hit "Sophisticated Lady" started to play.

"What is this?" Joshua asked, forgetting parts of their enchanting evening's plans.

"I told you I was gonna hook you up with THE REAL NATALIE COLE, man! This is her live joint, from 1978, man. She was on fire, man. I mean I didn't really understand why they kept talkin' about her and Aretha in the same breath until I got this album. Man, she was HOT!"

Joshua said, "Just let it play through dinner. It will be nice background music."

Elijah thought that would cool, because he wouldn't have to worry about googly eyes if they were listening to Natalie sing "This Will Be." Maybe they could have a moment and smile, but nothing too gushy.

Elijah hated it when cats tried to play him off as the hick country boy just because he had some manners and some style to him. Anyway, he thought "good choice" to himself, as Natalie's band grooved through "Lady" and she sauntered into her version of "Que Sera Sera," that jammed so hard that Josh came out of the kitchen and said, "the washroom is right there. Dinner's ready…oh, My God. This is Natalie Cole? I never knew she had that voice in her," Joshua said, in genuine shock, as Natalie wailed through the transition of the song, and took it through the roof!

"You have to make me a copy of this, please!" Joshua commanded sweetly.

Eli smiled and said, "This *IS* yours."

As Elijah passed the kitchen to wash his hands, he looked in and saw Joshua smiling and checking on everything. Their eyes met.

"Thank you again, Joshua, for having me over. This was an unexpected, but much appreciated surprise." Elijah leaned on the wall at the entrance of the kitchen. He looked at Joshua like he could do this every Sunday for the rest of his life. Joshua felt it. Joshua felt something.

"It's my pleasure Eli. And if you are going to be insistent about 'Eli' from me, then it's Josh for you, Mr. Monroe. Now wash your hands before dinner gets less than perfect."

As Eli turned, Joshua swatted him on his high, thick black man's rump, so that they would be no questions that WE are men, not **YOU THE MAN!** Plus, Eli's butt was just juicy and Joshua's wanted to return the gesture. Elijah looked at him, squared-eyed and smiled. He stepped to him so quickly that Joshua wasn't sure what his next move would be. To his surprise, Elijah C. Monroe got within an inch of his nose and whispered "Don't let you hands write a check that your hips can't cash," and he winked and left. His warm, caramel-colored eyes danced right there in front of Josh, putting on their own show of intrigue and delight.

He left Joshua standing there, dumbfounded and shaken, in every good way possible. His scent hovered in the air and Joshua could smell it, over and above the greens, roasted chicken, wild rice and coconut cake from scratch he had been preparing all day. He could smell Eli in the air, and hoped that his scent lingered long after the dinner was consumed.

As Josh put plates on the table, Eli reappeared, almost magically, directly behind him. "Can I help do anything?" Eli asked, standing and admiring Josh from behind, but keeping his distance.

"No, everything fine's Eli. Just sit down. Dinner's on the table and I don't know about you but a brotha is hungry."

"Amen to that," Elijah said as he pulled out Joshua's chair for him.

"Let me find out that Elijah Cleophus Monroe is a gentleman and a genius," Joshua smiled as he sat down.

"Gentleman, yes," Elijah said, taking Joshua's hand, "but hardly a genius." Joshua didn't hear that last part. He was still lost in the fact that his hand was now lost in Eli's.

"Why is he holding my hand? Why now, at the table? Can't this wait? What is he saying? I can't hear a thing except my heart beating in my ears. What? Huh?"

Joshua almost missed it until he realized that the lowering of his head signaled that Eli was about to say Grace.

"Lord God, we thank you this evening for the good food that has been prepared for the nourishment of our bodies and the strengthening of our spirits. We ask right now, Lord God, that you bless the home in which we receive it, the loving hands which prepared and the appreciative bodies who will partake of it, in Jesus' name. For this blessing and those that will be born out of the fellowship and friendship of tonight, Lord God, we thank you. Amen, Amen and Amen again."

They wanted to speak, but they didn't for two reasons. One, they were eating a sumptuous meal and we don't talk when the food is good. The other reason was because they were each spellbound in their own way. They smiled a lot. They acknowledged each other—Eli by continuously complimenting the food; Josh by commenting on each song on the cd. The silent was broken when Natalie went into "Mr. Melody" and its obvious jazz overtones surprised Josh. "Wow, she was doing jazz way back in the 70s, in the middle of all this R&B. That's hot. She really was ahead of her time. Thanks for this cd, Eli. You have great taste."

"Of course, I do. I'm sitting in an amazing home with great company and sho' nuff good food and I AM THE ONE with the good taste?" Elijah joked. "Man, this is really nice. The home, the night, the company. It's just what I needed." Eli surprised himself because the tone in his voice told on him.

"JUST WHAT I NEEDED" sounded like escape and refuge. He heard himself say it and then he looked to see if Josh heard him.

He had indeed.

"I really understand what you mean. With all this busy-ness and business going down all the time in the big city, I think we forget to stop and connect with people. Cell phones. Email. You could not see a person for months and still be up on every detail of their life. But I like good company and good conversation, but it's so rare."

Joshua was starting to get more comfortable and less constrained with Eli. He could tell that they could really talk about things and tonight, he would just go with the flow of the convo.

"At least you have your best friend here," Eli offered. "I saw the picture and I assume he's nearby."

"Yes, he lives in Harlem. His name is Carlton Bridges. He's a great guy. Fun, talented, crazy as a loon. But he's my ace!"

"That's so cool man," Eli interjected. "I just feel like I'm alone sometimes in the midst of all of this activity. No one knows how to slow down and stroll, cook a meal, have company without running to see what the end will be. I like Sundays, nice and mellow. Go to church and Praise the Good Lord. Come home and prepare a good meal that you have to put your hands in and just sit down. Josh, this is really nice man. I can't tell you how…."

He stopped. He really couldn't find the words and Eli was almost afraid to search for them aloud, concerned that what he was sculpting in his heart might be displayed before it was finished. He just smiled and the sparkle in his eyes met Josh's new glow and the room lit up.

"WHAT!? WELL ALRIGHT!" Natalie Cole saved them both. As she went into this funky romp of a song called "Party Lights," the groove was so hard that they were brought back to earth.

"Wait?! This is…"

"Yes indeed. Man, one day I have to tell you about this song. It sounds just like a groove from church. This is the joint that made me fall in love with the album," Eli said, as he began to play the "drums" along with the song. He was grooving, arms flailing all around, like he was onstage, behind the skins, tearing it up.

Joshua smiled. His smile and the something in it that made people stop, made Eli stop.

"Oh, man. My bad. I got caught up. I always do with this song. The groove is cold. Wait 'til you hear some of the other stuff on here."

Eli really wanted to know Josh now and asked, "So what would you say is your favorite album of all time?" The tone in his voice was open—20 Questions Meets

Blind Date—and he really wanted to just talk. Dinner was great and it just wasn't time for cake yet. They got their glasses and moved to the couch, a little stuffed, but happy.

"Hmmm," Josh began. "I listen to so much older stuff because of my Granddad's influence, but I like some contemporary stuff, too. But favorite of all time? Wow." As he contemplated, Eli just stared at him and gave him the room to think. Josh noticed and took it in and held that feeling. He was always expected to have the right answer, right now, so this breathing room was a lovely thing.

"I would say that the cd that I go to the most, which must be some kind of commentary on my love for it, is probably…"

Eli moved closer, like Josh was about to reveal the MegaLotto numbers or something. This answer held for him a mystery about Josh. A truth and a new level of him would come out with the title that was about to drip from his lips.

"I think we are just both old spirits, because I would really have to say that it's…."

Eli shifted in his seat. "Please don't pick something stupid or ultra-gay like some house joint that some guys absurdly call classics. This is important, baby…Think…Come on, say something…Brilliant." All of that was running through Eli's thoughts. This was really an important moment in their connection. Eli knew that he could be a musical elitist and he wasn't ashamed to say it. So, this moment could shape or sour the entire night. "SAY SOMETHING WONDERFUL," He tried to beam into Josh's head. It must have worked.

"Innervisions by Stevie Wonder. Everything on it is perfect man. ALL IN LOVE IS FAIR. LIVING FOR THE CITY. HIGHER GROUND. JESUS CHILDREN OF AMERICA. Just a perfect album, beginning to end. That stays in my car when I drive and I have another copy for my bedroom, so I know that it must be my favorite, because when I go there, I'm gone. I can listen to it loud and all day. So, is that okay with you Mr. Monroe. Do I get the big prize?"

"It's alright with me, Mr. Knight." Eli smiled and stood up. He couldn't believe he was about to do this, but the intro from Natalie behind the conversation told him what she was about to sing and he wasn't going to let this moment pass. He extended his hand to Josh, who was almost aghast because he could not believe that this man was about to ask him to dance, but there was his hand.

"I would hate to waste this moment. This is too perfect to not acknowledge," as Natalie chimed in with "Inseparable."

It enveloped the room and Josh didn't really know what to do, so he just allowed himself to be led. Eli pulled him to his chest and just let the song sing and they swayed. Josh put his head on Eli's shoulders and just drifted away. Safe, in these arms and this moment, he just let himself sway. As Natalie talked about him bringing out the woman in me, Josh almost moved, because he didn't want Eli to think he was about to become some housewife, happy she got a good man. But he didn't. He just stayed right there as she talked about flowers and trees and words and melodies of love. He stayed right there and felt Eli's chest rise and fall with breath and promise. He stayed right there and inhaled the scent of Elijah Monroe that was so intoxicating that he thought he would just allow himself to be free. If they left this moment and made their way upstairs and kissed and got naked and made passionate love and then showered and then slept and then rose in the morning, to guiltless smiles and afterglow, Joshua Knight would be just fine with that…in theory. But in truth, this moment scared him even more.

"It's so wonderful to know you'll always be around."

The song ended but the dance didn't. Neither knew how to break it. The next song shifted the mood for them, some rousing blue thing that she went into, so they just stood there. There was no sitting down and going back into the conversation.

"Dessert, maybe?" Josh offered, worried that if he didn't say something, he'd make the first move and he didn't want to look desperate. But he really did want to kiss those lips. Eli must have read his mind, because at that same moment, he bit his lips and moistened them, in preparation.

"Mmmm, that sounds great," he said and Josh didn't know if he meant the dessert or the thought in his head.

"Thank you for that," Josh said as he stopped and took Eli's face in his hands. "I don't know how to tell you how much I really appreciated that."

He kissed Eli.

He couldn't help or stop himself. Before he knew it, his strong jaw was in his hands and so was the next move. Eli was the one who got to be shocked this time, but pleasantly so. He kept his eyes open until he was clear that Josh intended to finish this moment.

Their lips met.

Joshua was not going to offer tongue, because that was just too sexual for the moment. He just wanted to kiss him to say 'I am feeling you. I like you. I want to know you, but not biblically just yet. I want to take my time, but I don't want to be coy, just careful.'

It didn't translate soon enough, because before he knew it Eli's massively thick tongue was in his mouth, sucking his bottom lip and taking his breath. Josh could feel Eli's hands on his waist and prayed that they didn't go further down. That would seal the deal and he really didn't want to move that fast, but....

Eli could feel the heat and the tension of the moment. He really meant it when he said SLOWLY! But Josh had started it and Eli was always one to face a challenge. But his challenge to himself was to make this one matter. "Don't palm his butt. Don't palm his butt." That was Eli's mantra to himself during the kiss that made him high and almost hard. When he felt too much motion in the ocean, he had to stop this. Not the evening. Not the feeling, but the moment had to slow down.

"This is not what we want. I know it. I know we have something more than just this moment. I can't blow this." Eli thought to himself as he moved his hands from Josh's waist and up his back and he pulled back.

"How about that dessert?" Eli asked, bringing Josh back to Earth and to the middle of the room where he had initiated a kiss and started something he really wasn't sure he was ready to finish.

"I'm sorry, Eli. I'm not usually that direct. It's...I just wanted you to...I am not normally....I...this is...we were...Natalie," Josh was speechless. He just stopped.

Eli completed the speech for him, "I know. Me too. Let's have some cake." Eli took Josh by the hand and back to the table.

He asked "Where are the dessert plates, cuz I know you have some." He was right. There on the counter were two plates, already waiting to be put to good use.

"Never mind, Ba….I found them, Josh." Eli stumbled through that and prayed that Josh didn't hear him almost say "Baby."

He heard him.

"Oh my God, he almost called me baby." Josh thought it was sweet and maybe a bit fast, but we aren't lesbians, so I don't have to worry about him moving in tonight, Josh laughed to himself. He looked around the room and thought that somehow colors were brighter, the music seemed clearer and was now some jazz odyssey of flutes and strings and guitars and perfect. Josh was ready for whatever happened, he told himself. He was ready for Eli to take him in his arms and carry him upstairs. He was ready for dessert.

"Dessert is served," Eli said and as returned to the room with a towel over his forearm, acting very much the waiter.

"Thank you kind sir," Josh played along. Standing tall, erect and delectable, the cake was three layers of coconut, butter cream and delight. It looked too good to eat. That didn't stop them.

They devoured it, probably as a gesture to consume the heat that was in each of them. Or maybe it was because they were both hungry. Hungry, indeed.

CHAPTER 7: THE CONFIDANTE

"Where, Tell Me, Where Do We Go From Here?"

"Wait. What do you mean that's it? You two didn't?"

Carlton squawked as his single finger on one hand and circular entrance on the other mimicked a 7th grader's display of sex.

"No we didn't Carlton. Man, I think he likes me, but maybe the kiss was too forward. I was ready, too. Oooo, I was ready. But after the dessert, it seemed like the heat was gone. No, it wasn't. It seemed like he made himself leave, like he had to, out of obligation. I mean we never talked about a lover or anything like that. Maybe he's with somebody."

"Man, Josh. You are doing it again. If you don't have all of the answers, you start providing them yourself,"

Carlton said, getting a little miffed that Josh was about to go into JOSHSPEED again.

"Slow down. Now, think about it. If he had a lover, how would we have available on a Sunday night, with no notice, for dinner? If he had a lover, would he have let you walk him home (and I am still tripping of that li'l high school gesture)? If he had a lover, would he be at home making you a cd? Come on, it just doesn't seem likely."

Joshua considered what Carlton was saying and breathed a little and then offered, as a retort, "Maybe he's out of town. Maybe they are long distance. Maybe he just didn't like the kiss."

Carlton was trippin'. It was 9:42 on a Monday morning, when Joshua Arrington Knight and KNIGHT IN SHINING ARMOR should be in full swing. With the new Coke account, they are probably buzzing like crazy this morning and NOW his normally *too* put together friend is coming apart at the seams. It was kind of cute. Just kind of cute. But it was also alarming, because he had never seen him like this.

"BabyBubba, breathe. Calm down man. Let it do what it do, baby," Carlton said, mocking Jamie-Foxx-as-Ray-Charles.

"Brownskin, I don't know what to do. I have never felt like this. I thought that after dessert, we'd talk some, kiss again and then, the dance would begin and we'd have to figure out how we discussed or didn't discuss going upstairs. But we ate dessert really slow and I think he started to feed me, but stopped himself. Then, he took my hand and said 'I think I need to be going. I have an early morning and I'm sure you do, too, with your new account. I don't want to overstay my welcome, so I think I should say good night while the night is still amazing.' What the hell is that?"

"It is what it is, man!" Carlton sounded flustered with Joshua and remembered his friend from before Gregory and how nervous he could get and how sweet it was, until he got too detailed and started to pick it apart.

"He said that the evening was amazing. He didn't want to overstay, which means he didn't want to finish it all in one night and you said that he was still looking back at you as he walked down the street, right?"

"That's true. We smiled and locked eyes and he walked backwards for two blocks, until he had to turn the corner. Okay, I'm tripping," Josh realized, but still offered "but who refuses sex in the city, Carlton?" Josh laughed at himself and the play on words.

"Who offered sex in the city? You act like your dessert and the kiss instantly means he gets the drawz. Maybe Mr. Country Gentleman is just that. I mean come on, flowers, a cd AND he was on time. Man, with most NY cats, that would have been seen as corny and he would have been written off as 'not my speed,' but he is just your speed and you forgot how you drive, that's all. Take your time, do it right. You can do it baby, do it BabyBubba," Carlton started singing his SOS, hoping it would make Josh lighten the hell up. It did.

"Okay, okay. Let me get on with my day. You would think I never kissed a boy before," Joshua offered, sounding as silly as he felt. "Thanks Brownskin. You are a rock! See you later."

Josh knew that he would. Josh and Carlton had a standing "check-in" dinner every Monday, which is partly why Carlton couldn't believe they were having this conversation. They would see each other in a matter of hours. But this was important. He hung up with Carlton just as Tasha stepped into the room.

"Good Morning, Joshua. I hope you finally got to enjoy some of that food from Friday. It was amazing. Your 10:30 is still a go, but I need to reschedule your 12:15. The Coca-Cola mockups will be here by 11:30 and I've contacted Mr. Woodruff about directing the commercials. He's on board. I also have some graphic designer portfolios for you to…"

Tasha's voice trailed off as she looked at Joshua. She couldn't tell what it was but he wasn't all there. There was a glaze over his eyes. There was a glow behind his eyes. Tasha knew Joshua too well.

"What's going on? What's happening? What's this about dear?"

Tasha went into the same Karen impersonation and Joshua realized that his two confidantes both knew exactly how to calm him down and break him up. Since Joshua couldn't have fallen in love, gotten into a solid relationship, moved in together, been betrayed and now become distraught, in 2 days, she knew it wasn't that again. But his eyes were registering that same sense of…lost. Tasha closed the door.

"It's nothing. I'm okay. Just an amazing weekend and now I don't know…."

Joshua thought too much and actually considered Tasha, the woman, the assistant, and thought, I am NOT going to share this much of myself with her. We are close, but come on. That's too much. I don't even know why I'm tripping, so I can't share that with her. Quick, change the subject, he thought. He did, partially.

"Really, just a lot on my mind. Oh, by the way, I almost called you over the weekend, but didn't want to bother you. Who supplied the music Friday? I was listening to it after you guys left."

"Oh, my boyfriend put together some mix tapes. He's a producer and has his own studio. He's very eclectic in his tastes and some of it is way too old for me, but he calls them classics and so I just let him put together something for a nice office function, so I told him no crazy lyrics and not too much hip-hop, just the LL, Ludacris, Common stuff. You liked it? I will have to tell him. But anyway, you're sure you're fine?" She smiled and gave him the double-take and he smiled in return.

"Alright, I'm watching. I will get R&D into the conference for our 10AM."

Joshua panicked.

Just for a minute. Okay, maybe for 3 or 4, he thought that that's why Elijah wasn't in his bed this morning. He doesn't have a lover. He has a GIRL! Oh my GOD! Joshua had never considered that! He was a gentleman. He was always taking the lead. He brought flowers. He's a DL brotha with a girlfriend! Damn, ain't that a…wait?

We talked about our lives at that diner and he said 'I knew that I liked guys in the 6th grade. I never had to experiment or ask. That's something I knew fa sho,'

Joshua remembered their detailed dialogue about growing up Black and Gay. He remembered loving Eli's story about the captain of the basketball team (Patrick Gibson) asking the captain of the football team (Elijah) if they couldn't maybe bring dates and then go off by "ourselves to do a little something, something," which pissed Eli off because the girl Patrick wanted to bring was Eli's friend and he didn't want to see her played like that.

Okay, so he's not married with 3 kids and a boyfriend on the side.

"So why didn't he stay last night? Maybe, just maybe he's not feeling me like that. Maybe he likes the romance part of us, the conversations and the company, but maybe that's all he wants with me."

Joshua was talking to Carlton now. He made his way up to Amy Ruth's, Carlton's favorite spot and since it was his week to pick, there they were. Joshua just walked through the day, through meetings and through the schedule of his life, waiting for dinner with Carlton. Joshua was pissed at himself for being this taken and for being this taken aback.

"Dammit, Brownskin, you KNOW I don't get like this. But I was ready for something last night, after taking the first step to invite him over and I can't believe that we didn't…."

"You didn't what, Joshua?"

Carlton was pissed and his tone told it. He only called him Joshua when he was upset. Otherwise it was 'BabyBubba," a nickname he gave him after Josh tried to do the Robot to Bootsy Collins' 'Bootzilla' jam at a 70s throwdown they went to years ago. "Brownskin" came from India.Arie, as Joshua's tribute to Carlton's always-warm heart and mad creative ways.

"You didn't have sex on a first date? You didn't take the first man that you have ever had in your home to bed with you? You didn't tear up the living room and go for Round Three in the kitchen, on the counter? Joshua Knight, that is not you. The kiss is still a surprise and the biggest step you have ever taken with a brotha, especially since Greg, but probably ever. Now, you are mad that he didn't tap that ass like you were some trick on the Pier? Come on, BabyBubba,"

Carlton had calmed down.

"This is already a pretty big deal for you. But can you at least get to a second date before you trip about second base?"

Josh looked into Carlton's concern and realized that he was driving his friend and himself crazy. Eli had to leave. Otherwise, the night would have been ruined by the awkward aftermath of moving too fast. Joshua felt his own stirring when they danced and the kiss brought up Eli's. Any man that brings flowers and arrives on time isn't about to be a Hit-It-And-Quit-It type of dude and that's what Joshua had been looking for and waiting to arrive. "So now that someone who seems like that is here, why am I tripping?" Joshua excused himself.

"I still look okay," he said to himself in the restaurant's eclectic bathroom with antique mirrors on every wall. Josh had pulled up his shirt and was checking out his 6 packless, but flat stomach. He liked the way his pants hung and the way his suit fit, his bald head look perfectly shaped and not too shiny. He looked good, so why was he having a fit? Maybe because he knew that everything in NYC was throwing itself at Elijah Monroe—male, female, trans—and he wondered "why me?"

Joshua Arrington Knight had stopped looking around in the crowd for so long that he had forgotten what it looked like when someone in the crowd looked back. He was thinking too much, again.

"You were in there tripping, weren't you? You think you don't deserve this cat. I know you, Josh. You described him to every detail and you did it with such eloquence that I could see you wondering with every word. 'Why not younger?' 'Why not more creative?' 'Why Me?' But here's why you, man. You are handsome and funny and smart and faithful and sincere, to a fault, and real and because you love love, man. Any cat that brings flowers is looking for a certain kind of dude and that's definitely you. You probably cut those flowers and put them on display by dinner, didn't you? Man, I know you and you don't need to be moving at somebody else's speed to feel like you are keeping up. If dude wanted some ass, he would have made a move, but you ever consider that maybe he chilled because he wants to be able to come back again? Maybe he's taking his time and trying to get to know you? Maybe, just maybe, he's trying to respect you? I know, cats hit it and then date, but he's a country boy and maybe he was raised a certain way, like you. Wait for Date Number Three before you start looking for faults, aiight?...Dayum!"

Carlton looked at Josh and laughed. Josh was still looking a little wound up but he was breathing.

"Can we eat now? Man, you know I'm feenin' for some greens and mac from here. Now shut up and let a brotha have some grub, please. Plus, I have to catch you up on Paris. Man, I could live there."

Carlton told Josh about jazz spots and poetry, artists on the streets and in the clubs, just doing their thing. He spoke about seeing every kind of brown and yellow and beige and caramel, just together. Carlton wasn't much of a romantic, like that, but since his Mom died, leaving him and his sister adult orphans, he considered what to do next. He hadn't made too many major moves in his life because he wanted to be there for his parents. They were older and had been good to him and supportive and he couldn't deal with a late-night call saying 'GET HOME' if he was in Europe, playing with his art toys and being free and adventurous. So he stayed. Now, Momma and Dad were together again. Sis was married and happy for the most part, except that her husband worked too much, but they had a nice home, sex was still good, but she just hated that they become Mom and Dad and forget to be Boo and Snook'ums sometimes.

So Carlton was considering a move, but couldn't tell Joshua that now. Not at the beginning of a love affair. Not if Josh was tripping like this at the beginning.

"Just get him married off and then, I'll tell him and I'll go. Paris. I swear, 'I'm coming back to you.'"

They laughed hard.

Carlton and Josh hadn't hung out for 3 weeks and watching the tables around the shift customers twice told you that. They ate and laughed. They laughed and Carlton told every detail of the trip. Pouring Libation for his Mom in the River Seine really wiped Carlton out.

"Man, I was torn up over it. I tried to go back to my hotel, but I could feel Moms all around me. I tried to sit down and she spoke to me. I tried to go for a walk, but the wind kept speaking her name. I tried to hide in this jazz spot and then the dude playing sax dedicated the song to 'anybody who knows what it feels like to lose your Mother.' Man, I was tripping. When I finally got back to the room, Josh, I just got on my knees. You know I don't pray like that, but I don't play like that. I talked to Moms mostly, but every once and a while, God would step into the conversation. I think something major is about to happen. But we'll see. So, did you and Mr. Elijah Mohammad make a second date? Or would this be the third according to Joshua Arrington Knight's Rules Of Engagement?"

"It's Elijah Monroe, Jigga! No, we didn't. I don't want to rush, so I think I should let him make the next move. I did the dinner-at-the-last-minute, spontaneous thing, so I think I need to give him some space, not room, I know what you're thinking. Just space, to do his thing and see what happens. I don't go for the Gay Games, so if I don't heard from him by the weekend, maybe, I'll call. But I have to leave him some room to make some moves, right?"

"Spoken like a true student of Carlton's Critical Thinking and Dating School of Love." Carlton said, glad that Joshua really wasn't as desperate or as despondent as he had sounded. He's just open. That's cool.

Carlton was glad to see him out there again. He really just wanted to see his best friend happy again, after Greg. Carlton still kicks himself for letting Joshua and Greg get as far as they did. Any man who would hit on your best friend, knowing who he is to you, is a dog and Carlton knew it. Greg says he was just drunk and playing around. But the way he tried to step to Carlton that night, with Joshua and Kevin in the next room, trying to connect, was foul.

⌘

"Come on Brownskin," Greg said, using Josh's nickname for his best friend to try to get him to loosen up. "I just never kissed lips like yours before. They all thick and juicy and I just want a kiss. I'm not trying to tap that. Just…."

"Look man, I don't how you and your boy Kev get down but me and Josh don't share our toys like that. These lips don't get kissed by just any cat who wants them. Otherwise, I'd be kissing brothas all day. So back up off of me before I have to use them to resuscitate yo ass after I knock you the hell out!"

"You guys okay," Josh asked from the living room, wondering why the beer and the best friends haven't returned to the conversation.

Carlton never really liked Greg after that. It's like he never fully appreciated Josh. Like he never realized how much he had with him, in him, and from him. Carlton even had to check himself on whether he was jealous and wanting Joshua for himself. He stayed away for 2 weeks, when Greg and Josh were first getting to know each other and getting serious. Joshua noticed. They talked.

Carlton realized that he and Josh were destined, like lovers, to be best friends. They know each other. They feel each other. They love each other. They support each other. They were never meant to sleep with each other. That was fine. But Carlton was protective of Josh when it came to guys, but he wasn't too tight about it. He simply watched.

⌘

"So, how are things with Donovan? I know you are keeping him at bay. You're not feeling him, are you?" Josh asked, feeling that Carlton was a little skiddish about Donovan and Carlton is never skiddish.

"No, it's definitely not that, man. It's like I said. I feel like something big is getting ready to happen and I don't know if I want to be tied down if it jumps off and it's something that makes me move or keeps me on the go. You know I don't like to be in it if I ain't in it. Not trying to be in a drive-by relationship."

"True," Josh paused.

"What do you mean 'if you have to move?' Is there something you are not telling me?"

"No man, just being open," Carlton said. "I don't know where I am going to end up in the next few months. Talking about a few projects with this major publishing house and maybe I'm just being independent for control's sake and not for authentic voices' sake. Penguin and Gotham have both been riding me hard, saying I can do whatever I want. They got the first 2 books and think I'm something that they are both lacking. Man, just being open. I will let you know if anything changed. You know that."

Joshua felt ease.

"So, what kind of stuff are you thinking about doing? That book about 'America's Chocolate Cities' (heavily populated Black cities and towns) or the one about Churches, Resurrected, after the church burnings? Both were cool topics, man. Very today, very focused and they would be crazy visual, like coffee table books."

"I thought about both AND a few other things. Workin' out in my head. I will run them by you when I sketch them out better. You know I respect your opine."

"Anytime. I know that if you go that publishing route, it's going to be because you think it's the best way to get it out there, so handle your business and…."

Joshua's cell rings.

They have a pact to normally turn their phones off for their dinner. Carlton leaves his on now, because he wants to reach his Sis if she calls, which has been much more frequently.

Josh just forgot, in his frazzled state.

"Oh Shit!" Josh never cusses. He wasn't really sure what to do. He looked at his phone and there it was.

*** *ELIJAH MONROE CALLING****

After the late night Saturday call, Josh stopped to put all of Eli's information into his phone. But he hadn't called since, which was only yesterday, so he never saw it on his phone. Right there. Plain view. Eli was calling and Carlton was looking at him.

"Answer it. See what he wants man…. Breathe. Damn, you are tripping. Breathe and…."

Carlton grabs the phone and answers it.

"Elijah, What's going on, man? This is Josh's best friend, Carlton. He's just in the bathroom and I didn't want him to miss you. He was telling about you and so I know that he wouldn't want to miss your call."

Joshua was shocked, and happy. Carlton really did want the best for him.

"Carlton? Hey man. I saw that crazy BEST FRIENDS picture the two of you took. Nice to meet you, kind of. Hopefully, we'll meet at some point, if I play my cards right. Just tell him to…."

"No, here he comes. He wasn't far. We're at Amy Ruth's, doing the best friend thing. Now, I guess I will let you do the Elijah thing."

Joshua covered the phone.

"Man, this is stupid. He's just a really nice dude I met and I'm taking my time to get to know him and I can't be acting like…."

"Ah, he's on the phone, man. Talk!"

"Aren't you full of surprises? Hello Eli. How are you doing?" Josh said, as he adjusted himself in the seat, like Eli had a camera somewhere on him and could witness his frantic state.

"Sorry to disturb your dinner. I thought I was gonna get your machine. Anyway, won't stay on long. I just got tickets to see…ready for this…Nancy Wilson at the Lincoln Center. It's her final tour. She's retiring from live performing and I couldn't let this chance pass me by. The tickets just came my way this morning. The show is sold out. Of course the first person I thought about was you. I hope I'm not crowding you, but I would love it if you would go, man. I know you love Nancy and you know I think she's the truth. So, all you gotta do is say yes, and I will get off of your phone and let you get back to Carlton and dinner."

You could hear Eli smiling through the phone.

"Yes, of course. When is it?" Josh asked, looking at Carlton with the assurance that he'd get details in a minute.

"Saturday night! Can you believe it? This is crazy. But I'm excited. So I will call you with details later, cool? Tell Carlton I'm sorry for breaking up the best friends' dinner flow, but I will bring him a T-shirt or something. Talk to you soon, Josh. Peace."

Click. The red button had been engaged again.

"So, he wanted to invite me to Nancy Wilson's Farewell Tour. She's retiring from live performing and she's in NYC on Saturday. That was really cool." Joshua tried to be flip and light about it but he was about to bust open and this IS Carlton.

"Man, please. You go all goo-goo about this dude and NOW he calls with tickets to see YOUR FAVORITE SINGER, on her farewell tour and you want to act brand new!? BabyBubba, you are talking to Carlton here. This is great. He's definitely coming correct. I just might like this dude."

Carlton really did like his style. He spoke even when surprised by Carlton's answering the phone. He was nice and observant. He was quick, knowing they were at dinner.

"Me likes," Carlton smiled at Josh. "Well, you wanted him to make the next move. Checkmate. He knocked it out of the park. Nancy Wilson. Saturday night. The Lincoln Center. That's gangsta."

Joshua couldn't hear him. He saw Carlton's mouth moving but all he could think of was Nancy Wilson and Elijah Monroe, at the same time, in the same building. It was almost too much for him to consider. He must have been so busy with the new campaign set-up that he hadn't heard about Ms. Wilson stepping down from the stage. But Eli did and thought of him first.

"That is so cool," Josh said, in a middle of something Carlton was saying for which 'That is so cool,' was neither the answer nor appropriate.

"Man, you haven't heard a word I said, have you?" Carlton said and he was right.

"Okay, you were right. Sorry, I was somewhere between here and work. What did you say?"

Josh lifted his eyes to the ceiling, trying to get some mercy from Carlton and to regain some measure of tact and decorum.

"Come on, Carlton, what did you say?"

"Man, never mind. It really wasn't that important. I just like the way this thing is looking on you. So can you come back down to earth or is it a rap?"

Carlton had never seen this side of Josh. Even with Greg, he never got giddy. Excited. Happy. Full. Yes, to all of the above, but never giddy. Then he tried to catch himself and stop it, like he didn't have permission to be happy, again.

"Josh, don't do it man. Stop all that over-analysis that you do so well. Man, you can be such a Virgo sometimes. Stop picking him and this and the future apart. Come here."

Carlton got stern and he lifted his finger and pointed to the very spot where they sat.

"COME HERE! Be here. Live here. Open yourself up, right here and stop trying to make every guy who ever looks your way have to be so good that he's too good to be true. This dude's name is Elijah. That's all he can ever be. Now, find out who that is."

Carlton was finished with the subject. If Josh was going to let Elijah into his life or even just into his schedule, it was up to Josh. Carlton had had enough to trying to get Josh to forget about Greg. The only fight that they ever had was about Greg. The only time their friendship ever hit a bump was because of Greg. Enough of Greg, he thought.

But that didn't stop Josh was living in the past. If he was going to move, it was up to Joshua and Joshua alone.

"Look, he's not Prince Charming and it's not his job to come to you perfect. So tell him about yourself. Don't make him be a psychic and guess and then punish him for not doing it right."

“Damn, Carlton, are you still upset about Stephon? He was nice. He just wasn’t my speed.”

Joshua could tell that Carlton was still upset that Josh didn’t give his boy a real chance. It was too soon and too new. Stephon was a little too sexy, with his poetry and foot rubs and the like. Josh was afraid he would have only been with him for sex and he couldn’t do that. He needed love. Joshua still almost cried when the next person Carlton introduced Stephon to seemed to get him and now they’ve been together since. Joshua couldn’t attend their Holy Union two years later. It would have hurt too much.

Greg and Kevin are happy and Stephon and Malik or Micah or Mecca or whatever his name is are happy and I’m still….

“You’re right, Carlton,” Joshua said as he seemed to sit up in himself. “I am going to really take my time to get to know Eli and see what he’s about. Even if we don’t work,” he said and then looked at Carlton, who’s left eyebrow went up like Dwayne “The Rock” Johnson’s.

“Okay, no matter what, I will just see what it becomes. Jesus.”

They both laughed but inside they both knew that that was easier said than done for Joshua. When his heart ached, it was a pain not easily repaired. But maybe, just maybe, time and a good love, could heal all wounds.

“I’m going to call him when I get home,” Joshua thought. “No time like the present.”

Just conversation, nothing more.

CHAPTER 8: THE WHIRLWIND

JOSH & ELI

Take Manhattan

SATURDAY
5:30pm

Joshua felt a little uncomfortable with the level of input that Elijah wanted to put into this date AND the lack of participation that Eli would afford him. He wouldn't let Josh do a single thing.

"But I drive, so let me come and pick you up," Josh offered and it was met with "Thank you, Mr. Knight, but this is my special night for you and I want to do things a certain way, if you don't mind. When it's your turn to handle the plans for the event, I will submit," Eli paused, making Josh smile at the play on words. "But I got this Josh. Let me do this for you, for us, for Nancy."

They both laughed because Josh knew that he wasn't going to win, so he just let Eli handle everything.

The great tickets. The sedan that picked them up for the show. The amazing dinner before the show, where Josh was so excited about seeing Nancy Wilson that he could barely eat.

The evening was perfect. As Nancy Wilson returned to the stage for her second encore, she cried and told the audience, "Please know that you will never be far from my heart and you will never know just how glad you have made me, tonight and every night, for the last 60 years."

With that, her band played "How Glad I Am" and Josh got so excited that he grabbed Eli's hand and leaned into him. He forgot that it was only a second date (technically) and that he was normally reserved and tentative. This was Nancy Wilson and that was his favorite song on Earth. He had thought that she would end the night and her dynamic performance without doing it. He would have been happy if she had done that, but hearing it now made him ecstatic. Josh cried as she did her thing as only The Wonder Wilson could. He never let go of Eli's hand. Eli never let go of his. He put his arm around Josh and let him inhale the moment. He spent half of the night watching Josh's eyes dance with every note and every lyric. Eli couldn't believe how handsome. That's not the word. Sexy? No, beautiful. That's it, how beautiful Josh was when he smiled. Eli had seen that look now and wanted to make sure he did his best to bring that look back to him again and again.

As Ms. Wilson bowed and received armfuls of flowers, Josh realized that he was holding Eli's hand. Their eyes met. Josh started to pull away, but Eli wouldn't let him and Josh really didn't want to, so they stayed in the moment. Josh leaned closer and Eli held him tighter.

"You will never have this moment again," Eli whispered to him. "Enjoy every minute of it, Josh." Eli was talking partly about the night and Nancy and the concert, but he also meant their connection, their vibe, their connection without fear.

Josh could tell that he meant it all, so he stayed in Eli's embrace for as long as people applauded and Nancy bowed and flowers flew. Their departure from the theater, their ride home, the rest of the night was a blur and they cherished every minute of it, all in the same lifetime.

They didn't talk much, they smiled awkwardly and a lot, and they found themselves in front of Josh's door at 11:43PM, after fighting traffic. Eli was going to simply walk Josh to his door and say goodbye. Josh was simply going to offer him a nightcap, nothing more.

"Thank you again, Eli, for the most amazing night of my life," Josh beamed. "I can't tell you how great that was."

"Your smile tells it all," Eli offered back. "I am just glad that I could give it to you. I spent half the night watching you watch her and it was nice." Eli wanted to come real but not too mushy and he was floating and didn't want to fly, not too swiftly.

The tension was palpable so Eli prepared to turn and return home. Josh stopped him.

"Would you like to come in for a drink or some coffee, maybe?"

Eli considered and reconsidered again, all in a moment.

"Josh, I really need to be at church in the morning and it's already midnight. But, please let me make it up to you. Let's have lunch tomorrow. I really hate for tonight to end, but I better get home before this thing turns into a pumpkin, man. Thank you for letting me injoy this evening with you."

Eli smiled and moved in to Josh, not sure just how much of a kiss he would plant, but knowing he was going to kiss Josh.

Josh just looked too good, too sexy, too sweet to not taste. Eli took Josh's face into his hands and just looked at him for a moment.

Josh trembled, anticipating. He wasn't really prepared, in his heart, to sleep with Eli but he really liked him and really thought that they could build something special. He also really wanted to be naked with Eli. But he knew he wasn't ready.

He also knew that he wouldn't know how to resist it if Eli pushed up on him the right way. Elijah Monroe was so much the man that Joshua had been waiting for, but the intensity of his feelings for him and about him and them and now and this made everything in Josh freeze up.

What if he hurts me? What if he's not really single? What if I'm not the only guy he's dealing with like this? What if he's...

All of that was flooding through Josh's heart, until Eli kissed him.

The kiss that made Josh's head swim. The kiss that made Josh's feet leave the ground. The kiss that made Josh grab Eli's back. The kiss that made Josh swoon under his breath. The kiss that made Eli lean Josh against his front door, but the lean was really so he didn't "accidentally" palm Josh's butt. The kiss that sealed their affection and their attraction. The kiss heard 'round the whirl. The kiss that took Josh's breath away.

"Are you sure you don't want to come in?" Josh tried to recover and not look needy, but really wanted to let Eli know he was welcomed to stay.

"It's not a matter of if I want to come in," Eli said.

Everything in him wanted to come in, and get in and be in Josh's space all night. But he knew that if he did this before he and Josh were ready, it could ruin them and everything.

"I just really need to be at church tomorrow. Maybe one day you will come with me. Anyway, let me get out of here before you go into negotiations and something tells me you are a great negotiator."

Eli looked like he wanted to stay but was fighting some secret, some thing he couldn't share. He also looked like he wanted to eat Josh alive, as he bit his lip and descended the stairs, shaking his head.

He turned again and said "Good Night, Mr. Joshua Arrington Knight. I look forward to seeing you tomorrow. Our spot? Two o'clock?"

Eli's reference to the diner where they first connected was clear to Josh and he went inside knowing that he would see Eli tomorrow, but just a little shaken by the kiss still and the fact that it didn't automatically move upstairs. As much as he wanted to take his time and get to know Eli and be more than just a sexual object to him, he still, somewhere in his body, wanted Eli to make the move and at least try to get him into bed tonight.

"Why?" he asked himself aloud, "Why would I want him to step to me like that when I know that if he did, I would have stopped him and then been pissed that he did? Come on Josh! Stop it. You asked for a gentleman and you got one. Breathe!"

Josh laughed as he made his way to his bedroom to shower and unwind. The shower became just the opposite for Josh. With warm water and hot thoughts, combined with body scrubs and shower gels that emitted the scents of musk, eucalyptus and peppermint, Josh became more aroused than he was in Eli's presence. Now, with his thoughts of Eli and his own naked body, Joshua came alive. Every fiber and nerve-ending in him seemed to be on fire and he could only smell Eli's singular scent in the air. Josh couldn't believe how heated he was getting in that shower, but he leaned against the wall and let himself feel every shiver and quiver of it. He let himself be sexual with the thoughts of someone new and someone he knew, instead of thoughts of Henry Simmons and a beach in Acapulco. This was a real man and a real kiss and a real connection. And, if only for one night, Joshua Knight was going to let himself feel it, all over his body.

SUNDAY
1:59PM

Josh and Eli actually arrived at the same time. They laughed at the irony. Lunch is great, and so is the conversation. They dined till about 5pm. Josh went to Eli's and listened to music and then they watched "The Color Purple,"—20th plus time for Eli; only the 3rd for Josh, including the time in the theatre and then once more with Carlton on a drunk silly night. Eli is amazed. They kiss. Josh left at exactly 9:30pm, because he had a very big meeting with Coke and he still had some notes to prepare. He hated to leave.

MONDAY
2:16PM

Josh enters his office after a kick-ass meeting with the Coca-Cola execs. It went so well that they increased the marketing budget by 3 million dollars for the year. He is overwhelmed. Not by that, but by the fact that there are congratulatory balloons and a dozen white roses on his desk. The card, when he finally finds it attached to the balloons that read "WELL DONE!" says:

> *"I heard that somebody did a great job today! Just wanted to send my best wishes! I'm throwing out all my Pepsi and buying some Coke stock today!*
>
> *Feeling Good? Eli."*

Josh closed the door to his office and fell against it. He felt the tears coming, but stopped them.

"Whatta Man, Whatta Man, What a Mighty Good Man!" he thought and the phone ringing stopped him from reading the card for the 12th time.

MONDAY
7:14pm

Josh calls Eli to say thank you. He doesn't answer his phone and he doesn't want to call his cell. He leaves a message.

MONDAY
7:18pm

Eli calls Josh immediately after his cell gets the page from his forwarded home phone. He listened to Josh's message twice before calling. He doesn't share that fact. Eli's in the studio, but takes a break for Josh. They talk until 8pm, when the artist reminds Eli that they are on the clock and back from break. Eli reluctantly hangs up, but say "I'll call you when I finish."

TUESDAY
6:43am

Josh went to sleep without hearing from Eli. While brushing his teeth, his phone beeps, announcing a new message.

> "Message received at 2:14am. (ELI'S VOICE) Hey sleepy head. I didn't want to wake you, but I wanted to keep my promise. The session went late. Sorry I didn't get to say goodnight in person. Knowing you, it's 6:45 and you are brushing your teeth. Good Morning. Have a great day. We'll talk soon." Josh almost drops the toothbrush in his hand.

TUESDAY
7:22pm

Josh and Eli call each other at the exact same moment.

"Hang up, that's me on your other line." They laugh and talk while they each make dinner—Eli reheats some Chinese from down the block; Josh just has some soup and a sandwich. They share their mutual love of LAW AND ORDER: SVU and those throwback PBS Oldies concerts. They eat on the phone and realize that their show is about to start.

"Man, it's 9:57," Eli says. "Time is really flying when you are having a great conversation. Talk to you on the other side," Eli says and hits the red button.

TUESDAY
11:01pm

"Man, that was off the hook. When he said 'I am greater than everybody! I am greater than God!' I knew that little girl was going to shoot him. That was one of the best ones yet!"

Eli was really excited about tonight's SVU and Josh loved to hear him when he was passionate. They recapped and said goodnight at almost midnight. They were proving hard on each other's sleep habits, until Josh realized that Eli was only about to go to work.

"I have studio time booked tonight from 1 to 6AM. Some of these singers are real night owls, but I love it, man. Anyway, I will talk to you on the other side. Maybe we can get up sometime this week?"

Eli asked and Josh said "I will call you sometime tomorrow and we can do the calendar thing."

"Good Night Sleepyhead," Eli said, in his sexiest midnight voice.

"Good Night Night Owl," Josh said, making Eli laugh and appreciating that Josh returned the tone, very sexy and come hither. The pause before the red button was hit was audible. They were like schoolboys and couldn't hang up the phone.

Josh finally did it first.

WEDNESDAY
11:19am

"Josh, there is an Eli Monroe on Line 1."

Tasha says, "He tried your private line, but it was busy. Shall I take a message?"

"No, Tasha, I'll be with him in a minute," Josh says as he returns to Carlton to say "Let me call you back. Eli's on Line 1 and I just need to confirm a time with him."

"So I am already being booted off the phone for dude? That's not right! That's not right!?," Carlton says playfully. "I will see you later man. Regular time or you gonna be late because of the project?"

"No," Josh says, "I'll be cool. We are actually right on schedule. So I'll see ya."

"Hello Mr. Monroe. Sorry to keep you holding," Josh says, with a smile in his voice.

"No problem at all, J," Eli responded with his new special nickname initial for Joshua. "The music was hot. That Verve Remixed project was on, playing some Shirley Bassey. So how you doing? Going crazy over there with this new project?"

Eli's question got a 5-minute synopsis of the project, its details and the marketing strategy. Eli loved that Josh was so open to let him into his work.

Josh thought he had gone too far and stopped himself with "Sorry, Eli. I really didn't mean to bore you with those details."

"It's really not a problem. It's cool to meet someone who's about their business and in such a different field. I feel like I could learn something from you and still appreciate your passion."

Eli meant that. He really liked the way Josh broke things down, like Eli was a client, but never being condescending or pompous. He was skilled at what he did and it showed, even in their conversation.

"Anyway, I was thinking that maybe we could have dinner on Friday night," Josh said, thinking that getting to the weekend would be nice without sounding desperate or rushed. He just wanted to be chill and sound like it. Eli didn't have those same concerns.

"So you want me to wait till Friday night to see you again. Lord, Jesus, you gonna kill a brotha."

Eli was kidding, kind of, but really wanted to see Josh, so he said "Friday is fine, J. That's good with me. We finished in the studio last night and I'm good till next week. So Friday it is."

Joshua was a bit taken aback. He didn't want to seem distant or plotting, he just didn't want to come off too needy.

Fridays are good, right? It seems like I want to see you when I got my free time back and it still leaves room for the weekend, if you want to expand the plans. Friday, yes, would be just fine. I would love to see him now, but Friday is cool.

"Well if you want, we can do something sooner."

Joshua covered his own mouth. ***What the who?!*** He couldn't believe he said it, but it was said now. He waited for Eli to say that Friday was fine and that would rescind his offer and things would be cool.

He didn't expect "Cool, what are you doing for lunch?"

WEDNESDAY
1:15pm

Eli shows up bearing Caesar Salads with Grilled Chicken, some hot tea and coffee, and a smile. They ate and conversed about marketing and business and entrepreneurship and community building. Tasha only stopped in twice and smiled, offering some bogus excuse to see Joshua happy.

They really connect on some subjects and have a healthy debate about young hip-hop artists and the flooding of the marketplace with clothes and shoes and not many job opportunities. They agreed to save the debate for another day when Tasha enters at 2:47pm to remind Joshua that he had a 3:00pm with BET News to make comments for their News Briefs segment.

Eli stood and went to extend his hand to Joshua as he left, wanting to be professional in his professional environment. Joshua appreciated the gesture and rewarded it with a kiss to the cheek as he pulled Eli to him and said, sincerely, "Thank you so much for lunch. I probably would have skipped it, worried about this interview if you hadn't done that."

Eli blushed and said "Momma said 'knock 'em out," as he left the office and looked back one last time.

"I'll talk to you on the other side. In-joy the rest of your day, J."

WEDNESDAY
8:12pm

"So how you doing, BabyBubba? You seem really chill these days. Things must really be cool with Eli, huh?"

"They really are, Brownskin. He's a cool brother but like you said 'I'm just gonna let it do what it do.'"

Josh said it, trying to be as cool as Carlton was when he said it. He succeeded. Almost. The lack of presence in his eyes told Carlton that Josh was busy thinking in his head, overcalculating and considering in that mile-a-minute-mind of his. Carlton figured he wouldn't address and just let Joshua stew in it and maybe he would check himself on whatever he was trippin' about.

"Cool, cool. So how's the project coming along? And remind me to tell you about something Donovan said the other day. Anyway, go. The project. Details."

Carlton and Josh did the best friend, check-in dance well. Joshua would take about 20 minutes leading the conversation, hashing about details and the like to Carlton, letting Carlton offer critique and criticism and Joshua really listened. Then, Joshua would listen as Carlton talked about the direction of his next book and the pros and cons of going with a major publishing house vs. staying indie, especially with new bookstores and the various online options.

They talked for hours and ate good food and remembered why they were best friends, all over again. They balance each other like that.

"So if we don't get up out of here we are both going to be exhausted tomorrow and you have an outline to finish, good man."

Josh hustles Carlton off because he really did need to get to bed and they really could talk all night, especially in person. Carlton really wasn't much a phone person. Eli was. Josh knew that Eli would be on his phone before he turned in for the night and he didn't want Carlton to see him get all flustered and excited. He wanted to be home when Eli called, which would probably be around 11pm and it was now just after 10pm. He hopped the train and was in Brooklyn by 10:30pm and walking to his door by 10:45pm, when, ring....

"Hello, Mr. Monroe."

THURSDAY
AM

Big meeting day for final details of Coca-Cola, but Josh couldn't get Eli off his mind. He told him how important the day would be, so they agreed to not talk during the day. Well, Eli agreed not to disturb him and Josh agreed because he would have answered if Eli had called.

Joshua lost all track of time.

THURSDAY
10:11pm

Eli just called to say good night and extend well wishes for tomorrow's big presentation. Josh thought it was really sweet, but he was also caught up in the details of preparation, so he was not really all there. Eli was preparing to say good night. Joshua was prepared to let him go and explain everything later.

There was silence.

Then, Elijah did something that shocked Joshua more than he thought it would.

He said, "Josh, I know that tomorrow is huge for you, because you have some major decisions to make. I will pray for you tonight, seriously. I really wish you well tomorrow, J. Do well, man."

Joshua heard the sincerity and the concern. It took him away when he heard Eli say he would pray. His mother always says that. Every time.

"I'm praying for you baby. I know that things get busy, but I pray for you everyday down there in that city that swallows people and their dreams whole. You keep keeping on," she would say as he said "Thank you Momma. I love you." "I love you too baby,"

she would close and say "and your father loves you, too. You know he's asleep already, God bless him. Night, son."

"Eli?"

"Yes, J."

"Do me a favor?"

"Anything for you."

"Pray with me now. I'm kind of nervous about this meeting. The executives from World Headquarters are flying in for this one, because Coca-Cola is slipping in the marketplace and they are really riding on being able to speak to the young, urban, hip-hop consumer. This campaign is going to be big, and I'm really feeling the weight of it. When you said you would pray, it really made me feel some ease. So if you don't mind, I'd appreciate it."

Joshua couldn't believe he had let Eli into that place. He couldn't believe he had told of his fear and his faith. But it was said and he needed it. He hoped that Eli's faith was more than just words. He hoped that he really could encourage him.

He picked the right man for the job.

"Let us pray, J. Lord God Almighty. Captain of the Battlefield and King of Israel. Lord of Lords and Host of Heaven. Precious King, we come before you tonight as humble as we know how. I ask right now, Good God, in this prayer of intercession, that you bless Joshua and all that he is being called to do in a mighty way. Bless his mind and his movements. Bless his thoughts and his theories. Bless him in the details and in the doing, Lord. Use him tomorrow, Lord, to do this mighty work. You see Lord, he isn't just selling soda to children in the cities, Lord. He's being called to project an image into young minds and hearts. He's being called to speak to a generation. He's being called to help rebuild a kingdom. He's being called to change lives through his company and we know that, in you God, he can do all things. Bless his business and his associates. Bless his clients and his presentation. Show your son favor tonight, Lord, that he might slumber without interruption and that he might rest and be renewed with the rising of the sun.

Bless him, Lord and let him know, through you, that all things are possible when we give it all to you. For this and all blessings, we thank you Lord God. For this and all victories, we thank you Savior God. In your name, we lift you up this day and always, Lord. Amen. Amen. Amen."

"That was," all Josh could get out before he excused himself and left Eli wondering if he had said too much, but feeling like he had really spoken to God.

Eli just waited while he heard water running in the background after Josh abruptly pardoned himself.

Two minutes passed before Josh returned to the phone.

"I'm sorry Eli. I don't know what happened, but thank you so much for that prayer. Wow. (Josh sniffs and Eli understands) I think I can go to sleep now. All the pieces are done and I just need to be ready come morning."

Josh had recomposed himself and was bright again. Maybe even lighter than before, because now he really felt like all he needed to do was rest and do his thing in the morning.

"Thank you for letting me pray with you, J. That's a real personal relationship, us and our God, and I'm honored that you asked me to do that."

Eli wished he could hug Josh right now, because he was full and humbled.

"Man, if I didn't know better, I would swear you were a deacon in an ol' Baptist church or something."

Josh really was overwhelmed at the tone in Eli's voice when he prayed. He clearly had some old church training and it really made the prayer feel like it was delivered with conviction.

"Thank you for reminding me of just how good God is and how much he's already blessed me, Eli. I am going to hit the hay. Talk to you tomorrow? I will let you know how the meeting went. Good Night."

"Good Night Sleepyhead."

"Good Night Night Owl."

FRIDAY
7:16pm

"You sure you are still up for dinner, J? Seems like you had a really long day." Eli was concerned.

Josh didn't call him after the meeting and he was being a little withdrawn. He didn't want to get together out of obligation. Dating is about injoying the company of someone and wanting to take a break, from the world, with them.

"I don't want to impose if you need to unwind and just do you."

Josh really didn't mean to be distant. It's just that his emotions were all over the place since Eli prayed. Not only did the meeting go brilliantly well, but also he mentioned to his Momma that Eli had prayed for him and she shouted on the phone. Not screamed. Not hollered. She shouted like she was in a Baptist church and the unction had fell on her.

She said, "The Lord heard my plea and sent you a strong church man. Praise the Lord."

This was crazy, because Momma was on the Nurses Board at Greater Love Cathedral and caught the shouters, but was rarely among them. She wept and asked Josh for details about Elijah ("good, strong Christian name…he must have a good mother," she declared).

Josh wasn't very forthcoming because he couldn't tell her that they had only been seeing each other for a matter of weeks and they were taking their time. Josh was also distracted because he was worried that Eli might be thinking that he was a bit too sensitive, since he did cry after the prayer. Josh was just all over the place, because he was really feeling Elijah Cleophus Monroe and he didn't know how to handle it.

⌘

He was trying not to act too excited while he rushed home, picked out his outfit, took a shower, stopped again because he couldn't believe how well the meeting went, thanked God, washed his face, called his Mom, replayed the demo of the commercial on his dvd player for the 12th time today, and almost missed Eli's call.

⌘

"No, Eli, I have really been looking forward to just unwinding, but I really don't care what we do. It's the company that matters."

He meant that. He really just wanted to see Eli and that was all. So that's all they did. Eli offered to cook at Josh's and they could just watch a movie or two. Josh was fully prepared to hit the train, but had to acquiesce when Eli mentioned pan-seared salmon, kale and collard greens and a dessert surprise.

Eli arrived by 8:30 with shopping bag in tow and a smile on his face. He walked right past Josh, exclaiming "Just give me 45 minutes in the kitchen and I'm gonna make you smack ya Momma."

Josh asked if he could do anything, got dismissed to the living room, came back, was dismissed again (this time with a kiss), set the table, poured some wine, put on some Liz Wright and still couldn't find anything to do but poke his face into the kitchen.

"Taste this," Eli said as he broke a piece of the salmon off and swirled it around in the mixture of herbs, tomatoes, scallions and seasonings that he prepared. Eli held it to Josh's mouth and said, "I hope it's not too spicy."

It was and it wasn't. At first Josh was prepared for the fire in his mouth, then he realized that it was spicy but not hot. It was amazing.

"You like it? Be honest." Eli searched Josh's eyes, looking for approval.

"Man, that is amazing. That's the best piece of salmon I have ever eaten." Josh wasn't kidding. Eli had put his foot in that fish and if the rest of it was as tasty, there would be a fight for seconds.

Eli rounded the meal out with garlic mashed potatoes and the surprise dessert was his Mother's banana pudding, which she sent him monthly, to keep him from getting homesick.

Josh was led to his seat at the table and Eli served him. The plate looked edible, because Eli had put some kind of spices on the dish itself and his presentation was restaurant quality.

"My Mother raised me to cook, because she didn't ever want me to just be with somebody because I needed a meal."

Eli laughed as he put his own plate down, and took Josh's hand and said Grace.

Two servings each.
3 glasses of wine, apiece.
The Diary of Mad Black Woman.
Claudine
(A sister who had a reason to be mad, but wasn't)
One heaping shared serving of
Mother's Banana Pudding.
Cuddling on the floor.
Playing with fingers, which Eli started, but Josh perfected.
Foot rubs.
One accidental butterfly kiss from Josh to Eli.
Cool night air.
One real kiss from Eli to Josh.
Great company.
They doze off.

SATURDAY
4:19AM

"Oh my God, what time is it, Eli?" Josh said as they looked up and found the TV staring at them.

"Oh man, J. It's after 4! Man, we had too much of everything. I am wiped out. I better get a cab. I'm not about to wait on a train this late. I'd be better off just walking across the Brooklyn Bridge."

Josh wasn't about to let that happen, but couldn't believe he uttered the alternative.

"Eli, why don't you just stay? It's really late and I would be up all night if you took the train and I would go with you if you tried to walk."

"Are you sure? I don't want you to think this was some kind of set-up to stay over."

Eli was being sincere. Josh appreciated it and added, "Of course you didn't. Unless you put something in my wine to knock me out, too. Anyway, let's just put this stuff away in the morning. I am exhausted."

As tired as he was, Josh still knew the impact of this moment. Stay over meant same bed, because he didn't want to insult Eli by offering the guest room.

Eli was prepared to stay there and wouldn't have been insulted, but didn't mind the prospect of waking up with Josh in his arms, or being in his. He hadn't really thought of those dynamics, except by size. But he would deal with that later. Right now, he's spent and ready for bed, but all of those spices are now kickin' in his mouth and he's got no toothbrush.

Josh is well prepared and offers toothbrush, robe, towel, wash cloth, slippers and shaving kit.

"Dang, J. I didn't know I was at the W Hotel. Way to go, baby. I feel like I got hooked up or something. I could use a shower right about now. I'm tired, but I feel grimy after that wine. Man, it's like the temperature dropped 20 degrees or something."

Josh had already moved to increase the heat. The fall vs. winter competition was beginning and tonight, it felt like winter was kicking autumn's leaves!

As they entered Josh's bedroom, Eli was a little overwhelmed at being upstairs, at being in so much space (he didn't see this kind of spot in NYC that often) and at the unknown. Not that he wasn't thinking about getting with Josh almost everyday. But it had only been a few weeks and he swore to take his time and he was really injoying getting to know Josh. But Eli was a man who was virile and very attracted to Josh. He loved seeing Josh's nice legs. The calves were thick and shapely and his feet were just as nice as he remembered that first day in Roadhouse. He didn't want to mess up and do something tonight that might mess up tomorrow, so he would follow Josh's lead. It was his home, so it was only fair. *You step and I will step indeed.* But if Josh acts reserved, Eli would have to release himself in the shower. He hoped for the former.

"So, I heard you say you wanted to shower. Feel free to help yourself. Be careful, it can get really hot, really fast. Everything is pretty apparent, so make yourself at...." Josh stopped himself, but the invite had already been extended.

As he sat on the bed, Eli entered the bathroom, taking his t-shirt off along the way.

"My God," Josh thought, as Eli's brown skin and broad shoulders and flowing locs all converge and made for an image of manhood that made Josh exhale. Eli got comfortable quickly and didn't bother to close the door as he disrobed, with his back turned. What a back indeed. The expanse of his back, with the locs and the big arms all made Josh know that there was going to be quite a vision when Eli's pants were removed.

Eli turned to check himself in the mirror and that's when he realized he had left the door open. He thought he caught Josh checking him out, but when he looked again, Josh was taking off his socks and paying him no attention. Eli closed the door and took off his pants and worried that he couldn't get himself back down to completely flaccid. He wasn't hard, per se, but he was apparent.

"Puppies. Sour milk. Garbage. Come on." Eli said to himself, trying to bring up a thought that would bring him back down. But the thought of Josh on the other side of the door had consumed him, so he hoped that the cold water would bring him some relief.

Eli got into the shower.

Josh took off his pants and t-shirt and considered for a moment if he should put on something because he didn't want his commando status in bed (he just didn't like wasting the feel of good sheets and a warm bed against his skin).

"Maybe some lounge pants will be enough," Josh thought as he heard Eli scream.

"Dammit, ouch."

Josh was in the bathroom before he realized he was nude and standing before a man who had only been seeing for a few weeks and who had never seen him naked.

"You okay?" Josh hoped that his question through the shower door would be answered the same way and Eli would never notice.

He was wrong.

"I'm okay. I just turned on the wrong valve and almost got scolded. But it's fine. I just…" Eli said all of this as he stuck his head out of the shower and then noticed that Josh was standing there, naked and innocent and looking as sexy as he ever thought he could be.

Eli didn't mean to stare, but Josh was sexy. His legs started at his waist and they were solid and strong, thick and sexy, and Eli could tell he had a nice butt, from the front. He was hairless and his nipples were much darker than his own skin, which made for a lickable contrast. Eli kept telling himself to stop staring and stop inspecting Josh, but he had spent so many days wondering what Josh looked like under those stylish clothes and now, almost burned and almost embarrassed, he knew.

Josh almost covered himself, but he thought it would look silly. They are grown men, and plus, he should just leave now and put on some pants, so that Eli would know that he wasn't trying to entice him into some tango they might not have been ready to dance.

Eli eased the tension and caused more by saying "You want to join me. The water's perfect now."

Josh was already naked and Eli and the water and his lips and the wet dreads and the prospect of seeing his body were all too much and before he knew it, Josh was standing in front of Eli, water hitting his back and Eli kissing his lips.

They turned so that they were both getting wet, but Eli stood taller than Josh, so he let him get closer. The kiss was intense, but not aggressive. Eli just wanted to kiss him. His groin gave off a different message, as Josh looked down and noticed that Eli's erection was pressed up against them.

"I'm just....excited to see you. It's not a pistol." Eli smiled and tried to cool the heat in the shower. Josh smiled. He wanted to touch it but that would have sent the wrong message. He didn't want to have a session with Eli or have him or finally hook up. Josh wanted to make love with Eli and he would wait for that, even with this hard-to-refuse offer pressed up against his hungry stomach. They kissed and fondled for what seemed like minutes. Eli took Josh's face into his hands. Josh pulled Eli's nipples and Eli opened his mouth with delight and drank water from the spraying shower. Josh cupped Eli's buoyant behind and Eli sipped water from Josh's collarbone.

"What do you want to happen tonight?" Eli finally asked Josh.

Josh didn't know what to say. He didn't want Eli to think that he didn't want him, because he was almost as horny as Eli. But he also didn't want Eli to think that he just wanted a quickie with him. Josh prayed and hoped he didn't get the Great Shrug Off after offering his heart, but he said it.

"Eli, I really want to just lay naked with you tonight. I know it sounds corny, but I really want you and I want to see where we can go. I don't want you to think it's all about sex because we both know better than that. I think if we can just lay naked tonight and still feel the same heat tomorrow, then we will have something to work with. If we decide that we can't stand the heat, then we still have time to get out of the kitchen. I just don't want to jump in too fast. I have been there and I want this to be special. Cue music and lights."

Josh couldn't believe he had said it but it was what he felt. Eli smiled. It was an audible smile, bordering on a laugh but never quite getting there. Eli agreed.

"Cool. I really do like you man, but I know what you mean. I want to build something and I know sex can make everything crazy. That naked-laying thing sounds hot and if you can deal with my obvious attraction for you knocking on the door of your thigh all night, I would love that."

They kissed again.

They got into Josh's warm bed with the nice sheets and the dance began. Josh thought he was ready for the feeling of Eli's erectness behind him. He wasn't. He turned.

"What's wrong?" Eli asked, concerned and a little taken because he was looking forward to at least getting to feel Josh's round bottom against him.

"Nothing at all," Josh said, trying to make Eli feel immediately appeased. "I just want to hold you. I thought I would keep you on your toes and plus, you're taller. That's too cliché." Josh hoped that his maneuvering worked.

It did, but only to a degree.

With Eli's broad back against him and his locs emitting their Eli-ness, Josh could barely sleep. He wrapped his arm around Eli's chest, which Eli then placed his own arm over. Their legs intertwined and Josh was almost shocked to realize that his hard penis was resting against Eli's cheeks. He hoped that Eli didn't notice. That was a silly thought.

Eli noticed.

Neither of them got much sleep, but they slumbered in peace, in a warm bed and safe arms, they shared their first night together and it was sweet indeed.

The next morning, Eli woke to find Josh already up. He wasn't out of the bed. He wasn't awake. But there was Josh, on his back, beside Eli, already up. Eli wanted to pleasure him awake, but knew that that wasn't the right thing to do, but it was hot to think. He wanted to just hold him, but with temptation that close, Eli thought it would be better just to let him sleep. Eli got out of bed and went to the bathroom to let out one of those morning pisses that can make you lightheaded. He returned after washing and drying his hands to find that Josh had turned on his side. Eli slid in behind him and took his proper turn doing the holding. He wrapped his arms around Josh and spooned right behind him, hoping that he wouldn't get too hard-to-handle in their caress. He put his nose against Josh's nape and let their toes tickle each other. Josh was awake now, but so injoyed the warmth of Eli that they just lay there for another hour, in complete silence.

Finally, Josh said "Good morning" and Eli replied with the same, but delivered directly against Josh's ear and with his massive leg draped over him. Josh almost moaned, but he shivered instead.

Breakfast led to a walk around the neighborhood.

The walk led to 4W, that shop with all of the artisans, selling their wares, that J didn't even know existed.

Then Courtney Washington, to get those pants they had held for Eli, and J picked up a few pairs of really nice linen pants that were on sale and definitely his style.

Then to the Nubian Heritage, where they got some oils and really nice soaps. Showering definitely agreed with them.

Then back home to Josh's.

Eli finally left at 6 or so.

Josh had 3 messages. They were all Carlton, wondering where he was on a Saturday morning.

Carlton came over and Josh spilled the beans.

Carlton smiled as Josh tried to act like he wasn't being turned out by each of Eli's gestures.

Their best friend banter turned to dinner and a movie.

Eli called and said "Thank you for the best shower and the best night's sleep I have ever had."

Josh smiled and said, "It's that Heavenly bed."

Eli retorted, "No I think it was the Angel in it."

Josh was going crazy, trying to figure out why this dude was single and so handsome and so sexy and so beautiful and not trying to hit it every time they got together. But, Josh stopped himself. "Damn, just injoy it and let it flow."

Maybe Josh would take his own advice.

Saturday
11:14pm

"Good Night Sleepyhead."

"Good Night Night Owl."

SUNDAY
2:03pm

"Want to meet for some grub?"

"Sure, I'll be at your house in an hour."

SUNDAY
11:42pm

"Good Night Sleepyhead."

"Good Night Night Owl."

MONDAY
11:42AM

"What are you doing tonight?"

"I don't know but hope it includes an 'us'.

MONDAY
12:02AM

"Good Night Sleepyhead."

"Good Night Night Owl."

TUESDAY
10:14AM

"I'm going into the studio tonight. Have some free studio time. Have some tracks I need to lay down. You are welcome to come if you like."

"I have this presentation to finish. I'm working on a commercial with Jada and Carol's Daughter. But I will come by and see you doing your thing."

TUESDAY
11:06PM

(LOUD MUSIC IN THE BACKGROUND)

"Yeah, baby…I'm gonna be here all night."

"Don't work too hard."

"I have to if I want to keep up with you."

"See. Listen to you."

"Good Night Sleepyhead."

"Good Night Night Owl."

WEDNESDAY
4:15pm

"I'm just waking up. Didn't get down till 7:30 this morning." Eli was exhausted.

"The Hardest Working Man In Show Business, huh." Josh laughed but smiled to himself because he liked that Eli was so committed.

"No, just doing my thing."

"So you are staying in tonight?"

"Yeah, I think I better. These late nights and cold weather don't mix. I think I'm coming down with something. Better chill tonight and let it pass."

WEDNESDAY
9:14pm

"What are you doing here?" Eli tried not to sniffle.

"You said you were getting sick and I can't just sit and let that happen. Back in bed, now."

"Okay, Florence Nightingale. Let me show you where…"

"I'll find it."

"So do all of your suitors get this kind of royal treatment?"

"Be quiet and lay down. And no. Just my Cleo."

"Very funny." (Coughs)

"Back in bed and be quiet, Mr. Sickly Man." Josh then pours a healthy tablespoon of some stuff that looks like liquid vapor rub or something. Without warning, he puts it in Eli's mouth.

"What is this stuff? It's awful!"

"It's medicine, man! It's supposed to be nasty!"

"This is burning my chest. Who ever heard of Buckley's? What in Jesus' name is that?!"

"It's going to make you better, that's what it is!"

"Wow, I feel it going down."

"Now, here's some soup, some juice, some water and some crackers. They better all be gone by the time I call you from my house."

"You are not gonna stay and nurse me back to health?"

"Then we'll both be sick."

"You're leaving right now?"

"Yes, but I'm going home, so I will call you in 20 minutes, so stop whimpering."

"Oh, so now I'm a baby?" Eli playfully pouted and tried to use batting eyes to gain sympathy.

"No. You were always a baby!"

"Very Funny, Nurse Ratchet!"

"I'll call you in 20 minutes. Now eat."

"Josh?"

"Yes, Eli?"

"J?"

(smiles) "Yes, E?"

"Thank you baby. You didn't have to do this."

"E?"

"Yes, J?"

"Yes, I did."

WEDNESDAY
11:19PM

"Feeling better already. That medicine was the beast but it's working." Eli sounds clearer already. He still can't believe Josh came over to nurse him. Eli had been waiting for a brotha who paid him this kind of attention his entire life. Not just physical adoration, but who was paying attention.

"See, Daddy knows best."

"So you got a Daddy thing now, huh?"

"Just with you, Daddy."

Eli laughed and noticed that he didn't cough, this time. "It really works."

"Yes, now go to sleep and let it."

"Good Night Sleepyhead," (yawning)

"Good Night to you, Sleepyheaded Night Owl."

Thursday
8:14AM

"You alone in the office?"

"Yes, why?"

"What are you wearing?"

"You are so racy in the morning. A blue suit, a white and blue-striped shirt and a cream tie with blues in it. Oh, and some really nice Kenneth Cole shoes. I remember how much you like his shoes. They do feel good on my feet."

"I wasn't being nasty. I just wanted to see you, to visualize you. Now, who's mind is really in the gutter, Mr. Knight?"

"You need anything?"

"No, just gonna chill today and get it all out. Call me later. Just wanted to hear your voice before your day got crazy. Good Morning Sleepyhead."

"Good morning Night Owl? That sounds weird. I will have to think of something else for mornings."

"Have a great day and my cell is off, so just call the home phone. Don't want all that ringing. Have enough ringing going on in my head."

"Okay. Sleep tight and I'll check on you throughout the day."

THURSDAY
11:16AM

"Feeling better?"

"A lot better, thanks to you."

THURSDAY
2:02pm

"Need anything?"

"No but thanks for the soup you left in the fridge. All I could keep down today."

THURSDAY
3:01pm

"Hey, turn on Oprah. She's talking to Stevie. I know you love him, so injoy"

THURSDAY
4:02pm

"Man, Stevie is amazing. I have got to finish that song I was working on so I can lay it down. Stevie just makes a singer want to sing, a writer want to write, a producer want to produce. Stevie reminds you of why you love music."

"Somebody sounds motivated." Josh loved to hear the passion in Eli's voice, even when he's not feeling 100%. He can just hear him sit up when he talks about music.

"Invigorated is more like it." Eli loved the way he felt supported by Josh. He loved the way he could dream out loud with him. Eli had a moment, right there, sick and still, where he really realized that he could be falling in love and it felt good. But, for the first time, Eli was the one feeling anxious. He really wanted to see Josh right now. He really wanted to feel Josh's touch. He also just wanted to see him, even though Eli felt like crap.

"I'm wrapping up here. I will stop by on my way home. Okay?" Josh really did want to see Eli and just be, with him.

"No, baby. I stink. My locs are all over the place and I really want to finish this song. Call me when you get home. Maybe I can shower by then and then you can come through. I just don't want you to go out of.....You know what, J, stop by. It was a nice thought and I didn't mean to shut it down. Please, it would be nice to see your smiling eyes."

THURSDAY
6:42pm

"You really do look a mess." Josh moved in to kiss Eli, without fear. He just wanted to kiss his lips.

"Oh, so now you got jokes? Very funny for an Ad Exec." Eli grabbed Josh and picks him up in his arms and just nestles his nose into Josh's neck.

"Oww, get off of me, Music man."

"Take it back or I promise you, you will never see your briefcase again!"

"No, not my briefcase. Take me. It's innocent. Please! TAKE ME!"

"You are as silly as me!" Eli looked at Josh and felt safe. He wanted to tell him something that would let him know that he loved him, was in love with him and wanted to love him forever. But he was…scared. He just didn't want to lay his whole heart out there again and be hurt. He knows that he is safe with Josh, but he's never felt this. He just kissed Josh again. He had to do something.

"You okay?" Josh thought he saw something come across Eli's face. Was he scared? Was he changing his mind? Josh had to let the thought go and just allow himself to be in Eli's arms. Anything else didn't matter. Not now.

"Yeah, I'm gonna try to work on this song, mostly lyrics. I have the melody already in my head."

"And when are you going to share this masterpiece?" Josh hugged him, still in Eli's arms, and kissed his nose. Eli looked at him like he was about to say something and he decided against it.

"When I know that it's ready." Eli kissed him back and put Josh back down on the ground. He had to. Otherwise, he would have held him for the rest of his life and he wasn't sure that either of them was ready for that.

"'You want me to get you something?" Josh wanted to do something. The air was thick and so was Eli's touch. He needed a distraction. He would be seeing Carlton soon, so he couldn't stay. Thank God. He would have given Eli his heart at any second.

"I'm good baby. Don't want you to get what I got, so let me blast the joint with Lysol after you go, so next time, you're safe."

"I'll call you when I get home from dinner with Carlton."

"Tell him I said hello."

"I always do and he always asks."

"Thanks J. You are something else."

"Finally, someone noticed. You're welcome, Eli. Call you later."

They kiss deeply at the door and Josh figures that any bug he catches is worth the feeling in his fingertips right now.

Eli knew he was in love. He just had to wait for Josh to catch up. Eli knew that he had found true love. He knew it because he had gotten the sign he asked for.

THURSDAY
11:16pm

"Good Night Sleepyhead."

"Good Night Night Owl."

FRIDAY
9:12am

"Feeling much better." Eli sounded alive, like he was different somehow.

"Good. You had me worried. I've got a long day ahead and that was going to mess with me all day."

"Well, no more stressin' about me. I'm actually up and already writing. Finishing this song, but some of the words still aren't coming to me. So let me get back at it and you do the same. We still on for later?"

"Of course. I wouldn't miss it for the world."

FRIDAY
7:14pm

"I have seen it a few times. I ***get*** all of the hype." Josh huffed at Eli.

"Hype? It's not hype. It's cultural relevance. It's history and emotions and struggles and community. It's us."

"So you are really going to walk me through 'The Color Purple' and teach me the cultural importance of each scene?"

"Yes I am, Mister. And you are going to like it or I am going to make YOU take some of that Buckley's cuz you must be sick in the head."

"Oh no, not the Buckley's. I gave it to you because you were sick. But that stuff is horrible."

"So now you tell me!?" Eli looked at Josh again, and he knew.

"Hey, I wanted you to get well." Josh felt it again and this time he literally shook. What was going on with Eli? Was he keeping some secret?

"Well, I want you to get Celie and Nettie and Shug and Mister, so grab the chips and then sit down, sexy."

Eli smiled as he smacked Josh on the butt and smiled, not believing that Fridays could ever be this sweet.

FRIDAY
11:42PM

"Man, you still don't have any tears for me?"

"It was good, but come on, I'm not bawling over a movie!"

"Your heart is cold, Mr. Knight."

"My heart is warm and fuzzy and cuddly, Mr. Monroe. It's just that I can't cry over a movie when I'm with you."

"So what, you can't let me see you cry?"

"No, it's not that. It's that when I'm around you, I'm much too happy to even think about crying."

The kiss that followed, so tender and so passionate that it seemed to last for hours, almost brought tears to them both.

SATURDAY
9:22 AM

"Did you get home safe?"

Eli was still naked in the bed. He really did like talking to Josh that way. It was sexual. He just liked feeling so free with someone.

"Sure did. Sorry that I had to leave, but I really need to pack for this trip. My flight leaves tomorrow and I haven't gotten anything together yet. This is a huge trip for me and I can't believe I didn't pack, like, a week ago. Look what you are doing to me."

Joshua couldn't believe that he wasn't just crazed by now. Being with Eli was making him chill out about all of the small stuff. Okay, everything except them, but they weren't a small thing. But Josh was a lot more at ease and everyone around him noticed it.

"Sorry. I didn't mean to make you happy, Mr. World Traveler. Bring me back a t-shirt." Eli really did mean that.

"You want a t-shirt from Atlanta?" Josh was thinking about bringing him a gift but then let it go. Eli was from the South and didn't need some little dinky trinket. He forgot who he dealing with.

"I want a Coca-Cola World Headquarters t-shirt, man! Anyway, I know that this is going to be a great trip and your idea is so hot that I think that it will really make Coke pop again, HA HA. You like that. Funny right? You can use it if you like!" Eli laughed at himself.

Josh shook his head, but had to laugh. He really did love Eli's crazy wit.

"But more than that," Eli kept talking "I think you might have started something big. This is going to be huge."

"You really think so, Eli? I'm not as nervous as I was, because we have gotten some great feedback and solid talent involved. But I'm still nervous about the presentation, but enough of that and my worrying." Josh exhaled audibly.

"I leave tomorrow at 8pm, so maybe, I don't know, we could have some brunch after you finish with church tomorrow? What do you think?"

Eli paused and really considered it before he offered his statement.

"I think you need to come with me. I thought you were really involved with church when you were in DC. What happened when you got here? I thought that there was a Unity in NYC."

Eli breathed hard, just because he knew that people and their relationship with God and going to church is really personal. He was hoping he didn't step on Josh's toes.

"There is," Josh offered, "but when they changed worship locations and got their own building, it was around the same time that the firm took off and things got…weary with Greg. I just got so caught that I haven't been back. I will have to do that soon. But not tomorrow, because I'm so behind it makes no sense."

"Aiight, baby. I'll come by after service, or do you want to come into the city? No, I think I know a great spot. I will come to you. Don't spend all day packing and repacking. Just try to chill and I will see you tomorrow. And you will do great!"

Josh couldn't help but smile, not just on his face but he could feel a smile in his chest, like some weight was leaving.

"Eli, you're wonderful. I know that sounds like some line out of a Sandra Dee movie, but you really are special."

"Who's Sandra Dee?" Eli asks, completely missing the reference.

"So I am supposed to be enthralled by 'The Color Purple' and you don't know who Sandra Dee is?" Josh offered, as if the two compared.

"I just didn't know you were THAT old, Mr. Knight." Eli smirked.

"Whatever, Mister man" Josh quipped, trying to play flip and coy. "You think you are the bomb-diggity, huh?"

"Oh so now you are trying to talk hip-hop slang to me. You are so cute, Mr. Knight. But I will see your 'bomb-diggity' and raise you one 'all that and a bag of chips.' Talk to you later, baby."

"OK, Eli. We'll talk later." *Did he call me 'baby' again? God, I love it when he says that. It sends chills up my spine, but maybe he means it like they use it today. I hear straight guys saying 'baby' all of the time. It's like the new 'dude' or 'brotha' sometimes. I can't believe I'm still this nervous around him sometimes. He's great and that smile is something from Heaven. How on earth is a brother like this single? Why on earth is a brother like this single? I guess we haven't had that talk yet. I wonder if he's dated much since he's been in NYC. I wonder if there's some ex out there or if he's just playing the field.*

Damn, I really do get on my own nerves sometimes!

That's one thing that Josh never did understand about New York City. It seems like everyone here is always on the hunt for the right man, but also still always looking. It's like nobody will commit because they are afraid that someone better will come along and they don't want to be attached when Tyson walks into the club or LL leaves Simone and strolls into The Hangar. It's so ridiculous, but such is the vastness and vanity of The Big City. You always see something good, and sometimes, physically at least, someone better, but you never know their hearts until you know them. Eli does have a great heart.

Eli Monroe is a good man, and I am really going to get to know him after this trip. It's time to put down these barriers and piss or get off the pot.

SATURDAY
10:14pm

"I'm all packed and packaged. All of my reports and stats and charts and tapes and everything are accounted for, and I'm ready to go."

Josh was so excited that he called Eli before he realized it. He didn't mean to but every time he had a great idea or a solid thought that he wanted to bounce off of someone, he was on the phone with Eli. That would piss Carlton off, but he and Donovan were busy doing their thing anyway.

Josh couldn't believe that it had only been a few weeks, but he and Eli were becoming fast friends and solid hanging partners. He felt easy with Eli, but he could tell him anything. Josh was always worrying that Eli saw him as a buddy, that was until Eli would pull Josh to him as he was leaving and leave a kiss that let Josh know that he had feelings for him and he was feelin' him.

"Then why isn't he acting on them? Why haven't we been intimate yet? Why am I tripping on this when I said I wanted to take my time? Maybe, he just doesn't see me like that. Maybe I need to make the first move or at least open the door for him to do it. Yeah, that's it. It's time for me to give Eli a taste of his own sexy medicine. First Atlanta and then, Eli!" Josh plotted with himself to put it on Eli. He had to own that he was really in heat around Eli and didn't know what else to do.

He was determined to change his ways with men and get over the hurt of Gregory. You would think that Josh was the only man who had ever been hurt or betrayed. You would think that he was the only one who had a heartbreak still hidden in his closet.

You would be wrong.

CHAPTER 9: THE LONGING

FRESH FRUIT

"Good Night Sleepyhead."

"Good Night Night Owl."

Eli loved the way it felt to end every night with Josh on the phone. He swore he was gonna take his time, because he had had enough of cats in NYC always trying to climb Mt. Elijah but never wanting to get to know Eli. He hated that he still felt this vulnerable, even after guy after guy showed that all he wanted was the dream deferred.

"Don't nobody want all that!" still rang in his ears, but it was "Damn, man. What do you think this is going to lead to, marriage or something?" that still ached in his heart.

Reggie Tisdale. Reginald Darrell Tisdale.

He said those words to Elijah Monroe more than two years ago and they still hurt.

Why?

Because Eli's parents have been together for 34 years and yes, he did believe that their year and a half relationship would lead to marriage or some homosexual facsimile. He didn't know if he was ready or able to stand up in a tuxedo with his Mom and Dad and family and friends and the cats from the neighborhood he grew up in, but he did know that he wanted something more than just shacking up and sex on demand.

When Reggie and Eli met, it was atypical for both.

It was atypical for Eli, because he didn't normally stop to talk to guys in public, like this, but Reggie's eyes kept catching Eli's while they walked through The Union Square Market. It was a beautiful crisp day outside and Eli had walked up from his spot in the Village.

For Reggie, it was not his usual haunt because he was satisfied going out for dinners several nights of the week, but tonight, he just felt like cooking, so he came down to the Market because his friends told him that the produce was better than that stuff in that little bodega near his apartment. But the real reason Reggie found himself there was that he was leaving some dude's apartment and decided to stop at Virgin Records to pick up Mariah Carey's 'Charmbracelet' cd and give the girl another chance. "She can sing, even if she is crazy. Plus, I really like that song she sang on 'Oprah,'" Reggie told himself and on the way out, he noticed the Market and remembered his friends' advice, so he stopped to shop.

That's when he saw him: Locs in a band, leather jacket, jeans and a smile that was on display for the lady he was buying fresh fruit from, but that hit Reggie the right way nonetheless. Reggie had seen Eli twice before Eli finally noticed Reggie in all of his sexiness. Reggie loved to accentuate his unmanly buxom bottom in some jeans. He would calm it down with a too-big shirt and a XXL jacket, so that he didn't look like he was on display, but if you were willing to follow The Yellow

Brick Road of the stitching of his too-tight Levi's up his thigh, you could dream a dream about what lies beneath.

Eli smiled at Reggie.

Reggie smiled back.

Eli went to pay for his fruit and turned to look at Reggie again, but he was gone.

Hmmm.

Eli looked around and didn't see him, so he let it go and went to find some fresh greens, some mozzarella and maybe something new. He turned to go down another aisle in the open-air bonanza and caught Reggie's eye again. This time they spoke.

Reggie was about 5'10", thick, solid, nice apple-shaped head and warm brown eyes. He looked about 26 or so and Eli thought that he was handsome.

Reggie would have devoured Eli right then if he could have been allowed such a public display of "HOT MANNERY!"—his phrase for men he found sexy. They exchanged numbers and when Eli turned to ask Reggie what he was doing for the rest of the day, Reggie was already gone.

Eli didn't think much about it until he tried to call Reggie the next day, Sunday, just to begin the conversation and see what he was about. Reggie didn't answer. Eli left a message. Reggie called him back on Wednesday. Eli thought he was just busy.

Reggie was at home when Eli called the first time. He just didn't want to seem too eager. So he waited, 3 days, and then returned the call. They made dinner plans for Friday and they had a good time. Eli thought Reggie was even sexier while they grubbed on wings and Texas Blues at the Dallas BBQ. They didn't want anything too formal or fancy, they agreed.

Just a first date.

Their second was just a movie and a walk. They found themselves back at Eli's and the sex ensued heatedly, quickly and voraciously. They went at it for more than 3 hours. Reggie knew that Eli would put it on him, but he didn't expect him to be so…tender. He kissed more than Reggie liked, but he was so on target at hitting each of Reggie's spots that Reggie didn't mind the kissing. He didn't mind it for almost 18 months. He didn't mind it until Eli suggested that Reggie join him when he went home for Thanksgiving. They had let the first series of holidays past by—Thanksgiving, Christmas, New Year's, Mother's Day, Father's Day—without much discussion. They were new and still finding their way.

But Eli figured that now that they had one of everything under their belt and had passed the one-year mark, it was time. Reggie wasn't feeling it. His mother would never understand her handsome stud of a son being "shacked up with some big ol' man" and he wasn't up for her mouth, again. So he begged off Mother's Day. He didn't know his father, so no holiday really came up for them until it was Thanksgiving again. They had been dating since July 12th of the year before and now, Thanksgiving was upon them and Eli just thought it would be nice for Reggie to Meet The Monroes. Reggie wasn't up for it and thought that just saying so would be enough. It wasn't. Eli was confused.

"So, what, you don't ever want to meet my family or for me to meet yours? I thought we were trying to do this for real, Reggie. I didn't know you weren't up for meeting my family and maybe moving in one day or something like that. I'm just not the kind of brother who can just live in a Gay Vacuum. I love my family and we are close and I thought it would be a cool time for them to meet this sexy dude that I'm lovin' up."

Eli wouldn't say that he was in love. Okay, he did, but every time he tried to share that with Reggie, he got "stop playin'" or "you so crazy" or "man, you are really deep." He didn't know what to make of it, but he finally started to realize that each utterance was met with a hot round of sex. Reggie never answered him, but used sex to imply that he agreed. Tonight, Eli needed to hear the words from his mouth.

"Man, I love you. I want to spend my life with you, Reggie. I didn't think that meeting my family would cause all this strife. What's the problem?"

"There ain't no problem, Eli. I have feelings for you too, man, but it's not like we are trying to do this thing forever. Damn, man. What did you think this is going to lead to, marriage or something? I ain't got time to be marching for rights like that. I'm just trying to do my thing."

"But what about 'our thing?' I thought we were about something and trying to do this thing together. What happened?"

"Nothing happened, Eli. I just think that your big ol' country ass came to the big city, thinking that you was gonna find some dude who thinks like you, loves like you and wants to live like you, but this is New York City, baby. We don't go in for all that. I like you a lot, baby. I might even love you, but I'm not about to bring you home to Momma and start going to group sessions at GMAD. That just ain't my thing. If that's how you want to get down, then good for you, but I like my spot in Harlem and some freedom. I thought we were on the same vibe, but you definitely on something else. The loving's been butta, baby, but I think you want something I can't give you. I'm going back Uptown and if you want some, holla, but I can't go to Louisiana. That's just not my thing. So, if you want to continue to conversation, then I'm out."

That was it.

Eli couldn't believe how cold-hearted Reggie was being. He wasn't mean or bitchy. He didn't throw a fit, a punch or even the keys in his face. He was stating facts. He wasn't the marrying kind. Eli was and had to face that.

As Reggie walked out, Eli wasn't sure if it was for the night or the last time. He thought about calling Reggie later that night, but didn't. He thought about calling the next day, but couldn't find any words. He thought about it a lot in the last two years, but could never find the words to say, "l love you but I need more."

Eli almost felt like he needed to apologize for expecting so much out of love or another man. Eli thought he was wrong to want that much. Eli never told anyone how much that hurt. He suffered his last hurt over Reginald Tisdale. He just wanted to be in New York, doing what mattered, with someone who mattered.

He got the first part. The second remained elusive.

Eli had been up all night.

"Damn. I can't believe that Reggie just walked out."

Eli hated that those thoughts had risen in his head again, especially with all of this joy in his heart about Josh. Maybe, just maybe, it was because Josh was preparing to leave that Eli was tripping.

"Damn, that's some crazy psycho bull! I can't be tripping about that!"

He said it to himself and then, he laughed. He laughed because that was it and more. He laughed because he was worried about where he and Josh were heading. The feeling of Reggie overwhelmed Eli, like he must have been thinking about him, too. Elijah knew that he had let Reggie go, but the truth is that Reggie let him go and he never got over just being dismissed, so casually. Reggie never reached back and with 8 million people around, they never ran into each other again. But Eli couldn't get over the feeling that Reggie was somewhere nearby.

He let it go and concentrated on Joshua and the present.

"So the car is scheduled to be here at 5pm, and I'll get to Liberty by 5:45pm, or so. I'm checked in by 6:15pm and ready to board. I am going to just read a book and I'll be in Atlanta in no time. But I'm going to…." Josh stopped himself.

He didn't want to sound corny and he didn't want to put the cart before the house. They had spent so much time together that maybe they needed a break. Maybe Eli was going to use this time to see other people or just be alone. But Josh was going to miss him. Eli was such great company and more than anything, that's what Josh missed. A good conversation that didn't have to lead anywhere or a good laugh that went from simple to silly without warning.

"I am going to miss you too," Eli added.

He couldn't let the moment go. It was too important and he needed to be able to let himself speak again, from his own voice. He had let other people choke his words in this throat for so long. It felt good to just say it.

"But we'll talk and you'll come back a millionaire. Or, at least PAID!"

"You are so stupid, man. But…I am going to miss you Eli. I've grown accustomed to your face." Josh said and then laughed at how old all of his song references were.

Eli noticed.

"You are from the 50s, aren't you? But it's cool. You wear it well. Anyway. I would hop on the train and ride with you or something, but this is better. Just wave by my door on your way to the airport, J. Have a great flight and really, Coca-Cola needs you baby, so do your thing and do it 'til you're satisfied."

"Thanks for the encouragement, Eli. I think I'm ready to do this."

Luckily, the meetings are not until Tuesday, so Josh had some time to breathe and stop. He couldn't remember the last time he was in Atlanta, but he knew that its reputation as the Gayest City in the U.S. of A. had grown exponentially since he last visited. Maybe he would go out, since he was there until Friday. But the likelihood of that was close to nil. He could dream though. Dream that he was a light and carefree Gay Man who took it all in stride and just did what the day let him discover.

But Josh would probably be in his hotel room, catching up on movies-on-demand that he had missed in the theatre. But he really was going to miss Eli.

Brunch didn't happen because he really had a lot to do, but he had an idea.

CHAPTER 10: THE AWAKENING

THE HUNTER *becomes* THE GAME

Josh didn't like feeling this open, this vulnerable, but he knew if he thought about it too much, he'd turn back. But he was already here.

"What if he's with someone?" he said to himself, as he rang the bell and swallowed his pride.

"Go for it. It's only going to be 5 minutes and you won't know 'til you know, so…"

DING DONG.

Eli had just gotten out of the shower and wasn't sure if he really heard the bell. He knew he wasn't expecting anyone, so he almost igged the sound, until "Ding Dong" rang out in the air again, stopping him mid-lotioning.

With just a towel on, Eli answered the door, sure that it had to be someone he knew, but expecting no one.

"Surprise. I don't have long. I just wanted to stop by and see…." Josh froze.

He's naked. He must be with someone else.

"Dammit. I knew it. I wasn't even out of town and he's already getting some."

Josh was pissed at himself for the thought and for the fear. But here was the proof. Eli was glistening and toweled up, like he hopped out of the bed to answer. Josh didn't know what to think, so he froze.

"I didn't mean to disturb you." Josh said it under his breath, ready to die and disappear, but Eli never heard it.

"Hey baby. WOW! You did this for me? I was only kidding when I said wave, but this is much better."

With that, Eli hugged Josh and pulled him into the house.

"I was just in the shower and gonna just chill and maybe watch some TV. I know you can't stay long, but this is NICE."

Eli reached to hug Josh again, just excited about seeing him, when his towel unfurled and dropped.

Josh looked down. My God, this man was a perfect presentation of Black male pulchritude!

Eli reached down and casually grabbed his towel, as if to say "stop me at any time," to Josh, but what he did say was, "Man, you better be glad you are in a rush, cuz I would PUT IT ON YA," Eli said playfully and a tad nervously. He didn't want to ruin the moment or the sweetness of the gesture.

Josh had stopped by. Eli's heart was racing in his chest, as he silently willed his groin to stay silent.

Josh could see that he wasn't erect and probably was just out of the shower. But Josh couldn't get over the feeling that Eli was so much of what he wanted that he couldn't believe that someone else didn't want it too, and wasn't in hot pursuit. Josh refused to sabotage his thoughts with the words, but they kept circling.

HE'S JUST TOO GOOD TO BE....

Josh would never finish the thought. To finish it was to state it and he refused to be that cynical.

"J, come in baby. Sit down for a minute. I know you only have 5 or so, but I am glad you stopped by."

Eli had forgotten he was naked already. He felt naked around Josh anyway.

"So, Josh, I really wanted to do something earlier, but I didn't want to do it unless I could see you. I know that this meeting means a lot to you. I know that you are expecting big things, but I also know you are nervous. So, I think this was ordained, but I really wanted to pray with you about it."

Eli took Josh's hand. Josh thought he had heard him right, but now, here, in just his towel, Eli wanted to pray?

"Um, okay. It's a wonderful thought, Eli." They bowed their heads. Eli really did have a preacher's spirit in him or at least in his blood. The Prayer brought Josh peace, as Eli closed offering traveling mercies.

Josh stopped at the front door and turned.

"Eli, I hope that someone has told you this before, but if they haven't, let me be the first. You really are amazing. Thank you for that and for being so...You. I will call you when I get settled."

With that, Josh leaned in to kiss Eli and this time, he really did let go. He didn't have long, but he took his time, letting lips and noses mesh, and tongues dance. As Eli reached around to grab Josh's waist, his towel fell again. This time, he left it. They kissed for a short time, but it was heated. Josh knew that because he could now feel Eli up against him. He pulled back to see Eli's joy, present and pulsating, wishing he didn't have to go.

But Josh needed to go NOW, or the flight and the night would take on a different course.

"Travel safe, J. We'll talk later when I tuck you in, Sleepyhead."

Eli stood at the front door, as he slowly reached for his towel, but clearly in no hurry. He wanted Josh to remember this sight of his naked, exposed self, saying I WANT YOU. He wrapped the towel around himself and waved, as Josh drove away, looking back and biting his lip.

Eli was sprung in more ways than one.

⌘

After an uneventful flight, Thank You God, Josh grabbed a cab and made his way to the hotel. The Renaissance was really nice, without being spectacular. It was stylish and Josh liked that he didn't feel like he was in a hotel.

He unpacked quickly and hopped into the shower. He was on fire the entire flight. Eli's naked body standing at the door was on his mind for the hour he had to wait to board, the 30 minutes before take off, the 3 hours and 42 minutes of the flight and the 17 minutes of the cab ride. Josh needed to cool off. He took a shower.

Afterwards, he flipped to the On Demand feature and sure enough, there were 4 movies that Josh had wanted to see, but missed. So he thought to himself "Great, one almost every night, so I'm covered," as he pondered staying in his space and not venturing into Hotlanta's clubs and nightlife.

"I'm here. It's a really nice hotel and I am going to make some notes before I watch a movie. What are you up to?" Josh was talking to Carlton, because he wanted to check in and check on. They had both been busy, so besides their weekly dinner, they didn't really talk much in the last few weeks.

"I'm good. Just decided that I am going to sign with Doubleday. I have something to say and I really want to get it out there as much as possible. They are going to let me have my own publicist, so I can still play a role in the marketing and publicity. I'm real good, man. How you doing? How are things going with Eli?"

"Things really were great," Josh thought. He didn't know which voice to use to say that. The HAPPY voice. The I'M TAKING MY TIME voice. The CALM AND COOL voice. He thought too much, he realized. Just say it. Carlton beat him to the punch.

"Man, just say it. You think too much and when you do that, you get too careful. So, things are good, huh?"

"Yeah, Carlton, they really are. I stopped by his spot on the way to the airport. I felt kind of silly, but he said 'wave as you drive by' which seemed like he could handle a little silly stop-by. He was in a towel when I got there and I am so glad I only had 5 minutes, because…."

"Because what?!" Carlton injected. "It's not like you were going to jump his bones, man. That's not your style. So stop playing."

"I know, but I thought about it, Brownskin. He smiled that smile and I thought about getting a later flight." Josh was serious. He never went there with Carlton, especially when talking about a dude. Josh was normally so guarded.

"Wow, Josh. You really must be feeling Eli. I'm glad to see you kickin' it with someone who makes you open up like this. I'm really glad to hear you say it. So, you going out?"

Carlton and Josh rarely did the club thing, but Carlton loved to dance, and Josh loved to see Carlton dance, because he looked like he was somewhere else, especially on the ol' school nights when Bohannon and Chic and Sylvester and MFSB take over the floor. Carlton drifts away in his own trance.

But without Carlton, Josh knew that he would stay in, especially until Tuesday.

"No, I'm gonna catch up on some movies and just relax. I could use the breather. Plus, you know I'm not going out without you and you know that I hate going out in other cities. It always seems like the perfect man for you lives hundreds of miles away and has been waiting on you to arrive. He always says the right thing, smells the right way, smiles the right smile and then, you consider a long distance thing that could never work with a grown man who's busy living his own life. It's nice to know that there are quality brothers in the world, but why do they all have to live so far away?!"

Carlton wasn't hearing it. He and Donovan met in NYC and thrive and survive in the Big City, so he wasn't co-signing the legendary myth.

"Good men have to live in the same city as you, otherwise, what are you saying about YOU?!"

They were NOT about to have THIS debate again. Josh let it go. He knew that he couldn't win a love debate with Carlton. He was just too focused and he didn't fight fair when it came to being open to love. It's odd, because you wouldn't take Carlton for the romantic type. But you would take him for a fighter.

⌘

Carlton Bridges doesn't look like he should be a writer, a poet or a lover of men. He's not DL. He's not closeted. He's unclockable. That's a word that people put out there about guys who don't "appear" gay. Carlton doesn't try to hide who he is. It spills over into his words and his conversations with almost everyone. Carlton didn't really mind it when he and his father got into an argument so ugly about his "lifestyle" that they didn't speak for almost a year. Carlton didn't know what to do when his sister told him that his father had had his first heart attack. He swallowed his pride and showed up at Mercy General Hospital and made peace with his father. They were never they same again, but they respected each other as men. That's all Carlton ever wanted. To be respected as a man. A man who loves men and isn't ashamed of that.

Carlton didn't feel like he had to "come out" to his parents or his friends in a dramatic, Movie-Of-the-Week fashion. Carlton just wanted people to respect his truth. So, at 19, after spitting rhymes at every local freestyle battle in town, and winning, and trying to round out his world with writing and poetry slams, Carlton still didn't feel like his voice was being heard. So he really thought about it and one day, he had the answer. August 23, 1991, he decided to take the stage at the NuYoRican Café and spit, from his soul, a piece called **MANenuf**. That's the first time Carlton felt free and he wasn't trying to make a political statement. He wasn't trying to shock and awe people with his frankness. He just needed to speak, that's all and there, in that legendary spot, with people who had already showed love for his prose and his promise, Carlton felt like he could tell the truth. He wanted people to see him, all of him. Yes, he was a regular brotha with a short fade, rockin' Karl Kani shorts and his favorite Adidas. He knew every joint by LL and DMC, Big Daddy Kane and, here's a trip for some…METALLICA. He likes their edge but his friends don't know that. His friends don't know that he bought Natalie Cole's "Unforgettable" cd and that's what's playing on his walkman when they think he's lost in hiphop and angst. But this night, he hoped that MANenuf would let them in and that they wouldn't hate him for just telling the truth.

Tonight, Carlton would stand before his world and finally tell the truth:

my whole life long
the voices told me that i wasn't enuf

man enuf to have nothin'

man enuf to go no where

man enuf to love nobody
or have love come to me

because it wasn't right to
love a thing like me

the voices keep saying things
of such a ludicrous and misguided nature
that i molested their children
that i had too many sexual partners to count
that i didn't like women
that i could only do hair and nails
and serve attitude and finger snaps

have they forgotten that i taught their children and loved their children and fed their children while they hustled on the streets, macked on the boulevard and just strolled about

don't they know that I looked for love in the arms of so many brothers, cause my own brothers withdraw his love from me...with their permission; at their suggestion

as for OUR women, I love and revere them...ain't nuthin' like a strong black woman, in her being, walking, sauntering, smiling, loving, nurturing, talking...sassy, sophisticated lady...I diva-fy her and help keep her strong while she loves his children and heads the household he should be sharing...

and they don't even want to think that I'm in the salon, doing the hair and nails AND I OWN IT; and that's not attitude, it's confidence...years and years of tried and true confidence, that I'm wearing in my stride...sure and sanctified in my own skin

and the finger snaps...the neck rolls...the sass...the sourness...all small gestures and cantations to subside the greater spells and dismissals that I might utilize to rid myself of them...it is for their own good that I simply snap...roll...dismiss.

they have had the unmitigated audacity to parade before me their images of manhood like badges of honor i would never wear

unaware that their basketball-dribbling, baseball-swinging, b-boy posturing, thug-inspired disillusions of male bravado have spent many a night at my house and with all of their madness, their lunacy

the voices have made me feel as though i had to

do more
give more
live more

i mean, if a brother or sister got to do it twice as strong to get on

imagine what machinations of overachievement are being thrown at me by the holier-than-thous of the world…the voices…self-hate; self-doubt; self-examination; internalized and imploding

messin' with my mind
i can't take this anymore

I've got lives to live
I've got songs to sing
I've got things to do
I beseech thee…
Voices please
SHUT THE FUCK UP!

Carlton dropped his head and wondered. The room felt like it was whirling 'cuz he couldn't see, couldn't hear, couldn't think. What do they think? What did they think? *How do I get up outta here without a fight? I don't. I fight.*

Carlton prepared to leave the stage, but the applause made him stay. The people standing, showing love, made him stay. The sistah who came to hug him made him stay. His sister pushing through the crowd to say that she loved him made him stay.

Carlton Bridges doesn't mind a good fight. But he did it with his words, because…words count. He might let you get away with a lot, because if you give your word to him, he makes you stick to it, because "words count."

⌘

Josh confirmed his original plans. "So, I'm in for the night. Going to watch a movie and just call it an early night, so I can spend all of tomorrow finalizing notes and making this presentation move perfectly."

"Let it do what it do, baby," Carlton laughingly added and "Good night, BabyBubba. Do your thing and you know you have all of the bases covered! Call me when you can. Peace and Power!"

Josh's conversation with Eli wasn't as short. They talked for about an hour. Josh told Eli about his flight and about the hotel and about talking to Carlton. Eli told Josh that he just put on some music after he left and never got dressed. He wasn't going anywhere anyway, so why bother.

Josh almost passed out realizing that Eli was naked while they talked. Eli was so comfortable in his skin, as he walked around the house and got in and back out of the bed, made some coffee and was sprawled out on the couch in the living room, all the time, naked.

"So, you miss me?" Eli was playing sexy and it was working.

"Yes, I do and considering that salute you gave me, I know you miss me, too."

Josh was tired and in the bed, and he really did wish Eli was with him. The tone of their conversation got more and more smoldering. They were talking about favorite songs and movies of all time, but they laced it with so much heat that the fiber optic wires should have been melting.

"LET'S GET IT ON"

"SEXUAL HEALING"

"I WANT YOU"

The conversation turned to Marvin Gaye and somehow they focused on the catalog of his works that were raw and sensual.

"The Hunger"

"Jason's Lyric"

"9 ½ Weeks"

Somehow they got on favorite lovemaking scenes in a movie. They got descriptive and detailed. They recalled the touch and the feel of each scene and Eli started to go crazy over the sound of Josh's voice while he talked about why he loved watching Allen Payne and Jada Pinkett's splendor in the grass. He talked about Jada's thighs and the way her legs wrapped themselves around Allen, while that lucky blade of grass clung to his butt for dear life, glad to be there. Eli got aroused. Okay, that's a lie. Eli had been aroused by the sound of Josh's voice long before the conversation took this turn. Josh is the one who finally let himself get aroused. He loved the way Eli listened and prodded him about what he liked and what he loved. Eli was stroking conversation out of Josh's mouth and Josh loved it. He lay in the bed and just listened and talked and talked and listened and he noticed that the more Eli prodded, the more erect he became. Josh had never, ever even thought about phone sex, because he thought it was so seedy. But here and now, with Eli, he thought to himself "if he goes, I'll go."

They went.

"I have never done that before, Eli. It was so different than what I expected. Maybe it was because of you, but that was so hot. Wow. Something else to add to the Life Experiences List."

Josh and Eli had been on the phone for an hour now and had covered everything from "Sounder" (Josh's favorite movie) to "Prince's Purple Rain Tour" (Eli's favorite concert). But the last half of the conversation had been new territory for them. They had kissed and they had held each other, but they had not dared venture into the sexual aspect of their attraction. But at least now they knew that there was heat and fire and passion between them.

Josh had already found a towel and had cleaned himself off. Eli just languished in the scent of it. He was in no rush.

“I'm glad we did that,” Eli added.

“Really? I am, too. I didn't want you to think that I was some kind of prude or something, Eli. It's just that I have...”

Eli stopped him.

“I understand, J. Believe me, I know what hurt feels like and I know what it looks like. I'm not rushing. Que Sera Sera, baby. We have a lifetime to get there.”

Josh felt at ease. Eli could always say the right thing. If he was from NYC or DC or something, Josh would be apprehensive to his “right answer for everything,” but something about his Southern manner helped to take some of the edge off for Josh.

Some of it.

At times, he was still just lost between taken and taken aback, because Eli was just so right. He was everything that he had prayed for and hoped for and asked for, but he didn't expect him to arrive in the middle of the biggest campaign of Josh's PR firm's short history. Josh was feeling overwhelmed.

“J, you better get to bed, so you can do your thing tomorrow. I know that you've got a lot to get done, so you call me when you can, aiight baby? I'm gonna be in the studio off and on this week. Need to lay some tracks down for something I have been working on. But you know, for you, I'm always around.”

Josh smiled. He couldn't believe that Eli had said something so simple and so sweet.

“Okay. You will be my break. I have most of it laid out. Maybe I will call and run it by you? Especially the music part of the campaign, if that's okay with you, Mr. Super Producer,” Josh offered laughingly.

"Call my agent, who will call my label who will call my assistant, who will call my manager and then I'll call you." Eli said, snickering the whole time, but trying to pull off the joke anyway. "But since they are all me, I'm sure you'll get through."

Eli loved to hear Josh laugh.

"Eli, are you still naked?"

Josh couldn't believe he asked, but he was intrigued. After they finished, Josh had wiped himself off with a wet cloth, put on his underwear and some lounging pants and sat up in the chair beside the bed. He never heard Eli move. He finally had to ask.

"Sure am, baby. Why? You wanna go again? BigDaddy always up for you!" Eli was half-playing and half-mass, so he was down.

"No, you are right. I better get to bed. I just wanted to know. Maybe the visuals will invade my dreams tonight." Josh was such a romantic. Eli loved that about him.

"Good Night Sleepyhead."

"Good Night Night Owl."

⌘

It was 3:20pm before Josh realized that he had buried himself in work all day. He hated that sometimes he could just lose track of time, immersed in his work. He had wanted to call Eli twice today, but that perfect sentence or hip slogan would on the tip of his tongue and he had to get it out first. Then, he would call. Now it was late afternoon and he hadn't called Eli once.

Josh wished that Eli had called him anyway, but he knew that Eli wouldn't. He was a man of his words and he knew that Josh was going to be busy today, so he left it in Josh's court.

"Hey mister. What are you up to?"

Josh just went for it. *It's a call man, not a proposal*, he finally said to himself while dialing. Eli answered on the 2nd ring.

"Hey baby. I was hoping I'd hear from you. How's it going?"

Eli seemed excited. Josh was really glad to hear his voice. Eli was in the kitchen, making some coffee and then heading into his home studio to do some writing.

"It's going. I was caught up in trying to figure out some demographical information, but I'm finished with most of it. How are you doing? I'm sorry it took so long to call."

"Come on, baby. You know I know. When I'm in the studio, it's like another world and you can get lost in it. I'm good. Working on some stuff. Trying to pull together some lyrics for something I'm working on. Lounging and listening to music when I get stuck, so Marvin Gaye's been playing all day. Thanks for the inspiration."

Josh almost swooned. Eli was so sensual. Josh loved his heat.

"Eli, you need to," Josh started to say before Eli stopped him.

"What, stop? I need to stop? You want me to stop, baby? You want me to stop talking dirty to you?"

Eli was being a bit much, but wanted to really see if Josh meant it.

"No, I just meant that. Okay never mind. Tell Marvin I said hi." Josh laughed and changed the subject, with the quickness.

"Anyway, I really want to do a CD release with this new campaign. I need to know the 15 hottest new R&B and hip-hip artists. I've been doing some research, but I don't want it to look like I stole the list right off of '106th and Park,' you know. I know that from what I've read, that's what all of the young urban kids are listening to everyday, but I want to give them something new, too. Not too over-their-heads Neo-soul or retro, but a little edgy. Like some India.Arie or Common or Anthony Hamilton and a little Keisha Cole and Trey Songz and Twista and Juelz Santana. I really liked some of it."

Eli dropped the phone. He couldn't believe his ears.

Josh heard the clunk and knew what Eli was doing. He waited patiently for the backlash.

"Wait. Wait. WAIT. WAIT!!!!" Eli said, after returning to the phone and the planet earth.

"Are my ears deceiving me or what? Damn, baby, when did you do all of THAT research? You sounding like a DJ now, talking all that talk. So what tracks are you feeling?" Eli asked as he braced himself.

"Very funny, Eli. Oh, so we can only have one music expert in the family?" Ouch, Josh thought. That slipped. Eli caught it.

"Not at all, J. We can both be music experts, as long as I get to still produce it all. You can do all the researching you like."

Josh changed the subject again, embarrassed that he had slipped and said that, but trying to recover.

"I love that new Common song. His style is definitely right on time. I think that I want to try to get him for the commercial. I love Jill Scott's voice and Anthony's songs and sound definitely make me think of being down South."

Eli applauded. "Wow, Josh. You have been busy indeed. Well, if you like, I can put together some cds for you to listen to. Maybe a little of everything and you can decide. That cool? I will overnight it to you, so you can have it while you're there. It's all already on my computer, so all I have to do is select some songs, drop them to a cd and bam, you're good."

"Thanks Eli. You really are the man, huh? Well, let me make these final notes and we'll talk later, okay?"

"Okay baby. Do your thing and I'll talk to you when you need a breather."

"Thanks." Josh loved that kind of assurance. It made him smiled.

8:14pm

It happened again. Josh got so deep that it wasn't until his phone rang and Carlton checked in that he realized the time. Their conversation wasn't long, but Josh needed a break. He lounged and they just caught up on each other's weeks and projects. Carlton asked about Eli and Josh asked about Donovan and the book and how Carlton was really doing, since they didn't touch on the "Mother" subject until Carlton was ready. He assured Josh that he was in a much better place since the trip. He thanked Josh again and they called it a night around 9:30pm.

Best friends really can talk for hours.

"I'll talk to you when you get back, Josh, unless you wanna reach out before then. This Doubleday deadline is a trip, so a brother is knee-deep in edits. Call me when you need me. Peace."

Josh was dialing Eli when his other line rang. It was Eli.

"I wasn't going to bother you, but then I thought about something. What have you eaten today, Josh?"

Josh got silent. He realized that he hadn't thought about food all day and now he was starving.

"Just like I thought. I was sitting down to grub and thought to myself 'I bet he hasn't moved.' So hang up and call Room Service. I am going to call back in 30 minutes and you better be eating. Don't make a brother come down there."

Red button.

"But, I..." Josh realized that Eli had hung up and was serious. He called Room Service and got some chicken and rice and wild vegetables. They said it would be 35 minutes or so.

Exactly 30 minutes later, Josh's cell rang and there was a knock at the door at the same time. He was saved from Eli's wrath, but honestly wondered if he would have come. He thought that it was sexy to even suggest it.

"I'm answering the door now and unless you are on the other side, it better be Room Service."

"Oh okay. I was just checking. You know a brother would have come down there if I thought you weren't taking care of you. But since you have things under control, eat. Call me when you finish. Take care of yourself baby, until you let me do it."

Again, red button engaged.

Josh was dumbfounded and could barely eat.

"UNTIL YOU LET ME DO IT?!" What's that supposed to mean? He started to call Carlton, but knowing that he was busy and not wanting to look like a fool, he just inhaled and ate.

"Man, he's just too good...." Josh dropped the thought. Elijah Monroe was who he said he was and Josh needed to stop tripping. Eli had showed no signs of being anything other than true and truthful. But neither did Greg, so.

"Damn, let it go, Joshua! STOP IT," he said aloud as he ate. He was going to finish dinner and call Eli and then get some rest.

"So you are ready for bed and ready for tomorrow and ready to take the world by storm. You really seem ready for anything, J. Good to know that."

Eli was clear about what he said and meant to leave it open to interpretation.

"I know that I am ready for tomorrow and for bed, but I don't know about the ready for the world part, and I'm still checking myself on the ready for anything part." Josh sounded tentative and he didn't mean to. "But I am ready for the next level, that's for sure." Josh said it and meant it. "So, when I get home, I need to make a few changes at the firm. All good, but better for me."

Eli thought he was going to include him in that next level.

In his mind, Josh already had.

They did the SLEEPYHEAD/NIGHTOWL thing and Monday drifted off to sleep and waited for Tuesday to awaken.

Josh's meeting was a great success and his new campaign was really making the execs at Coke feel like they had finally found a new direction to revive their market-share. They wined Josh and dined him and he didn't have one chance to breathe until almost 11:30 that night. He returned to his hotel so exhausted that he fell asleep in his suit. He wanted to call Eli, but it was late and he was spent.

Eli knew that today was going to be packed, but still he missed the nightly regimen. He called Josh anyway and Josh was fast asleep.

When he rose at 3:30AM to remove his suit and get into bed properly, he looked at his phone and realized that Eli had called. Josh took the phone in his hand and listened to the message three times before he would finally let himself go to sleep.

Three times, he heard:

> ***"J,***
> ***I know that it's only been a month and a half, but I'm feeling you and I know you know that. I think about you all day and I really hope that you and I can take this thing to the next level.***
>
> ***I am so proud of you and I wanted you to know that. I know you put it on 'em and I know that they now know what I am finding out more everyday. You are the best thing breathing, baby.***

Good Night and I hope that they wined and dined you right. I love you. Good Night Sleepyhead."

Josh was floating. He knew that it was on the cell, but he didn't mind that the first "I love you" wasn't in person. It came right on time. Josh was on top of the world and Eli's message was his axis. Josh went for it. He didn't care. He called Eli.

"Hello," Eli answered, voice gravelly and quiet, clearly awakened from sleep.

"Don't wake up, Eli. I just want to say thank you for the message and the words. I will call you tomorrow with all the details, but I wanted you to know that I love you, too. You are the best. Go back to sleep. We'll talk tomorrow."

Josh had said it. He had let "I LOVE YOU" escape from its prison.

"I love you too, baby. Good night Sleepy…" Eli had accidentally smashed the red button with his cheek as he drifted back to sleep.

When Wednesday rose, Eli woke up a little groggy, but didn't remember the conversation with Josh at all. No one ever called him in the midnight hour, because they either knew he was asleep or in the studio all night. Thankfully, he also didn't have anything in his life that warranted late night calls, so he never even thought to check the phone, especially since there was no message. He actually spoke to Josh and so there would be no "new message" from his phone to tell him that Josh was thinking about him.

He still thought that he hadn't heard back from Josh and just assumed that the day would be lots of meetings and handshaking to seal the deal.

Since Eli had vowed to take it slow, he was going to let Josh make the next call, not out of tit-for-tat, but just so he could let me the man.

Josh was grooving on a Wednesday afternoon. The Coca-Cola team was planning a huge dinner that night, but the day was wide open and since he had spoken to Eli late last night, he didn't want to wake him. Josh just thought he'd see Atlanta, drive around, hit a mall and just check out the city. He showered and just prepared to blow off some time, since dinner wasn't until 7pm.

Eli hit the studio and worked on a song that he had been feeling for a few days. He took his phone with him, just in case, but wasn't really expecting to hear from Josh.

Josh stopped to call Eli at 11:18am, but Carlton checked in to tell him that he had emailed a chapter that he wanted him to read.

Josh thought to call Eli at 12:46pm, but his Momma called to say that she hadn't heard from him in a while and that meant he was working too hard. She reprimanded him until 1:03pm.

Josh meant to call Eli at 2:11pm, but Coca-Cola called to say that they would be doing drinks and cigars at 6pm instead, and they would be sending a car.

Josh wanted to call Eli at 2:14pm, but realized that this gathering was a little more formal than what he had brought, so he had to find Lennox Square Mall, post-haste.

Josh intended to call Eli all day, but the day got away from him and he didn't mean to be this busy. But he knew that Eli understood and wouldn't hold it against him. The Day After The Deal is always filled with obligations and meetings and events to show off the new relationship. Eli understood that. Josh hoped that Eli could feel him thinking about him.

"God, I'm so sentimental sometimes. Just call him later. I will just call him later," Josh said to himself repeatedly and tried to take the angst off and just get ready.

Eli settled into studio at around 4pm and laid down some tracks. He played a few instruments and really wanted this thing to be right. Eli had just thrown on some sweats and tied his locs up, so anyone who knew him knew that this meant he wasn't to be disturbed, because he was in "go" mode. Eli looked the part of an artist right about now—papers thrown all over the floor, pen in hand and pencil in mouth, talking to him as he auditioned potential lyrics for his own ears first. Eli was focused like never before, because this was the first song, in a long time, that he was writing, for himself, the artist. He realized that he wanted to try to focus on his own thing, really, and see what could happen for him as an artist. This song, from his soul, was going to be a new direction for him and he hoped, for music. Every lyric had to say something and he wrote and erased, sang and re-sang and riffed and listened intensely. Before the world ever heard it, it had to touch Eli first. If he could feel it, they would. When he looked up, it was 11:04pm and for the first time in weeks, he realized that he would end the night without saying those words into Josh's ear. So he stopped and said them into the air.

"Good night Sleepyhead."

"Good night Night Owl," Josh said as he checked his watch at 11:04:18pm and realized that this function wasn't going to end anytime soon.

He was engrossed in heated dialogue with a VP of Marketing and an SVP of New Products and they weren't going to finish until they had an agreement on the best placements of commercials and radio and TV and the like. The Coca-Cola family was invigorated and Josh was happy, but he still missed Eli. He wanted to steal away, but every attempt to do so was met with someone finding him or fetching him to another quick exchange of ideas.

Josh had built this ship and now had to sail it into the harbor and he knew that everyone at KNIGHT IN SHINING ARMOR was relying on their captain to do them proud. Josh was on fire, handling every challenge and every suggestion with finesse and detail. He had researched music and clothing and hip-hop and rock and MTV and BET and regions and styles and was sure that what they were launching would be the biggest thing to happen to Coke since "The Real Thing."

Josh didn't make it back to his hotel until 2:29am. He was exhausted but psyched. Right now, at this very moment, all he wanted to do was talk to Eli. He wanted to share. He knew that Eli was either in the studio or asleep and he didn't want to disturb him in either case. He didn't want to believe that Eli was out dancing or drinking or just being single, because Eli never showed that kind of behavior, so why think he was doing that now. Josh was doing anything he could to not deal with the fact that Eli had said "I Love You," but he hadn't talked about it yet.

"I know he was asleep when I called, but he heard me and knows I love him, too. I am busy and we will talk about it, but he knows and he knows I know."

Josh was rationalizing again and knew that his half-assed attempt to justify calling Eli in the wee small hours of the morning and saying it back, while he slept was not what Eli deserved. He deserved to be awake and present and hear it at the same level that Josh had heard it same to him. Josh knew that he had to get home soon. He needed to take a big step to let Eli know that he heard him and he felt the same. The timing was right. Joshua and Elijah would make love when Josh got home. Not as some ritualistic sacrifice, but because he had realized in these 2 months that he really did love him, and want to be with him and that he needed to let his guard down and Eli into his heart.

"I get home on Saturday and I will be with Eli on Saturday night. Perfect timing," Joshua said to himself. He knew it was coming, but he wasn't sure of when. Eli's message of love and encouragement sealed the deal. But what did it mean, Joshua thought to himself. Just sex? Next level? What's the next level for 2 men who have been dating for almost 2 months, but spend every chance they can together?

"Certainly not moving in together! We are not lesbians and even lesbians don't do that anymore. Not after 2 months!"

But Josh knew it meant more than sex. It meant commitment. Joshua wasn't sure if he was ready for that. Not because of Eli, but because the last time he said commitment, he lost his heart.

This time, he wanted to be sure.

"But who can ever be sure," Josh said to himself. "Eli is a great guy and I'm ready and he's ready and we are adults. Whatever happens happens." Josh said and meant it, but wasn't sure if he believed it.

"Breathe."

CHAPTER 11: THE SURRENDERING

"I Get A Thrill... I Get a Chill... When You Touch Me."

Josh's flight landed early and at 10:16am, he is already on his way back home. He called Eli, who answered on the first ring.

"Hey baby! You have a good flight? Where are you?"

"I'm in the car, almost home. I'm going to grab a few things in a bag and I'll be there by noon. I've got so much to tell you."

Josh was excited and Eli was too. He couldn't wait to tell Josh that he was going to go for it and make his foray into being an artist, and see if his voice could be heard in the crowded landscape of music. Eli was nervous and really wanted to taste Josh's lips again. He wanted to do so much to him, but the kiss would do for right now.

Josh did just what he said. He told the car to wait. He ran into the house, grabbed a bag, two pairs of jeans, a sweater, 2 shirts, 2 t-shirts, some shoes and his travel bag, and was back out the door in 6 minutes flat.

He called Eli to report that he was on his way.

It was 11:14am.

Eli was making breakfast and was wearing a tank top and some lounging pants and slippers. He had showered, but just enough to take the funk off. He didn't lull in it, because he hoped that he could do that with Josh. He wanted to just Be today, nothing to do but be in each other's company.

At exactly 11:41, the doorbell rang and Eli turned the fire down on the homemade home fries and went to the door. He opened it and found Josh grinning like a Chester cat.

Before he could say "Welcome Home," Josh was already on him.

Josh grabbed Eli and kissed him so hard that he knocked him against the wall. Josh pulled Eli's locs and looked him directly in the eyes.

"I Love You, Too" he said, as he cupped Eli's butt in one hand while he still had a handful of hair in the other.

The kiss lasted for 2 minutes or so, until Eli and Josh smelled the onions and peppers and potatoes making their presence known from the kitchen.

"WOW! That was worth the wait," Eli said. Josh grabbed his own bag and walked in and placed it in the living room.

"I Love You, Baby," Eli volleyed back, as he scooped up Josh and kissed him again. "I didn't mean to leave it on your cell like that baby, but I was happy for you and proud of you and wanted to just send some love and I realized that the only love I could send was the love I have for you, so 'I love you' came out and I wouldn't take it back. Josh, I love you and I really hope that you know that."

Eli had a tear in his eye. He couldn't believe it.

Josh couldn't believe it, but there it was, and there they were.

Two grown men, feeling like teenagers, acting like kids. Josh wiped the tear with his thumb and then licked it.

"You can put me down now. I'm starved and those home fries smell like heaven."

They ate.

They kissed.

They showered.

They ate.

They laughed.

They watched TV while it watched them kiss.

At 4:17pm, it happened.

Josh was lying on Eli's shoulder while a TV Land rerun of "Good Times" came on, and it was the episode. "Savannah Jones" was the new girlfriend of "Sweet Daddy Williams" and he had commissioned JJ to paint her portrait as a surprise. As the show moves on, Josh choked up. He remembered that this was his favorite episode. It was also Greg's. Watching it was one of the favorite things to do. Josh prepared to cry. Josh prepared to rehash the past. Josh did the unspeakable for him.

Josh changed the channel.

"Hey, I was watching that," Eli huffed. "I thought you liked 'Good Times!"

"I do, but I'd rather have my own good times with you, James Evans, Sr.!" Josh said it and crawled on top of Eli while he kissed him. Eli wasn't sure where things were going, but he knew he didn't have time to get to the shower to relieve himself, so Josh had better be careful.

Josh wrapped his arms around Eli's head, with his elbows on Eli's shoulders, facing him while he kissed him like some new form of oxygen was concealed in Eli's lips. Josh needed Eli to know that he wanted him, now. He sat in his lap and stayed there, even after Eli made it apparent that to continue to do so would be hard on him.

They were only wearing boxer briefs (Josh) and lounge pants (Eli) when Josh stood up and took Eli's hands.

He tiptoed and kissed Eli's lips.

He moved downward and licked his left nipple.

Eli winced and grabbed Josh's butt.

He hoped that it would tell Josh that that was his spot and if he kept going, things were going to get serious.

Josh understood that.

Josh keeping going.

Josh licked Eli's right nipple and reached down and unraveled the cord of his lounge pants. They slipped open, but between his obvious erection in the front and ample buttocks in the back, the pants just hovered on his hips.

Josh helped them make their way home, to the floor, which is where they would be spending the rest of the night.

Eli stood there, naked, erect, aroused, excited and unsure.

Josh had been so coy and reserved when it came time for sexual stuff. He wasn't frigid, but he was never forward. Eli grabbed Josh by the arms and lifted him to his feet.

He searched his eyes and Josh told him, with a smirk and a kiss, that he knew what he was doing.

Eli wanted to hear the words.

"Baby, are you sure you are ready for this? I know you wanted to wait and I do, too. You know I want you so bad, but I don't want it to be our last time because things got awkward. I will wait if you want to because when it's on, it's on. I have been waiting for you a long time. Not just sexually, but in my heart, so if tonight's THE tonight, then say it."

Eli meant it. He wasn't trying to have sex with Josh this time and no other. He wanted this to be the first of many. He didn't want an odd dance afterwards that would then take away the friendship and the closeness.

They were worth more than the sex.

"Our closeness means too much to me to mess it up with a good nut. I want you, the right way, and I want you to want me, too," Eli quoted Marvin and knew that Josh knew the importance of those words.

That's when Josh knew that there was no doubt, that he wanted Eli, too and he said so, because he couldn't want any longer.

"Eli, you are more than I ever thought I could expect. I have been hurt and I thought that I would never feel love again. But this is something more than just that. This is new to me. I am not coming at you with past baggage. I turned that channel."

The reference to Greg and Good Times and the episode were lost on Eli, but he didn't care.

Josh was pouring out his heart and Eli was listening.

"You are an amazing man, and whatever we become, I want you to know that you,"

Josh stopped to kiss his right cheek.

"mean"

Josh kissed the left.

"the"

Josh kissed Eli's left nipple.

"world"

Josh kissed the right one.

"to"

Josh licked his navel.

"me."

Josh got on his knees and Eli pulled him up when it became clear that Josh was about to blow him away, with the act and his words.

They made their way to the bed.

Eli just didn't want head to be their first sexual act.

He loved it as much as anybody, but he didn't want Josh on his knees, before him. He had been worshipped like that before, and it wasn't sexy to Eli at all. He wanted to be on equal footing. He placed Josh on the bed and licked him from head to toe.

They negotiated their way around each other as Josh licked Eli's neck, while Eli licked his shoulder.

Josh, nipple. Eli, back.

Josh, abs. Eli, thighs.

Josh, pubic hairs. Eli, cheeks.

They explored each other for what seemed like hours.

When Josh finally grabbed Eli's hard hull, Eli almost erupted. He had waited for that feeling for so long with Josh. He had wanted to know how Josh would grab him and how he would feel in Josh's mouth and how Josh would use his tongue and knowing now was dizzying.

Eli let Josh have his way with him, while Eli concentrated on Josh's smooth, round, sculpted butt that hovered over his face. Eli had always fancied himself a cunning linguist and spread his unusually thick tongue to enter Josh and show him and his anus why they would quickly become best friends.

GASP.

While he was busy swallowing Eli, Josh wasn't sure what Eli was doing in his 6 part, because he was handling 9 just fine, thank you.

But when Eli opened Josh's cheeks and began to rim him, like his sweet ass was his own Momma's peach cobbler, Josh moaned out loud.

He was focused and sharp and aimed right for the hole every time, and opened it and slurped and licked and nibbled and Josh almost screamed for something.

Eli was so good that Josh rolled onto his back, dropped Eli's lethal weapon and let Eli have his way.

Mr. Control Freak surrendered control and let Eli devour him.

It was marvelous.

Eli rimmed Josh for at least 30 minutes and Josh thought he would pass out. He finally grabbed Eli's locs and pulled him up for a kiss.

"If you don't stop that, I might have to let you," Josh surrendered as he reached for a condom on the nightstand.

At some point, Eli had put oil and lube and condoms on the nightstand, and safe sex was clearly the course of the night.

Josh was glad because they didn't have to have that awkward conversation about protection. He was prepared to, just fine, but he was glad that Eli had really heard him when they talked about responsibility and sexuality in one of their free-for-all chat fests.

So now, in the thick of it, Josh fellated Eli again and then rolled the condom onto his hardness.

Josh was more than relaxed enough to take Eli, but Eli grabbed some lube nonetheless. Josh wasn't sure what to expect. It really had been a long time.

Eli could tell and planned to be gentle.

He entered Josh with ease.

Josh moaned softly and Eli bent down to kiss him.

Josh wrapped his legs around Eli and controlled the pace with which he entered.

As Eli kissed him, Josh guided Eli into him and the feeling was euphoric.

Josh opened his eyes and found Eli staring at him.

Eli worked his rhythm into Josh until they found their dance.

It was magical.

Josh was trembling from the sensation, as Eli entered and kissed and entered and licked his neck and entered and sucked his nipple.

Eli was gentle but forceful.

They continued their dance for a sweet while, until things got hot.

It was Josh who turned their oven to broil.

Eli almost jumped when Josh grabbed his chest and pushed him backwards. Before Eli was sure what had happened, Josh was on top and Eli was under.

Josh made sure that Eli never slipped out of him. He felt safe with Eli now and Josh let all of the sexual inhibitions that he had been holding onto go.

Josh rode Eli like he was a Texas Bronco. With his hands on Eli's strong chest, and Eli's hands palming his butt, Josh let himself go. He was floating and dizzy, excited and scintillated as Eli throbbed within him and hit every spot he encountered.

Eli was thick and not huge, but large. His large hands held Josh just right and he felt like he was protected and could be free. Their lovemaking lasted for 2 hours.

By the time they had finished, everything had been explored.

Josh had rimmed Eli.

Eli had taken Josh on the floor and in a chair.

Josh had taken Eli in the shower.

The sheets were on the floor and they had sweat like the bedroom had become a sauna.

Eli was still so hard that he ached and Josh couldn't even touch himself without shaking.

They were almost afraid to touch.

They did anyway.

Josh placed his head on Eli's chest and Eli ran his hand down Josh's back.

They didn't speak.

They couldn't speak.

The only conversation they were having was one heartbeat to another. They could hear each other loud and clear.

They had ascended.

Josh lifted his head just in time to catch Eli's eyes.

They kissed. It was real.

They had passed the sexual threshold and both quietly wondered.

CHAPTER 12: THE MORNING AFTER

NOW WHAT?!

Josh was so nervous that at times he found himself staring at Eli as they went through their day. He was waiting to see if things would change.

He felt stupid at times, like he thought Eli would move away from him or think differently of him. Josh hadn't allowed himself to be this open to someone in so long, and the truth is that the sex was the least vulnerable state.

It was the tender "I love yous" and Eli's consistency that really shook Josh.

Eli was a good man and Josh needed to let to himself realize that and stop anticipating drama, cuz you get what you ask for. Josh came to this revelation as he and Eli walked around Eli's apartment all day, naked and unconcerned.

They cooked. They watched TV. They danced. They talked. They never got dressed. It was nice.

Josh stayed all day and didn't have a care in the world. Eli was attentive and open and sweet and forthcoming about everything. Everything except that phone call.

At about 6 o'clock, Eli got a phone call that took him into the bathroom for privacy. When he emerged, he was clearly and visibly a little shaken. When Josh asked him about it, he said, "it was just some family stuff," but didn't want to elaborate.

Josh and Eli had spent very little time talking about family. They had discussed size and responsibilities, relationships and roles with their families, but never the clans themselves. They knew that would come later. Eli wanted to tell Josh that his Dad was sick and he needed to go home to visit, but he didn't want Josh to think it was a half-cocked invitation to get him home to meet them.

Eli was still raw from Reggie's tone when he wanted him to meet The Monroes and didn't want to broach the subject too soon with Josh. They would have time. So Eli decided to not mention the details of that call.

That omission made Josh edgy, just for a minute. But when Eli scooped him up and asked if he was hungry, the edge slipped from Josh's mind.

Eli and Josh remained in their state of naked bliss all day and much of the evening. When Josh suggested that he should go home, Eli asked him to stay the night and just go home in the morning, when Eli left for church. Josh agreed and they spent the rest of the night laughing and lulling, kissing and contemplating—life, love, hopes, dreams, they covered the gamut.

Josh finally fell off to sleep on Eli's stomach at around 1am. Eli just turned off the lights and let him rest there.

They slept 'til sunrise.

⌘

The layout of Eli's place let so much sun into the room that it was visually impossible to sleep in the morning, unless the windows were covered and Eli didn't cover them. He likes the light and he likes morning, even though it conflicts with his night owl lifestyle.

A tender morning shower, breakfast, and eight perfectly timed kisses made up their morning. Josh had packed his things and was ready to go, while Eli got dressed, looking so handsome in his slacks, a navy blazer and a cool navy and brown tie. He was going to a church that was cool in his dress code, but he was a Southern church boy and you always get dressed for the Lord.

As they waited for a cab to reveal itself on a quiet NY Sunday morning, Eli turned to Josh and said "Thank you for one of the greatest nights of my life. I can't tell you how much I've wanted to hold you in my arms. I hope this feeling never ends, baby. You got a brotha sprung."

Eli took Josh's face in his hands and kissed him tenderly.

Their romantic moment on the curb was interrupted by "You need a cab?!"

On most days when you want a cab, you can't get them to stop, but this morning, with two tall black men kissing on the streets of the Naked City, one magically appeared and took the heat out of their curbside cavorting.

Josh got in the cab.

"Call me when you get home from church."

Eli ducked his head into the cab and kissed him once more.

Josh was exhausted. He barely slept all night. He would wake up and see Eli sleeping like a baby and Josh would just smile and stroke his thigh or kiss his face and try to just injoy the moment. But now, at home and solo, Josh realized that he didn't sleep much last night. He got into the shower and the heat of the water brought make recent memories.

Josh recalled every detail of finally making love with Eli and he trembled when he remembered how tender and forceful, sexy and sensual Eli had been all night. Josh knew that his relationship with Eli had taken a new turn and he hoped that he had made the right choice. Josh had never been so assertive, but he knew that Eli was a gentleman and he would have waited until Josh said something.

Josh figured actions spoke louder than words.

Now, so fresh and clean, Josh realized hadn't spoken to Carlton, but he knew if he called, they'd be on the phone all morning. So, Josh got into bed and figured he would just call Carlton after a quick nap.

Josh was awakened by Eli's call at 2pm. He looked at the clock and couldn't believe he had slept that long.

"Hello," Josh said, still clearing his voice.

"Baby, did you go to sleep on me?" Eli said, just chipper and clearly energized. "I thought you slept well. You didn't like the bed?"

"No, it wasn't that at all," Josh said. "Just tired from the long trip and the long ride," he said, playfully. Eli got the joke.

"So what you doing? Maybe you just need to take the day and chill. Get some rest and I know your boy Carlton is wondering where you are." Eli was on point, as usual.

"Why don't you just stay home, handle your business and call me when and if you get a break. I'm a little spent myself, so I'm gonna grab a nap, hit the gym later and maybe watch a movie. So, call me later and we'll see what's up. I love you, Joshua Knight. Thanks for being in my life."

"I love you, Eli Monroe and thank you for bringing me back to life."

The line was silent.

Neither could find the next word, but they knew that hanging up wasn't what they wanted to do, yet.

Eli offered, "I might have to go home this week. No big deal, just need to check on my Dad."

"Is everything okay, Eli? Do you need me to go with you?"

Josh was being sincere, but knew that getting away would be impossible. But he still wanted to be there for Eli if he needed him.

"No, baby, it's okay. I know you are bogged down and he's okay. Just not feeling 100% and Momma wants me to come, cuz I always kick Daddy into high gear. I think I will only be a few days. But, we'll see."

Eli tried to make it all seem really casual. Any inflection in his voice would tell Josh that he was concerned and Josh might make plans to join him. Eli was concerned that Josh would then have too much time away from the project, then something would happen and BAM, whose fault would it be that Josh was away.

Thanks, but no thank you.

I will go on my own and things with Josh and me can stay cool. Eli hated that he was drawing conclusions for Josh, but he didn't want to mess up their flow. They were clicking on everything and Eli did know in his heart that if he needed Josh, he'd say so. This just wasn't that big a deal. *You meeting my family in a time of crisis is not that big a deal. We'll save that for somewhere down the road, and better timing.*

Twenty minutes later, Josh and Eli realized that they could talk all day.

"Baby, I better get to the gym, cuz otherwise, I'm gonna lay down and right about now, I'd be out for the count. Hit me up later and get some rest yourself. Love you, sexy!"

"I love you, too, Eli. Go and keep that thick country body tight, because I am not about to go Low-Carb, so we have to work it off the old-fashioned way. I'll talk to you later."

Carlton rang in as they were hanging up and they talked for the next 45 minutes. Carlton got every detail, from Josh' assertive first move to Eli's tenderness. They shared without heated details, because Josh was discreet and Carlton didn't care about those things anyway. He wanted to know how Josh was feeling and what this meant for their relationship, or was Josh just testing the waters again.

Josh was so in love he couldn't speak it. He couldn't wrap his heart around how Eli made him feel, and he was scared to death.

"I have been so buried in work and avoiding love and trying to protect myself and my heart and my self-image that I don't even know how to be comfortable in this skin. I want to be open and spontaneous with Eli and not worry about old stuff." Josh had said it and now it was out.

"Spontaneous? Weren't you the one who packed a bag and showed up at this brother's door with the intention of putting it on him!?" Carlton laughed.

"But that wasn't my original intention. I just wanted to see him and the rest just happened." Josh was trying to innocent, again.

"What do you think SPONTANEOUS means, man!?"

They laughed and talked about next levels and relationships and fear and hurt and past and then, finally, Greg.

"I just really want to believe that that's not the marker by which I judge relationships. I mean Greg was sweet and funny and nice and yes, he made a mistake. But if I don't see how that happened and what I was doing in it at the time, he will always be the perfect man who just happened to slip and that didn't just happen. Besides, we fit almost too nicely. I think he liked the adventure of Kevin and I get that. Greg and I were so bent on being Mr. and Mr. Black SGL that we almost forgot what it felt like to just let go. We were on the right Boards, at the right gatherings, supported the right causes and it was all so nice, so sweet. But we never spent an entire day naked, just alone. And, Greg never dreamed with me. He would set goals, but he never dreamed out loud. He never just spoke it, no matter how big or possible. I like that Eli just talks about his career and his dreams and his songs, even before they came to pass. I used to be like that. I had forgotten that spark in myself."

Carlton was surprised to hear Josh be so frank. He could feel Josh bearing his soul through the phone and knew that his buddy didn't need to be alone right now. Josh was thinking too much, even in all of his openness. Carlton had to head him off at the pass.

"Man, why don't you come up to Harlem? We'll go to the Shabazz Market and just hang. What do you say?"

"Sounds like a plan. I could use some air anyway."

Josh was dressed and on the train in 30 minutes. He didn't want to think too much. He just wanted to love and be loved and stop thinking too much. Josh was noticing so many brothas and papis noticing him on the train and he wondered why they noticed him now that he was in love.

Then he realized it. They probably always were smiling and nodding and trying to say hello. It wasn't them that had changed. It was Josh. One thick Latin brother stared at Josh from 14th Street to well past 106th. He slipped Josh his number when he got off at 116th. Josh looked and smiled, because sexy Rico had included his email and was still looking at Josh through the window as the train pulled away. Josh still had it, but it was all for Eli now.

Wait, was he getting exclusive already? They really hadn't had that conversation and Josh realized that they needed to, sooner rather than later, just so he knew. But that was thinking and he wasn't doing that right now.

Right now, he was going to meet Carlton, hang out and hopefully make it back home with a find or two that only Harlem could offer.

When he got to Carlton's, they hit the street. They didn't even go upstairs. Carlton came down and they walked and talked. The tall buildings and busy buzzings of Harlem passed them on every corner. Books. Oils. Black and brown people, making their way, passing the day, in Harlem. They passed the old storefronts that made Harlem rich. They passed the new megastores that were getting rich in Harlem. They commented on the state of change that was thick in the air in Harlem.

They went to the Malcolm Shabazz Market at 116th and Lennox Ave. and Josh picked up some really nice mud cloth fabrics. A visit to Booth 51 introduced Josh and Carlton to HEGWEAR, a brother who specialized in African-inspired luggage. The brotha noticed Josh's fabrics and told him that they would make great suitcases. Josh thought he had found some new throws for his couch or maybe some wall hangings. But James, the proprietor had changed his mind. Josh was changing and Good For Me, he thought. He placed his order and left his fabric, allowing him to continue to venture through Harlem without…baggage.

They walked around until they were near 135th Street and stumbled across HATS BY BUNN. Josh had seen the brother's work recently when he was honored on TVOne.

"Let's stop in here. I like this guy's stuff."

"Here? A hat store? Wow, you really are opening up to new ideas, aren't you?" Carlton stared at Josh, as he grabbed the store's handle.

The shop was stylish and brimming with colors and hats and creations that only colored folks could appreciate fully. Josh locked onto a Fedora-styled hat that he thought his Granddad would love. He tried it on.

"Now that looks gangsta on you," Carlton suggested, but Josh said "I was thinking about it for Granddad."

The hat was black on the brim and white on the top half and had a black, white and silver meshed fabric around the center. It was stylish, indeed. Josh would definitely get it.

"But I got a little something different for you," the milliner offered. He was a light-skinned brother, with locs and a warm smile that lit up his ageless face. He crafted each hat by hand and looked at each like his child. He studied you before he offered advice, so Josh was intrigued to see what he would see in him. Bunn left and returned in about 3 minutes.

"WOW."

That's all that Josh could get out at first. It was turquoise and brown and olive and while the colors almost made Josh want to run, the style and the sheer workmanship on that hat made Josh feel like he had to at least try it on.

"Look at you, looking all sexy and Damon Wayans," Carlton said, all surprised at how good Josh looked in the hat.

"Man, I can't wear this hat. It's too much. I look like I'm trying too hard."

Josh said it and didn't believe it himself. He couldn't believe how good he looked. It hit him just right everywhere. The colors matched his skin. The fit matched his personality. The look matched his dreams. Josh always wanted to look like this guy he was seeing in the mirror—assured, confident, strong.

"Wrap it up before I change my mind, Bunn!" Josh was sold. Carlton didn't look around much. He was just happy to see Josh make a new choice.

They shook hands with the owner and then made their way near the Schomburg, which wasn't open. But Pan-Pan's was. It's a small diner on the corner that made chicken that would make you call your mother to share your joy. They injoyed some chicken and waffles and good service and great conversation. The place was a landmark that would suffer a tragic fire years later. But this fall day, it was home.

Aunts and Mommas were taking orders and giving them, too.

"Now, I know your elbow ain't on my table."

"Sorry, Ma'm."

Josh and Carlton laughed and ate and left a great tip. Their waitress kissed them.

Only in Harlem.

"Brownskin, I better get home. Man, I'm tired and I might end up taking half of Harlem with me if I don't get out of here."

They hugged and vowed to keep their weekly dinner.

Josh was home in no time and walked in just as the phone rang.

"Hey baby. What are you up to?"

"Not much, just spent the day with Carlton. Why? What's up?"

"I was wondering if you could come over. I need to ask you a big favor. I won't keep you up all night, but it's important."

"Sure. Give me an hour."

Josh didn't bother to change. He just brushed his teeth and headed for the train. He was walking before old Josh kicked in and started thinking.

"What does he want to ask?"

"He can't be asking me to marry him this soon, could he?"

"He is going to tell me about some other lover, isn't he?"

"No, he asked for a favor, so maybe he's going to ask to bring someone else into our thing. Guys are always trying to have their cake and eat it, too."

"No, he doesn't seem the type, but who knows?"

Josh laughed out loud and stopped himself.

"You will hear what he has to ask when he asks!"

Josh boarded the train and let his thoughts center on his new hat and the one he brought his Granddad and hoped that his luggage was cool when it was finished; anything to not think about Eli and what he wanted to ask.

"Hello Stranger," Eli said as he opened the door and his arms to receive Josh. "Come on in."

"Man, it's getting cold out there. It's definitely not Indian Summer anymore."

Josh and Eli bantered for a little while, before Eli sat in front of Josh and took his hands. Josh had no idea where the conversation was going and almost missed it when Eli talked about knowing Josh's crazy schedule and the big campaign and the like, but this was really important. Josh braced himself and almost shook while Eli looked at him so intensely. Josh really wasn't sure what Eli was about to ask. So he listened and stopped trying to guess.

"But this studio is something I have been trying to pull together for months and now that I have to go home to see Dad, they are ready to do the install. If I miss it, I don't know how long I will have to wait. So, I was wondering, since you are so comfortable around here, if you could stay here Tuesday night and be here to let them in Wednesday morning and check everything afterwards? You don't need to hang around. I trust the crew, worked with 'em before. But I don't trust'em with my keys. So, since you already work near here, you could get to work sooner and then, I could have the engineer come by your office and you can sign off on everything for me. I know it's a lot to ask, but I have been working on songs lately and having a real studio at my disposal would make writing so much easier. Please, baby, please baby baby please, say yes!!"

Then Eli got on one knee. That's when Josh finally said yes.

"So, you will only have to sleep here one night. I'm leaving Tuesday morning and I won't be back until Friday. I'm sure that Dad's alright, but Mom's gonna ask me to fix things and do this and that, so I might as well build the time into my visit. But I would love to hold you before I bounce so if you want to come and stay tomorrow night that would be sexy."

Eli's eyes told Josh that he really wanted him to stay. Josh wanted to anyway and he was right. He was so close to Josh's office and not being in morning rush hour on the train for 2 days during this campaign would be great.

"Thank you baby. So, here take these now, so you have them."

It seemed to be happening in slow motion. Eli reached into his pocket and pulled out a simple silver keychain, that looped like infinity, with two keys on it.

"Josh, here. Josh? Baby, you okay?"

Josh was frozen for a moment and Eli noticed.

"What's wrong?"

"Nothing, honestly. Just tired and my mind's all over the place."

Eli gave Josh the code to put into his phone for the alarm and that was it. No proposal or request for a kidney. Just open the door.

Josh and Eli watched "Family Guy" and just cracked up from its bawdy tone, but they both loved it. Josh knew he had better get home before Eli put his arms around him the right way and Josh was there again, all night.

"Baby, I'm going to get out of here before I end up staying all night."

"I wouldn't mind that at all."

"I know and neither would I, but I know tomorrow is Monday. I need to update the team on the ATL trip."

"So I will see you tomorrow evening?"

"Yes, you will Eli." They kissed and Josh made his way home to an uneventful night, where he turned in early to get ready for Monday.

"Good Night Sleepyhead"

"Good Night Night Owl"

The exchange had become so much a part of their ritual that Josh would reach for the phone in the dark and speed-dial Eli without even thinking.

Wow, that's a change.

Monday started early and lasted long. Josh had 14 meetings before the day was over. He had a videoconference with the graphics guy. He reached out to Common's manager, Derek, and they planned to meet later, but agreed that all involved were interested. Josh was a brilliant multi-tasker, but all of his thoughts were taking 2nd place to his thoughts of Eli.

He couldn't believe that someone had become such a part of his routine. He was always thinking about Eli and he didn't mind at all. He was looking forward to staying the night and just being in his arms. Josh coasted through the day, checking each task off of his To Do List with fervor and finesse. No one would have known that he was a nervous wreck.

He couldn't figure out if he should use the key to Eli's place to open the door.

THAT was his major dilemma of the day.

Josh stood outside of Eli's spot for almost 5 minutes, immobile. He didn't want to seem to eager or forward. The key was for when Eli wasn't there, but he was home now, right now, in there, waiting. Opening the door and declaring, "Honey, I'm home" was too reminiscent for Josh and too familiar. But he liked the idea that Eli trusted him with his space and "JESUS, JUST OPEN THE DOOR" he kept saying to himself, while he stood at the bottom of the stairs. He then freaked over the idea of Eli having to run some pointless but necessary errand and finding him there, frozen.

Josh finally moved.

"I was wondering where you were," Eli said innocently.

Josh had called to say 'I'm on my way," partly as a courtesy, but in his mind, just a smidget of it had to do with giving Eli to give out any signs of debauchery that would ruin his image of the man of his dreams. Josh was officially tripping.

"I was gonna cook something, but I didn't know what you were in the mood for, so I figured I'd wait until you got home…I mean here."

Eli smiled at his unintentional intentional faux pas. He really loved the way his place felt when Josh was in it and didn't mind alluding to that.

"Whatever you want to cook is fine with me, Honey. How are the kids? How was work?"

Josh joked as he grabbed Eli and kissed him like a housewife from the '50s.

"That's all I get," Eli pondered coyly.

"Okay, but remember you started it," Josh said, as he took Eli in his arms and tried to dip him. Eli's considerable height and thickness variance over Josh made that virtually impossible. So Eli just flipped the script and finished what Josh had intended. He took Josh's briefcase and placed it on the table. He grabbed Josh close, planted a kiss firmly on his lips, while he held his lower back and dipped him. Josh knew it was coming, but the sensation of it still made him dizzy.

Eli didn't lay a simple little kiss on him. He kissed Josh like he was hungry and Domino's had long missed its 30 minutes or less guarantee. He devoured Josh and Josh swam in the intensity of Eli's kiss. His hands moved down to Josh's butt and they stayed there as they kissed, when Eli brought his back up and while he said, "I am so glad you're here."

Josh moved closer and said "So am I," as he reached down and grabbed Eli's butt in return, mostly because Eli has a dynamic posterior.

"Why, Mr. Knight! If I didn't any better, I would think you are trying to induce me!"

"Don't you mean 'seduce' you?" Josh corrected.

"No, I meant 'induce,' cuz you are gonna start it, but I guarantee you, I'm going to finish it!"

"Okay, Mr. Monroe. What would your Mom say if she heard you talking like that?" Josh was being cute, but he was also getting a little heated and wanted to lighten the moment.

“She would say that I learned well from my Daddy!” Eli said, sternly, as he stepped closer to Josh and kissed him again.

“So what do you want to eat or are you not that hungry now?”

“Well, since it’s our last night together, let’s go out and have let somebody else do the work. Either that or we can just hang out there tonight and injoy each other’s company. I will leave it up to you.”

“Well, baby, I really don’t feel like sharing you tonight, but I feel you on letting someone else do the work. So why don’t we compromise and do both. We can call somewhere and get a delivery and then we don’t have to cook but we don’t have to leave either.”

“Great idea. I thought I was the idea man in this relationship,” Josh said it and then almost regretted it. He had said ‘relationship’ too soon and didn’t know what Eli thought they had or what he really wanted. Josh’s chagrin was almost visible.

“Come on baby. We are both the idea men and the creative men in this relationship. That’s why we get along so well. We think differently but alike. We balance each other out.”

Eli wasn’t even concerned about Josh’s fear or his flub. He was testing the waters and Eli wasn’t afraid to swim in them. He almost regretted not asking Josh to go with him. Even if he couldn’t, Josh would have appreciated the request. Eli realized that now and didn’t know how to correct it, so he called his Mom. He figured that he would introduce the two by phone and that would let Josh know that he didn’t want to keep any part of himself out of reach.

While Eli called one of his favorite eateries that were stored on his cell, Josh and Mrs. Monroe had a nice chat. They talked about his upbringing, his parents, his business and his feelings for her son.

“So you and my Eli have been seeing a lot of each other, Joshua. He’s a wonderful young man, isn’t he?”

"Yes, Ma'm. He really is. You raised a remarkable son."

"Yes, we did. His father was a little rough when he first told us that he was, you know, only attracted to men. But when his Daddy realized he wasn't going to change him and that he hadn't changed, they were fine. We hope to meet you soon, Joshua. You seem like a wonderful young man yourself. I will have to get your Momma's number, so she and I can talk soon. We might be related someday, so I should get to know her."

Joshua almost fell on the floor. This Southern Black woman had talked about her son and him like marriage was the natural next step, although there weren't even legal stairs for their relationship. Josh appreciated her tone, though. The law might not recognize their love, but Mrs. Lois Monroe did and expected them to take some logical and biblical next step if they were going to be together. But right now, she just wanted to know his mother and his people and what they did.

"Yes, Ma'm. I will have to put the two of you on the phone someday soon."

"Yes, Joshua you will. You can give her my number. Anyway, let me speak to my Elijah. I have a roast in the oven and need to get off this phone. Nice to meet you, baby."

"Thank you Mrs. Monroe. The pleasure was all mine."

"I am sure it was. Take care, Joshua. We will talk again soon."

Josh handed the phone to Eli, who smiled as his mother said some very sweet things about Josh. Josh couldn't hear what was being said, but Eli's eyes, which kept darting over to him and winking, coupled with the air kisses Eli kept blowing, let him know that he was "in" with Mom.

"She really liked you. I think you are the first person I have let her talk to like that. She met a guy or two that I was seeing, but they never seemed comfortable talking to her. You just charmed my Momma, Mr. Knight."

"I know my way around Southern Mommas."

"Apparently, and that's not the only thing you know your way around."

With that, Eli grabbed Josh and started to kiss him again. The kiss got passionate and just when Eli thought he'd have some Josh for dinner, the real meal arrived.

"Saved by the bell," Josh said, pulling his shirt down and his pants up. Eli had only tried to lick him all over, and his expert tongue was so skilled that it made Josh weak. He was ready to submit, when the doorbell reminded them both that the night was young.

Steak, lobsters, baked potatoes and broccoli made up their impromptu dinner and it was excellent. Eli had ordered from some nearby place that knew how he liked his food.

"My goodness, that was excellent. We have to go there again sometime. That lobster was so tender."

Josh almost licked his fingers, but Eli reached over and did it for him.

"Man, you better stop before I pour some melted butter on *you*."

Josh couldn't believe how forward and frisky he could get around Eli. He felt strong and aggressive and sensual and alive.

He also felt like it would all end at any moment. At those times, Eli could see the fear in his eyes and would do something—a nibble, a lick, a kiss; a smile, a whisper, a wink—to say 'I am real, baby. Now breathe.' Josh was getting more and more comfortable around Eli and Eli knew that he had been good to wait. Waiting made their time together more grounded and more balanced. They had moved past roles and expectations and were just, well, good together.

"Come on Cletus. You walk over here, but you limpin' back." Eli did his best Grandma Klump on Josh, who fell out laughing, because it was so unexpected.

Eli grabbed him and sang "Put a Little Sugar in My Bowl" by Nina Simone and that had become Josh's 2nd favorite Nina Simone song since buying almost everything she had ever recorded. That was a weak spot for Josh and before he knew it, they were naked and deeply ensconced in Round Two.

"Eli, let me ask you something. I hope it's not too deep or too soon or too anything, but I need to ask."

"Okay, baby. Ask me anything. I mean that. Fire away."

"Okay. Today, right now, what are you looking for?"

"With you?"

"Or with anyone in a relationship," Josh added, to give Eli the room he needed to not feel trapped.

"Well, first, I am looking to build a relationship with you, Josh. I like you. I love you and you know that those two don't always go together. I think you are brilliant and witty. I love being around you and I love the way I feel around you. I feel alive in my skin around you and I want to be more of a man now, so that whoever put that hurt in your eyes will see you one day and know that love healed it. There is this song by Aretha Franklin and George Benson from the 80s that talks about loving all the hurt away. That song says it for me. I want to be with you and hopefully, we will keep growing and living and loving until we have loved all the hurt away and all we have is Our Love. I was a little scared to say some of these things to you, Joshua. I mean you are what most cats in NYC are killing each other to find. You're handsome, smart, you own your own business. Sometimes I look at you and wonder how you could have ever been single. Sometimes I look at you and Thank God that you were. I just know that I'm beyond feeling you. I know that I love you and if I get lucky, you are the last person I will ever say that to in this lifetime."

Josh didn't mean to do it.

He was there, inches away from Eli, naked and exposed, vulnerable and stunned. Eli had said everything he wanted to hear a man say. Josh thought he would hug him or kiss him or even thank him. Josh didn't expect to do it, but he did. With Eli right there, and his own manhood on the line in his mind, Josh lost it.

Josh cried.

These weren't just "Oh, aren't you sweet, Honey" tears. These were "Oh My God I Have Been Waiting To Hear That My Entire Life" tears and Elijah almost got concerned, except that, at some level, he understood. Okay, he overstood. See, Eli could always see that hurt in Josh's eyes and he consciously vowed to never do anything to make Josh hurt again. He didn't say cry, because he knew that he might do something one day that would bring Josh to tears, but he didn't think that was for months or years to come.

Josh just cried, almost without air, over the words and the sentiment and the love in Eli's eyes when he spoke. Josh was in there, trying to stop himself from purging like this, but the safety of Eli's arms and his own need to finally get all of this STUFF off of himself, out of himself, had overtaken him and Josh needed to let it all go.

How would he explain this to Carlton or anyone else, when he could barely explain to himself? He asked Eli what he wanted and Eli spoke from his heart and soul. He said things about Josh, not just about relationships, that Josh had always wanted to hear someone say and now, here he was, lying naked in a bed with a man who was so sexy that sometimes he made Josh nervous, still. Josh really did think that the next guy that he dated would be some compromised version of what he wanted and he would have a "less than" relationship just to feel safer about love and trust. He didn't expect or at times feel worthy of Eli and all of his kindnesses.

Eli is such a gentleman and a gentle man, and he is such a friend. Josh just couldn't fathom all this in one man. He had no idea and apparently didn't hear Eli say that he had found all of that in him. Eli understood and would probably have cried himself, but he didn't want Josh to think he was patronizing him. Anyway, this was Josh's purge and Eli just held him until Josh finally, some 20 minutes later, finally caught his breath.

"I don't…."

"Baby, you don't have to say a word. I'm just glad I was here to hold you when whatever fell off of you finally fell."

"Eli, I love you in ways I can't even comprehend. You are so good to and for me and I don't ever want to let what I have been through determine what we can do or be or have. If you ever see me holding back, push me. I mean that. I don't mean fight me, but call me on it and maybe, just maybe we can love all the hurt away."

Eli took Josh into his arms. As much as Eli wanted to make love to Josh that night, he knew that more than anything he needed to hold him. Their legs and arms and souls intertwined that night. They had become one.

Unbreakable.

Inseparable.

Nothing could stop them now.

But that didn't mean that something wouldn't try.

CHAPTER 13: THE SHOWDOWN,

PARTS I and II

JUST when YOU*thought* it was SAFE...

Josh stayed with Eli all night and even offered to ride to the airport with him. He just felt so connected that part of him didn't want to let Eli go.

But go Eli did, to check on his father and do some things for his Momma and tell her how in love he was and how happy he was and maybe that he was even going to spend the rest of his life with Josh. He would tell her these things while he was putting in the new dishwasher and finally hanging that new screen for the projector TV that he had sent his family. Dad's eyes didn't always act right, so Eli figured he would make the TV bigger. But everything he did while there made him think of Josh.

Josh was no better in New York.

He went through the day feeling almost giddy. Tasha saw. Carlton heard it in his voice. Even the lady at the little bodega near the office commented on it when he stopped in to get some water and some gum. Love is Visible and Audible when it's really love.

Josh went home that first night and Tuesday never seemed so long. He tossed and turned. He only spoke to Eli once, because he was so caught up in family that he didn't get to really call that first day. They did talk for about 20 minutes, but much of that included his sister, his Mom and several cousins saying HI to Josh and telling him that they looked forward to him coming down for a visit. Eli finally went onto the back porch and that gave them a few minutes of peace.

"I miss you already, baby."

"I miss you too. I don't know how I'm going to sleep tonight, but I am sure I'll dream about you."

"You sure know how to touch a Black man's heart, J. Thank you, baby, for letting me love you."

"Thank you, Eli, for waiting, so patiently. I could see it in your eyes that you knew that I was scared, but you didn't push or grow impatient with me. I will love you for that for the rest of our lives."

"Man, you better get off my phone before I get on a plane tonight and come put it on ya!"

"Bring it, baby. I am not afraid. Come on, Cletus."

Eli had to laugh at Josh adopting one of Eli's favorite lines.

"Let me get back in here to these Monroes before we end up staying up all night. I love you, Josh. Good Night Sleepyhead."

"Good Night Night Owl. I love you too, Eli Monroe. Really, I do."

"Hey. Save those last two words. You might need them again, if I have anything to do with it."

Josh couldn't speak another word. Eli had silenced him with the possibility of marriage and that was the deal-sealer. Josh had hit pay dirt, with the perfect man.

Josh barely closed his eyes that night or the next few nights. He thought of Eli and could relive every touch. He lay naked in his sheets and for the first time, he could tell the difference between naked and nude. Josh had slept in the nude for a long time. Tonight, for the first time, he slept naked, and vulnerable and open. He liked it. He felt like he was breathing new breath. But he didn't sleep much at all that night. He kept waiting for Eli's touch on his back or a kiss to his forehead. Every thing in Josh's body was alive and vibrant. He had finally awaken from what felt like a lifelong sleep. Maybe even a daily coma. He was functionally comatose at some level and Eli had resuscitated him.

He knew that those were big words to put on someone, but they were even bigger emotions to feel. Josh had to breathe and let each new breath remind him that he was alive and this was real.

Wednesday was pretty uneventful at work. The campaign was moving along brilliantly. The commercial shoots were coming out really hot. They were sleek and edgy, and the new recording of the Coca-Cola "I'd Like To Teach The World to Sing" was done and featured many celebrities, recording artists and military parents, holding pictures of their children. The song was also being released as a single, and all proceeds were going to the USO.

So many people say that they support the troops, no matter their stance on the war, so Joshua thought what better way to do that from all angles than to offer a song that spoke peace and helped to bring some relief to the troops. The idea was the talk of the advertising and music industry.

Mary J. Blige, Busta Rhymes, Omarion, Keisha Cole, Fantasia, Nick Cannon and others had all signed on.

Josh got the biggest surprise of his life when he got word that Mariah Carey would produce the track. While many love Mariah's voice, Josh had always liked her as a producer and songwriter as well. One of the few contemporary artists that he would listen to was Mariah and she wanted to help, since she was a big supporter of the USO. All in all, today was a good day. Thursday and Friday both moved with the same High, But Not As High As My Heart moments, were Josh was happy, but still holding back, because Eli wasn't there.

He didn't want to disturb him and he really did want his family to have their time. They would only talk at night, when Eli had some space, time to breathe. They would blow kisses and make wishes and speak of how sweet Saturday would be when they were together again.

Josh thought he would end the day by going by to check on Eli's place and just be there for a bit and then go home. He thought to himself that he might just stay, because it was closer and maybe he could sleep tonight, in Eli's bed. It was so hokey that Josh laughed out loud. But he still considered it. He figured he'd make up his mind when he got there as to whether he'd stay. Josh reached into his briefcase and pulled out the simple keychain and the 2 keys that would get him into Heaven Here On Earth, also known as Eli's place. He didn't like feeling out of control and would never normally display such emotion, even (and especially) to himself. But being with Eli made him realize that he wasn't in control in the first place.

If that song hadn't played and he wouldn't have gone to all those shops looking, only to have something tap him on his shoulder and show him to Roadhouse Records, he and Elijah Monroe would never have met.

It was destiny and he had to let that truth ring in his ears and live with the beautiful consequences of it.

NEWS FLASH NEWS FLASH NEWS

Joshua Knight

is not in control of the Universe.

He smiled and exhaled.

The day ended for Josh at about 7pm, and he made his way to Eli's.

Eli had called him in the middle of the day, which was odd, especially since he didn't leave a message. He also didn't answer when Josh tried to call him back. Josh got a feeling. He stopped to get a sandwich, because he thought it was be crazy to wait until he got home to Brooklyn to eat, when Eli's was closer and he was starving, still operating much of the day on little food. Some habits are hard to break.

After he got a turkey, provolone and LMT wrap, Josh made his way up Eli's steps and thought that he had turned the lights off when he came by to check on the place on Tuesday. The living room was alive with lights and movement. He knew he hadn't left it that bright. He thought for a minute that a burglar might be in the apartment, but realized quickly that they would have to be stupid to bring that much attention to the act of thievery.

Then, Josh got excited.

The next thought that hit him was that Eli had come home early to surprise him. Josh got happy, but then felt bad, because he hated that their love took Eli from his family. They hadn't seen him in so long and he really hoped that he didn't sound so pitiful that Eli felt he had to return a day early.

Josh could hear music as he prepared to open the door. It had to be Eli.

He opened the door and the smell of that vanilla candle on the dining table hit him. It had to be Eli.

He listened and heard Natalie Cole inviting him to "La Costa" and since that stayed in Eli's cd player as their personal love song, Josh knew his baby had come home. It had to be Eli.

Josh put his briefcase and the sandwich down and wanted to surprise Eli with his own surprise. Josh would get naked in the living room and open the door already nude. It had to be Eli.

Josh removed his suit and debated leaving on the tank and boxer briefs to give Eli the pleasure of peeling them off of him. It had to be Eli.

Josh decided against it and let it all hang out. He would open the door naked and nude and let Eli have his way with him and then, after a night of lovemaking, he would make him get back on a plane for Louisiana, so he could go back and be the man of the family, since his Dad wasn't well. His mother needed him and so did his family. Josh pushed that thought aside and allowed himself to be selfish. He would deal with the trip back home for Eli later. Now, Josh was hungry for Eli and Eli was on the other side of that door, waiting for him and Josh wasn't going to make him wait a second longer. It had to be Eli and knowing Eli, he would be rock hard, laid out and looking like he was already ready.

Josh turned the knob and when he saw the face and body of a man he had never met, he almost fainted, again.

Josh had such instant flashbacks of Gregory and Kevin and their apartment and the demise of their relationship and the death of all of his dreams and all of this in a blink. He couldn't hear what the dude was saying who got up out of the bed and approached him.

"Who are you?"

Reggie rolled his eyes at Josh and looked him and his naked body up and down. Part of Reggie wanted to push Josh out of the room where he had poised himself to take back Eli. The other part of him wanted to push Josh—though he didn't know his name yet—down onto the bed and get some of what he had heard of making Eli so happy.

Reggie had kept tabs on Eli, even though he had walked out on him.

After a few rolls in the hay with every Tomas, Ricardo and hairy Arab, Latino and Asian he could get with over the few years, Reggie realized that he wanted something steady. Not necessarily committed, but just someone to come home to and to kick it with him he got bored. He figured that that was a good enough reason to be in a relationship and so his thoughts brought him back to Eli.

First, he tried to call, but could never reach him. Eli had changed the home number, only because some of Reggie's tricks came out of the woodwork and kept calling, even after Reggie bounced. But his cell, Eli kept that the same. He had to because that was his main contact for gigs and he didn't want the drama of having to contact all of his contacts. Yet, Reggie would never dial it.

He probably knew that Eli would curse him out and tell him where to go, so Reggie conveniently never dialed those digits. Reggie would be at one of his sex parties or with whatever dude he could lasso on the train, at the gym or in the club and he would have a flash of Eli in his mind. He hated it because he had to admit that Eli was an expert lover. If only he would put away all that corny mess about commitment and long-term and meeting the Monroes. They could still be kicking it. But Eli wanted something real and consistent. Eli was always steady.

Remembering Eli and his sense of same, Reggie decided he would check something out. He dug around for about 4 days before, one day, in the door in his kitchen, there they were—two keys, dangling from a simple keychain. Reggie debated it.

He called around and asked some of their mutual friends what was going on with Eli. Okay, they weren't mutual friends as much as Eli's friends who had put up with Reggie. An engineer at the studio Eli uses a lot was surprised when he heard from Reggie. It had been a while and he knew that they had broken up, though he didn't know about Josh.

So even though D-Money knew that Eli told him during one of their late night sessions that Reggie wasn't a steady thing and how he thought he was creeping on him anyway, he agreed to meet Reggie at the studio.

Reggie knew that D-Money liked him. He had caught him checking his tight jeans when he dropped by to see Eli once or twice. They even had a moment in the studio bathroom that could have gotten hot if one of the background singers didn't come in before they got into a stall.

D-Money didn't get down like Eli. He had a girl and 2 kids, but didn't mind getting sucked by an expert mouth and he thought that only a dude could really handle another dude when it came to head.

"No matter what a chick does, she don't know the spots, so she always fumbling," he thought. He also thought that tonight, before he gave Reggie any info, Reggie would have to give him something.

Reggie wouldn't mind obliging. He knew it and walked in and grabbed D-Money's crotch before he even spoke.

"First, I think we have some unfinished business," Reggie said as he got on his knees and sucked D-Money so well that he almost thought about tapping it. Somehow, though, D-Money knew that if he ever went further with a dude than some head, he would be in trouble, not just with his chick, but chicks in general. He knew he didn't want to travel that far down the road. So he just erupted and planned to blow his girl's back out when he got back out of this ecstasy that Reggie had backed him into, up against a wall and moaning and hitting all the spots.

Reggie quickly got the info out of D-Money and left. There was nothing to say that the blowjob hadn't already spoken. Reggie had to decide what he would do next.

Eli was out of town, with his damn family in Louisiana, and he knew that he had some time to think before he had to act. He asked around and found out about Eli and Josh, but couldn't find out details, except that they hadn't been together that long. But one cat in the circle revealed the secret that put Reggie into motion. He told Reggie that Eli had told him that he "was waiting for things to be right with this dude," and whoever this dude is, they haven't kicked it like that yet. They hadn't had sex, he thought. Dude didn't know about Josh's impromptu pounce on Eli after his trip.

Reggie almost laughed. He knew that if he put it on Eli before Eli got some with this new dude, he would be IN again. So Reggie plotted.

He called the Super in the building, who remembered him because a) Reggie was there a lot and b) Reggie had sucked him off once or twice, okay 7 times, to get access to Eli's apartment before Eli had given him keys. The Super nervously told Reggie that Eli had never changed the locks. The Super was nervous because he didn't want his wife to see that talking to Reggie made him hard. He was ashamed, not because he didn't want his wife to see it, but because he was hoping that another visit from Reggie would get him what his wife never did, saying "civilized women don't do that." Well, maybe you don't but that black guy who visits downstairs does and maybe I'll get lucky. The Super smiled, and so did Reggie on the other end of the phone, as he hung up and plotted.

Reggie had plans to execute, but his plans had not taken into consideration one major factor. Joshua Knight.

⌘

Reggie faced him believing that he was this puritanical rarity in NYC who wasn't in touch with his sexuality and was a prude. Reggie assumed that meant that Josh was also a pushover and a punk.

Josh's well-spoken inquisition proved Reggie's point as far as he was concerned.

"Who in the hell are you?"

"I'm Reggie. Who are you?"

"I'm Joshua Knight, Eli's…boyfriend."

"So, what. I'm supposed to be impressed? Man, I was with Eli for 2 years and I'm the best he ever got. I heard you weren't doing your job and putting it on Eli right, so I thought I would come home and break him off a little something. See, that's what's wrong with you siddity bitches. You always messin' it up with all this talk about marriage, unions, gay politics and this and that. Some of us just want a thick dick and a good man who knows who to use it. You probably waiting for him to ask you to marry him before sex him, right?

Well, I have already done that to him 719 times, baby. We used to keep a tally. So why don't you just put on some clothes and pick your face back up and back out of my Boo's apartment. Nice body, but I guarantee you, you can't put it down like me, so go quickly before he gets here and we have to have a contest because I promise you, you would lose."

Josh didn't know what to do. He was butt-naked and Reggie was talking so much junk that he thought he would hit him. He disrespected Eli's house and he disrespected their relationship and he disrespected him, and Josh wanted to hit him. Josh was never much of a fighter, even throughout grade school and the like. His parents agreed that fighting was the desperate resort of a desperate person. So Josh never fought much. He did have to fight Jerome Robinson when he called him a "faggot" after Marsha Brown said no to going to the dance with him because she was going with Joshua. But never again. Josh didn't like the sense of lack of control that fighting made him feel.

Then Josh remembered that he wasn't in control. He held his breath and left the room, to gather his clothes and his senses.

What was the guy doing in Eli's apartment?

How did he get in?

Were they still doing it on the side and is that why Eli wasn't pushing him?

Was Eli still having sex with his ex and justifying it because they had shared a relationship?

Josh wanted to hit something, but he would remain calm.

Josh turned to leave the room.

Reggie followed him.

"So you really are a bitch. You just gonna walk away from me? See, you can't hang."

"Shut up."

"You probably thought he was holding back because he was in love with you. He probably got a piece down in Louisiana, too. Probably banged out some thick country-fed brotha while he been gone."

"SHUT UP."

"Who you think you talkin' to? I ain't thinkin' about you and your li'l attitude. I get down in front of Eli and hoover him and you are a memory."

"SHUT UP!"

"You really think that a dude like Eli wouldn't be getting some after all this time? He's way too sexual to be holding out for some prissy queen who probably was devastated by some break-up with some other bourgie nigga and now you are saving yourself. Save it, bitch. You lost. When Eli gets home, I'll have him naked and hard and humping before he even has a chance to breathe. Ain't no need for all of that talkin' and 'how was you day' that you like. He need some sex and I'm gonna give him what you obviously can't."

Josh hit him.

He didn't really want to, but Reggie just wouldn't shut up and the noise of his voice was getting on Josh's nerves. Before he knew it, Josh had balled up his fist and focused all of that anger and rage that he was feeling, not only from Reggie's hateful words, and Eli's possible betrayal, but all of the energy that he had swallowed after Gregory and Kevin got busted. He remembered looking at Kevin at one point and even to this day, Josh swears that Kevin smirked at him. Like "finally you know and you can go." Even as Kevin tried to do the right thing and say the right things in front of Greg, he seemed like he smirked at Joshua. So Josh saw Kevin's face and Reggie's face and Jerome's face, when he reached all the way back to 1985 and that fight in high school, and hit Reggie with such force that he flew off of his feet and into the wall. Reggie was shocked. Reggie was shaken. But Reggie was also ready for a good fight. He grabbed his bleeding lip and prepared to go for it.

"Oh, bitch, you wanna tango? You want some? Then, let's go."

Reggie swung like a wild animal, barely connecting with Josh, except for Josh's blocking gestures. Joshua knew that Reggie was fighting against the fact that he had been hit, and not about passion. He knew that if he wanted to, he could knock Reggie out and be done with it. Joshua was on fire. His nostrils flared as

Reggie did more talking than swinging and Josh hit him a second time, just for good measure, before he again turned to leave. Reggie hit him but Josh felt nothing. He was enraged and the force of his blows made Reggie scared.

'This bitch is tryin' kill me over some dick?!'

Reggie backed up. Josh smirked this time.

"I'm getting out of here before I really hurt you."

Josh heard himself say it but couldn't believe his own rage. Josh looked at Reggie's swollen lip and eye, feeling bad for a moment—Only a moment! He brought it on himself. Josh had gotten dressed and it was time to get out of here. He would deal with Eli later. If there was an explanation, Josh wasn't trying to hear it right now and Reggie surely wasn't the bearer of it. Josh turned while Reggie screamed wildly behind him.

"That's right, you punk ass bitch. You need to leave and leave Eli alone. He ain't trying to get with no stiff board like you. That nigga likes a freak like me! You need to stop trying to be a lady and act like a man!"

Josh contemplated finishing what he started and knocking the taste from Reggie's mouth, but he left it alone. If Reggie had followed him, Josh wasn't responsible. He turned and Reggie was quiet. Somehow, Reggie knew better. All of his elaborate threats remained at a safe distance.

Josh could breathe now, because he was outside. But he couldn't breathe because he was outside, and not in Eli's bed, waiting for him to come home tomorrow. Josh wasn't in Eli's apartment, walking around, being familiar and getting ready to have a good night's sleep for the first time in a week. Josh couldn't breathe because what if Eli was still having sex with Reggie and Josh wasn't enough and it was all a dream, a fantasy that would never come true.

Josh couldn't breathe because he had done it again. He had invested his heart in a man who talked all the right talk, but when asked to walk, always headed to the hoes. Josh wasn't even devastated this time. He was pissed.

Josh was pissed, and sad because he really did want to believe that everything that Eli had said was the truth for them both. He wanted to believe that Eli was the one…no, The One. But Reggie and Eli had dated for two years and he should know better. The sex with Eli was ridiculous, like the man was insatiable, so that fact was already proven. When Josh and Eli made love, it was relentless, so Reggie's comments held some water with Josh and some fear for Josh. Of course they did it 719 times. We have already done it 6 times and we have only been together that way a little while.

But right now, Josh was pissed. His sandwich was still on the table in the apartment and he wasn't going back. He had remembered his briefcase, but forgot the sandwich and he was furious and ravenous.

Reggie was glad, as he ate it, wishing that Josh would catch him. Reggie found all the right reads when Josh had left the building.

"Bourgie Bitch thinks he can take my man?! What I look like? I'm Salt and Pepa and I'll take YOUR man, Miss Prissy!"

Reggie was talking to the air between bites.

Joshua just walked and tried to breathe. He couldn't believe how horribly the events of the night were going. He would have never expected this to happen and he was pissed. He swore that the night couldn't get any worse.

He was wrong.

Joshua was distraught. He almost wanted to go back and finish what he started. He needed to finish SOMETHING that he had started as it related to his personal life. He was aching and reeling from this. Why did Eli even bother to keep macking him and trying to get next to him if sex is all he wanted?! Josh knew that his radar was pretty accurate and that Eli was a pretty decent guy. Okay, he was more than decent. He's an amazing guy, but my eyes didn't just dream up this Reggie. He was naked and in Eli's apartment, already aware that he was coming home early.

"DAMMIT!"

Josh just stopped and screamed it to the top of his lungs, and then, when he heard it, he apologized because he was worried that that was exactly what he was about to do. To damn this relationship before he had a chance to breathe and to consider and yes, eventually, once his head cleared, talk to Eli.

Josh didn't want to go home. He wasn't ready. It wasn't his plan for the night, so he turned away from the subway and headed toward the Pier. It was still early enough that the area wasn't littered with young gay boys vogueing and being free like they couldn't be at school and home. Now, there were probably all manner of couples there, and some breathing space. Josh just needed to breathe and get this anger off of him. He wandered. He walked. He wondered. He was mad at Eli, at Reggie, at himself, and at even Teddy Johnson, his first crush. If Teddy had acted right, they could have been married since Jr. High and all of this foolishness wouldn't have been necessary.

Josh had to laugh at that, but his laughter was immediately seized as he strolled the Pier and happened upon a couple in love.

Because the area was so gay-friendly, you could see all kinds of couples just lounging in the park, being. The Pier looked like a park now and gay couples have so few places where they can just be, without a cover charge and loud music. So there were all kinds of couples lying out in the grass, just injoying a rare mild fall night. The weather had opened up that day and people came out of every neighborhood to just take in the evening's repose.

Josh was just strolling, trying to blend and breathe and get his head right. He needed to just get his bearings back and not think about what had just happened at Eli's. Josh just wanted to get that off of his mind. Seeing Greg and Kevin snuggled up in the grass, Kevin in Greg's lap, did it.

Eli was no longer on his mind.

Josh didn't normally think like this, but he couldn't help but think that he had done *something* to piss God off. First, a naked man in my man's apartment, then a fight and now this! Josh looked around and wanted a way out. He couldn't keep going forward because they would surely see him. He couldn't turn around because, well, he just couldn't. So he froze. Josh just stopped, dead in his tracks.

That seemed to make more noise than any other action he could have taken.

The flow of people to and fro, passing you by when you are chilling in the grass with your baby, seems to just keep your peripheral vision on alert. In NYC, you are always on alert, even when you are in chill mode. Greg was.

He always seemed to notice every dude who looked out of place at Pride or at the meetings that he led about Black Gay Male Issues and Involvement. He had been like that since the tall, young brotha came into a meeting at The Community Center some 12 years ago seemed to be fine being there. He was warm and interactive, until Greg stood before the group to speak. Something about talking about planning an event and men in love and Black Gay men loving each other that made the brotha snap. Maybe he didn't like Greg doing the talking or maybe seeing a Black man in front of the room reminded him of the neighborhoods and secrets he was trying to escape. Be that as it may, he snapped.

The lanky cute kid lunged at Greg liked he was his enemy. If Greg hadn't turned and seen him coming, out of the corner of his eye, the tall terror would have hurt him. The room went into a frenzy. Greg was shaken. The thug was apprehended and arrested. The young man behind all that pain was in therapy, with a gay counselor for months. One day, almost a year later, that same young man approached Greg. This time, he offered a hug and an apology. He didn't understand why he had been so angry, especially with Greg. But he was better now and sober now and clear-headed and sorry. Greg hugged him and forgave him. They talked about his past and his coming out struggles. He talked while Greg listened. By the time they finished, Jimmy had become a volunteer at the program and often helped Greg pulled meetings together.

But Greg still looked, even when he wasn't looking.

That's why he saw this guy, out of the corner of his eye, who was walking and just abruptly stopped. Greg waited a beat before he looked to see if it was just a moment or if he needed to act or react. He thought he might just be somebody checking them out. He thought it could be someone taking a picture of them. He thought that perhaps it was just someone thinking that they recognized him or Kevin and couldn't be sure. He didn't know what to expect.

He didn't expect Joshua.

Greg fumbled. He almost knocked Kevin's head out of his lap. He didn't know what to do. Greg was acting like he got busted again, but the truth is that he and Kevin have been together for 2 years now and he knows that they should have been all along. Greg's only regret in life is that he hurt Joshua.

Now, right before him, stands the only thing he ever did wrong.

In living color, lost and clearly upset, Josh just doesn't know which way to turn. That's evident to Greg, who is used to Joshua having it together. He hated to think that seeing him and Kevin together would still unnerve Joshua after 2 years. But, there he is, rattled at seeing them together again, and Greg doesn't know what to do. He taps Kevin, who then realizes why Greg was fumbling.

"Oh damn," Kevin blurts.

He thought he had Greg and that their relationship was solid, but Kevin always saw that regret in Greg's eyes. Many times he thought that it was Greg longing for better days. Sometimes, Kevin was clear that Greg just didn't like the way things ended. There was Josh, looking broken, sad and there was Greg, clearly prepared to stand up and react. Kevin didn't want to jump by his side, but he didn't want to look passive and unconcerned. He remembered that look he shot at Joshua the night it all hit the fan.

Kevin didn't mean to smirk, as much as he meant to say 'what can I say?' with his demeanor. He had always loved Greg and knew that Greg and he would be together someday. But Kevin hated that things happened like they did as well, so he didn't want to seem funky with Joshua. Joshua was good people. Joshua had a good heart. But right now, it looked like that heart had been broken all over again. Kevin prayed that it wasn't because Joshua was seeing them again, but there they all were, together again.

Joshua spoke first.

Okay, Joshua opened his mouth first. He tried to say something, but no words came forth. It even looked like he was about to cry. Greg's heart was aching inside.

"What have I done?!" Greg thought as he watched Joshua's eyes become void and lost. Joshua was in there, somewhere, dying and Greg couldn't let him drown, not again.

"Joshua, what's wrong? What happened? You look like you've seen a ghost?"

Kevin and Greg looked at each other and both hated that choice of words. They were the ghost. They were the Spirit Of Relationship Past and it was not a Merry Christmas for Joshua.

They walked him over to their resting place and sat him down. Neither knew what they were going to say, but they knew that they couldn't leave him to his own devices. He looked a mess and didn't need to be left alone on the pier or in this state.

"Joshua, talk to me. I know that I don't have the right or the privilege of knowing what's wrong and it's not like we have maintained a friendship, but I am here for you. You look like you're lost. What's wrong?"

Josh wanted to say

**"THIS IS WRONG!
YOU AND THIS BASTARD BEING TOGETHER
INSTEAD OF YOU AND I!!!
THAT'S WHAT'S WRONG!!!!"**

He wanted to, but he couldn't because it wasn't the truth. Although Joshua adored Greg and always would, he knew that there was something sweeter and truer between Greg and Kevin. They could be boys together and friends together and silly together. They always seemed to be injoying each other's company, no matter what they were doing.

Joshua was always so cerebral with his best friend, Carlton. Carlton would often comment on how Josh would give him the Book Report version of his life, instead of the truth. Josh was always trying to save other people the trivialities of his life, but the truth is he didn't like to speak them because then he'd realize how trivial his life was. Joshua wasn't living with passion and would rarely let himself be free, spontaneous or just open. It had to be organized and structured or there was a chance for failure, so he kept a list. Joshua's life mantra was:

"If You Fail To Prepare,
Prepare To Fail"

Joshua never wanted to fail, his parents, his people, his friends or even his staff. He never put himself on that list. He didn't think he belonged. When people talk about being on your own list of priorities and preferably at the top of it, Josh just shrugs it off as advent of a selfish culture.

"If you do for others, you will be blessed." Joshua lived by that and got it so ingrained into his psyche that he couldn't bring himself to do for himself.

Even now, with Greg and even Kevin looking really concerned, Joshua didn't want to disturb their evening.

"I really don't want to bother you two. I know that you were having a nice romantic time and here I come, the sad ex, looking like I'm devastated at just seeing you. It's not that at all. I just…."

Joshua couldn't believe himself. He was fumbling to find the right words.

"Before you say anything else, let me say something. I'm sorry. I am so sorry for hurting you. I am so sorry for betraying your trust in me. I never meant to hurt you or do anything to destroy your trust. I haven't able to fully commit in this relationship and take it to the next level because I needed to ask for your forgiveness. I came to your office once, but you were out of town. I called you a few times, but I couldn't find the words. So, when he asked me to marry him last week, I told God that the only way that I could say yes is if God gave me the opportunity to speak to you and apologize. I am sorry for the hurt that our being in love caused you because you didn't deserve to have things end like that. No one did. Please forgive me, so we can all move on."

Josh and Greg looked at Kevin like he was a stranger.

He was so sincere and so emotional in his apology to Joshua that Joshua's mouth fell open. Greg looked at Kevin and he almost hugged him. He wanted to say "WOW BABY, WHAT A BRILLIANT SPEECH" but he couldn't because Kevin had done what Greg had yet to do. He asked for forgiveness.

"Kevin, I really can't tell you how much I appreciate that. I know now that you and Greg were always in love and that doesn't cheapen what he and I had, but your love for him has always made me jealous. Thank you, though. Thank you for saying that and for letting my heart know that the man I loved is happy with the man he loves and the man who loves him back."

Joshua and Kevin started to hug and then both stopped. It was a bit too Lifetime for them both. They shook hands and held that moment, hand-in-hand for a long time. They didn't say anything and, to Gregory, it seemed as though silently, they were transferring energy or love or something. It was like Joshua gave any and all of the rest of the love he held onto for Greg to Kevin. They could feel it and they knew it was the right thing to do. Kevin smiled and said "thank you." He meant it.

"We were on our way to dinner. You want to join us?"

Greg said it before he really thought, believing it to be a sweet gesture. Kevin didn't really mind, but Joshua did. He didn't want to be a fifth wheel. He smiled and begged off. He still needed to clear his head. He was still lost; just now it was only about Elijah.

Josh really did lay his burdens with Greg down, by the riverside—The Hudson River, that is. Joshua got up to leave. He had been brought down to the Pier for a reason and that reason was revealed and completed. No need to wear out his welcome. Joshua said goodnight to them both and said to Kevin, privately, "move in with him."

Kevin smiled.

Finally, so did Joshua.

He knew that their apartment wouldn't remain some mausoleum to their long-lost love. He knew that Greg, too, had to move on. Even though Greg and Kevin had been together the whole time, Kevin's eyes told Joshua that something had been missing for them. That missing thing was closure with Joshua. Kevin and Joshua locked eyes and spoke words between them that Greg would never know.

Greg had his own conversation to have.

"Maybe I should take a walk?" Kevin said, sensing a need for a conversation between Joshua and Gregory that didn't need to include him.

"No. We're fine." Joshua really didn't think anything else needed to be said. Gregory felt differently.

He asked if he could walk with Joshua and Joshua looked at Kevin, Kevin looked at Greg, then Joshua, and they all agreed that the 2 exes needed a moment.

"I tried to call you for months afterwards, but I was scared. I was scared that I would hear the words 'I hate you' from you and that would have killed me. Joshua, you are amazing. I swear, I don't think you realize that sometimes, but you are. Kevin and I were reading a magazine one night and we saw one of your ads…yeah, I do know YOUR stuff…and Kevin said 'Josh really is good, isn't he?' We just stopped and stared at each other. You have been the Pink Elephant in the room for 2 years now. We almost broke up twice, because he thought I was still in love with you and I thought he was trying to live up to some image of you. But now, I realize that I have always been in love with Kevin and that I was afraid. So I put him in like and moved you into love. I'm sorry for that. I really did love you. But tonight, for the first time, after Kevin said what he said, I realize I am with the right man. But, Josh, you are doing it again. You are sacrificing yourself for somebody else's happiness. You are hurting and it's not about Kevin and me. You showed up hurting and lost and seeing us only distracted you from that. What's wrong?"

Joshua could tell that Gregory meant it and meant well, but he couldn't possibly talk to him about this. Not about another man and another betrayal of trust. Joshua couldn't find the words, so Gregory found them for him.

"Do you love him?"

"What?"

"Josh, do you love him? I know you well enough to know that only one thing would put that kind of hurt in your eyes. Now, I don't know what went wrong or what he did or what you are thinking, but you deserve to be loved. So, if you love him, work it out. If you don't, then bury him and this, but don't let it eat you up, Joshua. Go home and chill and tomorrow, call him and talk. You deserve some answers, but more than that, Joshua Knight, you deserve love."

Gregory looked back at Kevin and Kevin had just, in that very moment, looked up at Greg. Joshua saw it and that's when he knew that they were meant to be together. He saw that connection and knew that he and Greg never shared that. They shared a love and that love was good, but it's gone. As Barry White sang to Glodean after they ended—"WHATEVER WE HAD, WE HAD."

Joshua and Gregory finally ended that night. Joshua and Gregory finally had some closure and Kevin had some peace. He and Greg would later move into a completely new place in Harlem. They needed to start over, too.

Gregory and Joshua didn't hug or cry or even shake hands. It was finished and it was good. That's when Josh realized it. He realized that the reason that he didn't want to fight Kevin for Greg that night is that Kevin would have won. Kevin would have been willing to fight for Greg. Joshua realized that he wouldn't have. He would have been fighting for love and commitment and fidelity and monogamy, but he would not have been fighting for Gregory Marshall. He let him go. Josh also realized that he was in love with Elijah and now, that realization hurt more than ever. Josh was in love with a man whose ex was naked and in his apartment.

Josh was lost.

He walked the Village for about an hour. He found himself in some funky little shops and he knew that if he bought anything, it would have been a pity purchase. So, Josh left it all alone. He didn't need anything from the Village right now. He just needed to walk.

Josh didn't even realize where he was until he heard Lena Horne singing "Yesterday When I Was Young" and he looked up. Roadhouse Records was still open and Mr. Henderson was still helping somebody find the song and the singer to ease their pain or express their joy or exorcise their demons. Tonight, he would strike the right chord in Joshua, too. Tonight, Mr. Henderson would give Joshua a spoonful of sugar after the heaping helping of medicine he was about to dole out.

The Christmas-like bell announced Joshua's arrival and Mr. Henderson smiled when he looked up. He knew that "Sad Eyes" would be back one day and he was glad to see him. He had hoped that that young man that he talked to for an hour that day would have taken that sadness from him, but nope, he still looked sad.

"Boy, what's wrong with you? I thought after you found your song, you would have found your way. But you look as sad, if not sadder, than that day you walked up in here. Sit down a spell and tell me, who done ya wrong?"

Josh was off-put. He didn't expect Mr. Henderson to even remember him. But he did and he was watching that day when Joshua and Elijah met for the first time. Mr. Henderson was a very observant man indeed. But Joshua still didn't think that some old Black man who lived through civil rights and assassinations, world wars and the Tuskegee Experiment really wanted to hear about 2 men in love. Josh tried to hedge around the subject and solicit Mr. Henderson's advice without being forthcoming.

Mr. Henderson laughed.

"You don't think I saw the way you and that young man were looking at each other? You don't think I know what love look like when I see it? Let me tell you a story boy, and listen up good, you hear me. Listen up good."

Mr. Henderson pulls out a chair for Joshua as 2 customers mill around the shop. He leans in close, with a mixture of discretion and privacy and tells Joshua the story of his life, in 10 minutes.

⌘

"I went to war in late 1967. When we first heard we was going to the Vietnam, most of us got happy cuz we had never been outside of our own backyard, much less overseas.

I met this young man when we was in boot camp and took a quick shine to him. I didn't know nothing about the world and I thought we was just two young men on the journey of our lives. We were, in more ways than one. See, when I first laid eyes on Thurston, I thought he was like nobody I had ever seen. He was tall and strong and solid and looked like a grown man, which was odd cuz most of us looked like boys fresh off the farm. When we talked, I found out that he was 19 and had been working on his family's farm since he was 11. He was taller than the moon and had a smile like hope. I thought I could never say nothing to him about my feelings, cuz for one, I didn't understand them myself and for two, if I did, he might beat me into a inch of my life for being that way.

So we just became friends. We ate together. We fight near each other and took every leave together for about 9 months. We was close.

Then, one night in Hanoi, the big city, we all went out drinking. We had some time to just run around and get some fun in us. Well, that night, Thurston got so pissy drunk that I had to get him back on base without nobody knowing. He was so tall and so big that I could barely move him. He kept laughing real loud and I just knew we was gonna get caught by the MPs and two black boys would have ended up in the hole. But we made it back to our barracks and I tried to put him to bed. He pulls me on top of him and he said 'I see the way you look at me, Seymour Henderson, and I likes it.' Then before I could even respond, he kissed me.

He kissed me like he was trying to change my life. He kissed me like he wanted to share a secret with no words. He kissed me and said 'why you never tell me that you was that way? We could'a been together a long time ago.' I didn't know what to say. So I said nothing. I pulled away from him and I ran.

I ran into the night air, hoping it would change what I was feeling. It didn't. I knew that I had loved him from the minute I first saw him and we both realized we had the same name. I knew I liked him but I was scared. It was 1967 and black boys didn't act like that. I avoided him for the rest of the week. He tried to smile and I look away. He tried to speak and I would move. I was just nervous around him."

Joshua couldn't believe how forthcoming this stranger, this beautiful older man was being. He was telling his whole life, to a stranger, and he was only getting started.

"Finally, that next Saturday night, he confronted me after everybody else had gotten away.

'If'n I ain't' good enough for you, just say so. But don't just ignore me like I'm some slow dog on da porch. I got feelings and I shared 'em with you and you just leave me hangin', like laundry on the line. I thought you liked me, Seymour Henderson, and I thought you'd like that I liked you. I guess I was wrong. I'm sorry.'

That's when I finally spoke da truth to him and to myself.

Saturday, August 23, 1967, I looked into the eyes of Mr. Thurston B. Henderson and I told him 'I love you and I reckon I got scared, but I don't want you to think you ain't good enough. You perfect.'

Then, I finally kissed him back. We were inseparable after that.

We got so close that people started to tease us. 'So I guess y'all really are married, huh, Henderson and Henderson?' See, both of us got the same last name and that's why we noticed each other in the first place.

I got discharged in 1970 and he didn't come out until '72. I thought I was gonna die. We wrote each other, but by then I had left the South and made my way to

New York City. He said he didn't think he could leave his family and that they wouldn't understand. We tried to act like it was fine and that we would be okay, but I was destroyed.

I saw so many pretty and handsome men in Harlem, but not a one was as fine as my Thurston. So, when he said he wasn't coming, I thought I was gonna die.

But one day, it was June 17, 1973, I was getting ready to take out the garbage and go down to the Village just to have a night out. I put the trash into the can on the street and I turned to head for the subway. Just as I turned, I walked right into this tree of a man. I looked up into his eyes, cuz he was at least 3 inches taller than me, and he said 'Hello Mr. Henderson.'

I couldn't speak, but I could only hug him. Finally, I said 'Hello to you, Mr. Henderson. When did you…?'

He just covered my lips with his big 'finger and he said 'Shhh. Just show me where we live, Mr. Henderson.' From that day to this one right here, Mr. Thurston B. Henderson and Mr. Seymour L. Henderson have lived in that same Harlem brownstone.

Every day, if I am blessed, lucky and paying attention, I get to see the look on Mr. Henderson's face that I saw on your face when you first heard that boy sing that song you were looking for that day. If you are smart, you will not waste that, because if you do, the rest of your life will be full of 'What If' and 'Should Have Been.' Don't play with your heart or his. I almost did that when I tried to run from love. I don't know what I would have become if I had let love get away from me. Don't you find out."

Joshua looked at Mr. Henderson and saw that love in his years. More than 30 years later, he spoke of him and Mr. Henderson's eyes still lit up, just thinking about…Mr. Henderson. Maybe God was so insightful that he knew that if they didn't have something to draw them together from the beginning, they might not have been willing to come together. They share last names.

"What do Elijah and I share? We both have both our parents, Thank God. We both love music, but different eras. We both like to cook."

That's when Joshua realized it for the first time. He had Elijah both had biblical names. Maybe, just maybe…never mind.

Joshua tried to brush it off. Not the biblical names thing, but rather his feelings for Elijah altogether. He was furious because he wanted to just go to Eli's and talk, but Reggie was there still. Okay, and Eli wasn't. But Josh was still furious. That's all Josh could think about.

That's all he could think about as he hugged Mr. Henderson and thanked him for being so open with him. That's all he could think about when he went towards the subway to go home, finally. That's all he could think about as he looked up and realized he was in front of Eli's apartment. There he was again…and the light was still on.

Before he knew it, Josh was back in the building and heading towards Eli's apartment. He could hear the television and realized that Reggie had no plans on leaving. So he would be asked to leave. Forcibly.

"What are you doing back here? You finally decided to be a man about yours and…"

That's all Reggie got out before Joshua threw his clothes at him and opened the door.

"You have 30 seconds to get dressed and 10 to get the hell out of here or I swear I will not be responsible."

Reggie looked at Joshua, who looked at peace in his return, and he didn't know what to make of him. Reggie was used to street brawls and ugly name calling and loud fights. Josh wasn't screaming or even rolling his eyes. Reggie didn't know what to think about this Joshua dude. He didn't have much time to decide.

Joshua grabbed Reggie's arm and pulled him from the chair where he was watching some "Law and Order" rerun. Reggie pulled away from him and looked at Josh.

"Please, make me. Make me whoop your ass. Make me show you that I ain't giving up my man, without a fight. Come on. Please. Make me."

Reggie looked at Josh and noticed that his fist had been tight the entire time. He didn't care that he might have to fight Josh for Eli. He cared because he wasn't sure if something was in Josh's hand. Reggie wasn't beneath a tactic like bringing something in your hand and maybe Joshua had more street in him that he realized. But when Joshua realized what Reggie was looking at, he opened his hand.

"Oh you think I brought something up in here with me? Not necessary. All I brought with me was my love for Elijah and that's all I need."

Before he could make any more of his declarative and definitive speech about love and commitment and working through hard times, Reggie hit him. Reggie just blindsided Joshua and punched him in the mouth.

Joshua laughed because he knew himself and he knew he wouldn't be able to fight without provocation. Well, now he was provoked.

Josh hit Reggie so hard that he fell over the chair that he was standing beside.

"Oh, see bitch! Now you gonna make me!" Reggie thought he could easily take Joshua. They were from two different worlds, and Reggie's world was the survival of the fittest. He didn't know that Joshua's world was just about survival. Joshua had not come this far to give up over somebody who had a good thing and wanted back in. Elijah Monroe wasn't the reason Joshua was whooping Reggie's ass like he stole something. Joshua was beating Reggie because he was the last person that would stand in his face and tell him that he didn't deserve something that he had. He deserved to be happy and if all that was standing in his way was Reggie, then Reggie was going to have to move.

Reggie swung at Joshua and connected a blow to the chest.

It knocked the wind out of Joshua. Joshua hit the wall this time and that knocked some sense into him. He had to be willing to fight this fight or just stop. This wasn't about thinking. This was about doing.

Joshua got himself together just in time. Reggie was ready to connect another blow, and the look on his face showed that he was about business. Joshua blocked it, cocked it and hit Reggie so hard that blood splattered from his mouth.

The noise of the fight attracted the super.

He came into the room and just barely avoided the vase that Reggie threw at Joshua and shattered against the wall.

"Stop this nonsense. What are you doing to Mr. Elijah's apartment?!"

Joshua looked up at the super and then over at Reggie, who just looked mad that he wasn't going to get to finish the fight and realized that it was enough.

"I came in and found this intruder and I am simply removing him. Mr. Monroe is due back tomorrow and I just came by to make sure everything was okay. I have no idea how he got in, but I can handle this."

Joshua was stern and felt that there was no need to get loud. That just wasn't his demeanor.

Too bad the same couldn't be said for Reggie.

"What?! I got in cuz I got keys. I got in cuz Eli wants me and not you. So why don't you just…"

Joshua didn't even realize that he had balled his fist up against, but Reggie noticed it. Reggie noticed it and realized that "this crazy bitch" was going to fight him as long as he had to for Eli and it wasn't worth it. Reggie was just feeling lonely and it was a Friday night and he was in the Village. He could find somebody with a lot less drama to take away the loneliness. So he gathered himself and figured he'd do the bars until he found what he was looking for.

He passed Joshua in his pursuit to pounce and Joshua had no words. Just a gesture. He opened his hand.

Reggie wasn't sure what that meant, at first. Then he knew by the glint in his eyes that Joshua wasn't playing. Reggie dug into his pocket and there they were.

Two. Silver. Simple chain. Not as nice as his but nonetheless, there they were and Joshua realized that he wasn't the first man to get keys to Elijah Monroe's apt. He worried that Reggie represented some conclave of men who would come out of the woodwork. He was ready to panic about this, too, until Reggie showed who he was.

As Reggie passed the super, he figured he'd get the night started right. He reached down and grabbed the super's crotch, right there in front of Joshua. The man winced and looked around like he was instantly considering a place to let the deed be done. He closed the door as he smiled.

Joshua wasn't sure what he would say to Eli about the state of his apartment or the state of his own heart. He wanted to stay and clean up. But he had so much on his mind. He wanted to do the right thing, but right now, the right thing was to leave.

CHAPTER 14: THE SUBMISSION

deep WATERS

Reggie.

Ex.

Eli's apartment.

Fight.

Greg and Kevin.

Forgiveness.

The Misters Henderson.

He didn't know what to do, so he did what Josh did best when he was overwhelmed.

He retreated.

Eli wasn't around and Josh would do what he had perfected in an effort to protect his heart. Josh isolated. It was great timing, because the weekend was here and he didn't have to worry about getting it together until Monday morning.

For the next 48 hours, Josh prepared to cocoon himself and his feelings and just hide. But somebody said it and it's as true today as when they first spoke it:

**"You Can Hide Your Head,
But Your Feet Will Show."**

Joshua's feet, and the long, lonely walk that he had been taking in them, were now showing.

⌘

Josh was stirred by the ringing of the phone.

He knew he wasn't going to talk to anyone, so he didn't even bother to check his caller ID. It was Saturday and Eli was supposed to be home today. He didn't know if he would call and he hoped he wouldn't. Josh didn't know if he could talk to Eli today. He didn't want to own his pain. He didn't want Eli to hear him struggling and he wasn't even sure why he was struggling. Either he trusted Elijah Monroe and he was going to move beyond this or he didn't and it was finished. Point blank. Clear cut.

But Joshua was never that precise when it came to his own heart. He wanted to know why Eli would do something like this. He needed to know how Reggie came back into Eli's life. He was scared to find out how they would move on in their relationship with such an albatross in their way. He also was frightened to find out what was wrong with him that he kept drawing all this drama to himself.

Josh was overwhelmed.

He slept.

Josh drifted in and out of sleep and just couldn't seem to get it together. He would use the bathroom and return to bed.

Shower, then back to bed.

Brush his teeth.

Wash his face.

Turn on and off the television some 12 times, but always back to sleep. He drifted in and out of reality, because there he would have to answer the phone, which was ringing incessantly.

In the realm of reality, Josh would have to face Eli and he wasn't prepared for the lie that Eli and Reggie have cooked up overnight or the truth. Josh was really afraid that Eli would tell him the truth, which was "we were never exclusive" and "it was only sex," and Josh would have to hear Eli make him feel like a fool for putting the emotional cart before the realistic horse. Cliché as it sounds, Josh thought that they were exclusive, but the fact is that Josh was elusive. He didn't want to have the conversation because he didn't want to know if he wasn't Eli's only choice, because for him Eli was his only chance. If this didn't work, he was done. He was afraid of what he would look like without love in his heart and no possibilities in his future. Josh also didn't want Eli to think he was fragile.

Josh was just open, for the first time in a long time, and he didn't like the way it felt. He didn't like that he had fought somebody over a man like a common street urchin. He didn't like that he wasn't ashamed of it and would do it again. He didn't like that he screamed in the night air, because of something somebody else said.

Josh knew that he really needed to talk to Eli. But he couldn't bring himself to answer the phone. He couldn't bring himself to hear Eli's voice because he knew that he would lose it and the tears would flow and he would feel like a fool.

So he slept.

The phone rang.

Again and again, it rang and Joshua ignored it. He tried to ignore the banging at the door, but it wouldn't go away.

Josh put the pillow over his head and hoped that the Girl Scout or Jehovah Witness would get the message and get away from his door.

That's when he finally heard the door open and "Joshua Arrington Knight, get your ass down here now!" rang out from the living room up to his bedroom.

Josh jumped and realized that Carlton had let himself into the house and was in *BEST FRIEND SHOWDOWN* mode.

"Josh, I know you hear me. If you were sick, you would have answered the phone and let me know. So either you are hold up there with some man, since Eli isn't around, or YOU ARE HIDING! Whichever it is, get here NOW! Cuz if I come up there, it's on and poppin'!"

Josh appeared at the top of the stairs and Carlton almost gasped. Josh was always well groomed and pulled together. But there, at the top of his stairs, he was disheveled and sullen. He looked like he hadn't slept at all, but that's all he had done. His eyes sagged. His bald head was filled with his half-risen hairs waiting to be cut.

"He's Come Undone," Carlton said, trying to lighten the moment and when Josh didn't immediately laugh, Carlton knew something was dire.

He knew that something in Joshua, his dear friend, had finally broken.

After making some coffee, opening the blinds and just making Joshua get up, get dressed and get downstairs, they talked.

Joshua couldn't find the words at first and then when they did come out, they spilled. He had taken in so much shame, with his breakup from Greg, with last night's events at Eli's, from a comment he heard his Dad make—"I guess I ain't going to have to worry about grandbabies from him"—with a nasty snarl, after he came out.

Joshua was so heavenly bound on being perfect that his life had been hell-bent on self-destruction. Joshua had lived his life more concerned for everyone that he was for himself.

"Dammit, BabyBubba. Why do you keep doing this to yourself? You keep believing that your life is going to dissolve before your eyes and you have just been waiting for it to happen! Greg wasn't the love of your life and YOU KNOW IT! So you can't be upset about seeing him and Kevin or about them being together in the first place. What you are upset about is that he is happy and you think he couldn't be happy with you. But guess what? YOU WEREN'T HAPPY WITH HIM! You were settling and trying to make pretty pictures with your life and you deserve more than that."

Carlton continued, "I can't say if Elijah is the love of your life, but I know that he has brought life into you and you deserve that. Now, some sissy is in his spot, naked and he's not home and you want to blame him. Look, if he did you wrong, I will handle him my damn self, but he wasn't even IN THE CITY! You know that this dude is his ex and who knows what dude had planned, but he didn't include Eli in his plans, because he wasn't there. The reason you whooped up on him and didn't even think about touching Kevin or Greg was that you knew you didn't want to fight for Greg. You couldn't because you didn't love him like that. But you fought for Eli, and more than that, Josh, you fought for yourself. You want Eli. You deserve Eli. You earned Eli. You fought for Eli. Now, fight for Joshua."

Joshua wanted to cry. Joshua wanted to disappear, to just evaporate. He wanted to not be here to have to hear these things about himself. But Carlton was relentless.

"I am not going to stay up in here all day babying you and letting you wallow in this drama, man. Get up and do something or do nothing, but you can't keep doing this. You are a Superstar in your business life and a shrinking violet in your personal life. You are not doing the Universe, God, yourself or the world any favors by being less than away from work. You can be all that here and there! You are scared that if you are too happy, it's going to unravel. That's a lie. You are scared that if you are too happy, somebody's going to ask 'WHY YOU!' The answer is simple! WHY NOT YOU!? You worked hard to build your company.

You lived well and deserve a love that loves you back. You bought this house and everything in it, with your hard work and good heart and if somebody's doesn't like it, show them the door. But you can't just give up on life and on love because somebody saw that you had a good thing and came after it. Eli told you about Reggie and told you that they hadn't spoken a word in TWO YEARS. So because dude finally realized that he had a good thing and tried to get it back, you are going to let him win. Man, you need to listen to what you are doing and stop. Now, I don't know what it's going to take for you to clean up after this Pity Party, but enough already."

Joshua looked over at Carlton and couldn't believe that he was just so tired of dealing with his stuff. It was all over Carlton's face. He was tired of Joshuadrama and he clearly didn't have much patience left on the subject.

"I am sick and tired of watching you live this great life, with no light in your eyes. Maybe you need to get back in church or something. You need a center, man. This is crazy. You asked for some clarity and now you don't like how it showed up. Well, too bad. It's here now and so is Eli and so is success with your company and so is forgiveness with Greg and Kevin. So, now what? Now what, Josh?"

They talked for about 2 more hours.

Josh poured out his fears and Carlton countered with his triumphs.

Josh tried to run, but he couldn't deny it anymore. He was afraid to be too successful, too happy or too blessed. He thought that it was arrogant. He thought that people would hold it against him. He thought that somebody would talk about him.

"See, I heard your girl say something in an interview once that I would have thought you held onto like gold. Nancy Wilson said in an interview once, years ago, 'As Long As They Are Talking About You, They're Thinking About You.' Man, that's a classic quote. You gave me the damn interview to read and you didn't even take it to heart. People talk. It's what they do. You gotta give them something to talk about, like a good life and you are doing that. They talk because they want to know how you do it and the ones who really want to know, they just ask. So, take yourself a shower or something and let's go get something to eat. It smells like Past in here and we need to air this joint out."

Carlton always had a way with words, but by the time he finished today, Josh was naked and exposed. Carlton hit every button and made every point. The bad thing about telling your best friend everything is that…they know everything.

Carlton had had enough of Joshua trying to not be happy, so that some other not-so-happy person could feel like he was accessible.

Carlton was doing all of the things that he had going on—books, writing, relationship—because of Josh's encouragement and he was downright pissed to find that Joshua Knight hadn't taken his own sage advice. But that was over now. Josh and Carlton lit a few candles and prayed pain out of that house that night. Josh didn't even know that Carlton could pray like that, but he talked to God like they were old friends. Josh opened his eyes at one point and found Carlton crying as he prayed. Josh had never seen Carlton cry, and now that he had, it was for HIM. It was because of him.

When they finished, Joshua was reminded of how many times Carlton seemed to want to talk about something and he moved himself aside to take care of Josh. Now it was Joshua's turn.

"What were you going to tell me the other night? You said that Donovan had said something that you wanted to tell me. What was it?"

Carlton had no idea what Joshua was talking about. He had forgotten their conversation at the restaurant. Joshua hadn't.

"You said that you wanted to tell me something that Donovan had told you and of course, I hogged the night. What did he say?"

Carlton smiled. Joshua WAS paying attention and this was a pretty cool time to remember, because what Donovan said was a pretty big deal.

⌘

Carlton wasn't even thinking about love or relationship when he met Donovan. He definitely wasn't thinking about it with a brotha like this. Carlton was very brothaman from Uptown, with his denim and Diaspora, tight fro and broad philosophy. He almost didn't notice Donovan. He wasn't his type.

Carlton had stopped at one of the vendors on 125th Street, trying to see what good books were out. Even though he wrote, he was a voracious reader, too. He didn't need oils or incense, because a good book was all the mood Carlton needed. He was going through the Terry/Connie/Benilde section and knew that he wouldn't read that stuff, but respected the way that the sistahs were doing their thing. He wasn't a snob. He just liked to read about political and social matters, race matters and Cornell West, Ralph Wiley and other button-pushers. He figured he'd grab a book or two before he went home for the night. He almost didn't even notice Donovan.

But Donovan noticed him.

Even though Donovan was raised uptight in Upstate NY, he loved the city. He came to pursue his degree at Fordham University and would go on to teach at Hunter College. Donovan thought that he was inconspicuous. With his wire rimmed glasses and corduroy blazer, complete with patches on the sleeves, he thought he was a non-presence, in NYC especially and in Harlem particularly. But he loved being around Black people. Where he was from, he was lucky to see a random few at public events. In Harlem, colored people—Black, Caribbean, Latin, African—where everywhere and he loved the rhythm and the rise of seeing himself everywhere. That's probably why he noticed Carlton at first.

They were both looking at books and Carlton and he reached for a copy of "HOLLER IF YOU HEAR ME" by Michael Eric Dyson and they just did the black man nod. Carlton was going to let the professor have the copy, since he seemed so erudite and ready to read it. Carlton just needed something to pass time.

They spoke.

Carlton thought he had done enough to just say hello but Donovan extended his hand and offered it to him. Carlton thought he was kidding. He wasn't.

"Maybe you can recommend something. I'm always trying to find a good book or two to pass the weekend with. You seem to be comfortable around these books. I'm just fumbling. Any suggestions?"

Donovan smiled nervously.

Carlton noticed it. Carlton loved it.

At first, he was dismissable. Nerdy brother, uptown, trying to blend in with the people. But he kept looking at Carlton for guidance, for insight and for a friend.

"So where you from man?"

"Buffalo," Donovan replied, clearly glad that the brotha wasn't going to just blow him off. "I teach at Hunter College and I love to come up to Harlem every chance I get. Black people around these parts just don't know how lucky they are. Get's really lonely when you are looking for yourself in a haystack that's stacked against you."

Carlton liked his honesty. Carlton liked his way with words. Carlton really liked his smile.

Donovan had this nervous way of taking off and putting on his glasses. He would take them off, look around and, with nothing else to do, he simply put them back on his face. Carlton loved it. He kind of liked making someone nervous. Being nervous didn't stop Donovan from asking him "for coffee. Maybe there's somewhere around here that doesn't have Barnes or Noble attached to it where we can just talk."

Carlton was almost about to say 'thank you, but nah.' But then the glasses came off and he wanted to answer him before they went back on again.

"Sure, man. I know a spot. That would be cool. I'm just gonna chill at home anyhow."

With that, Carlton and Donovan, Cornell and Dyson all made their way to a cool little spot just off Lenox Avenue and they talked for about 2 hours. Donovan kept removing his glasses. Carlton kept noticing, and loving it. They exchanged ideas and numbers. They debated politics and personal ideologies. They were a perfect fit.

Carlton couldn't believe it, but this nerd—about 5'11, warm brownskin, light brown eyes and a regular fade, an average build and a beautiful mind—was really touching him in ways he didn't think he would ever have to worry about.

He's been worried about it for almost two years now.

When Carlton got back home from Paris, he was clearly…different. He seemed freer. His writing, which could get stagnant sometimes in the bustle and blah of New York City, was rich and alive and flowing like the Nile. Carlton seemed different and it didn't take Donovan long to notice and to know why.

One night, while they were at Donovan's, reading and relaxing, eating and just engaging each other's minds, Donovan asked him a question that made Carlton know he was definitely going to have to reconsider this man and this relationship.

"Would you like to move to Paris?"

Carlton realized that Donovan was really paying attention to him. He had seen the change and was willing to support this bold, brazen and beneficial move, all for Carlton.

"What are you talking about? You can't leave Hunter. You can't leave here and your family." Carlton was shocked he was being so reasonable.

"I am a grown ass man and I can do what I want." Donovan could tell that Carlton didn't expect that, by the way he jumped back, just a little and tilted his head to the right. "I have done what everybody else has wanted me to do my whole life. The school. The major. The job. I'm tired and I need a change. I see what it did for you and maybe a move like that can do the same thing for me. So, I'm asking you again, Carlton. Would you like to move to Paris?"

Carlton could only hug Donnie, for being so sweet. That's the night Carlton realized that he was in love with a brotha named Donovan, who loved it when he called him Donnie, because nobody else did and who let him have it when they debated and could do so while he rubbed his feet.

⌘

Josh knew that he had to do better. Josh knew that he deserved better. Josh was glad it was Saturday. Sunday couldn't come soon enough.

We need to talk.

CHAPTER 15: THE SUBMISSION

LET US ALL GO BACK TO THE OLD LANDMARK

I stood across the street as the people gathered and hugged on the street. I wasn't scared of Unity because I had been to a place like this before, in DC, but that was a church building. I can't believe I'm feeling like this about walking into this huge warehouse of a building that bore the sign UNITY FELLOWSHIP CHURCH OF CHRIST on Brooklyn's Atlantic Avenue.

The truth is that in a church with a steeple, I can hide my stuff. But here, with people like me and safety and Sanctuary, I think I'm afraid that it would hit too close to home. I have always been a bit scared when it came to black church. As much as I love the singing and a good word and the fellowship, when it gets rowdy, I get…timid. Honestly, part of me thinks it didn't take all that and part of me worries that it just might and what if I don't have it or can't find it to give. I'm not going to let that stop me today.

So Joshua crossed the street and went into service.

"Good Afternoon Brother. Welcome to Unity."

The usher was so warm and inviting. She handed me a program of the service and took me to a seat. The male couple on the same row said "Hello."

"Hello."

Then, since service hadn't started yet, I looked around and really liked the feeling of the place. People are hugging and smiling and for a minute, I felt upset, because he had been missing this kind of kinship since he left DC, but he never found it in NYC.

I found Greg and love and we stayed at home, making Sunday "Own Day" instead of a chance to worship. I can't blame Greg or anybody else. I haven't been to church because I lost my priorities.

That's when Joshua realized that he had been holding so much against himself—Greg, success, being cheated on, being single, not being able to give his parents grandchildren, losing the Spelling Bee in the final round in 8th grade, disappointing Marsha Brown when she realized, in 11th grade, that Jerome was right and Joshua was a "faggot," and so much more.

Joshua had taken on the weight of the world and now, in this Sanctuary, he just wanted to be fed. Service was about to begin.

"

WALK IN THE LIGHT

BEAUTIFUL LIGHT
COME WHERE THE DEW DROPS OF MERCY
SHINE BRIGHT
SHINE ALL AROUND US
BY DAY AND BY NIGHT
LOVE IS THE LIGHT OF THE WORLD
"

The choir led the way, as the preacher and other robed clergy marched into the worship space. They were reaching out and touching and hugging people as they came down the aisle and you could feel Love, not just love, in the building. Joshua needed this kind of energy today. He was so spent, so drained and just really needed to breathe and receive today. He didn't really come with expectations but he knew that he needed. He wasn't really even sure what he needed, but he was sure that his own reserves had been tapped out and that he was on empty—emotionally, spiritually, physically.

The warmth was enough. If he didn't get any answers or any relief today, at least he got kindness. No one needed him to do anything or fix anything or answer anything or create anything. Today, Joshua Knight just got to be.

After the welcome and something called an "affirmation," people got up and hugged each other again. "They do a lot of hugging here" Joshua thought as he was being hugged by tall brothas and gorgeous sistahs, elderly women like the ones he remembered from back home and young kids who looked like they were straight from the pier just hours ago. Brown and Black and short and tall and friendly and fearful, Joshua couldn't help looking around at all of the diversity in the crowd. He knew that this place was cool and wondered if Eli would come with him one day. Ugh!

He thought about Eli, when he really didn't want to, because he didn't know what to do. At some point, he would have to talk to Eli. He would have to face Eli and get the truth about the Naked Ex. Joshua didn't have time for this right now. He was in the House of The Lord and wanted to just hear a good word.

Joshua loved it when the choir sang. Like many folks, Joshua didn't mind some good music and the small but powerful choir picked 2 perfect songs for Joshua, as if they had taken requests: "STAND," the song that propelled Donnie McClurkin to the top of the charts and onto Oprah and "I SHALL NOT BE MOVED," a funky house gospel song that really got the church going, especially the young people and some of the adults, and set the stage for Pastor Jeff's sermon.

The Pastor seemed like a young man, and he was lean and of average height, but when he took the pulpit he did so with the gusto and fervor of a seasoned Baptist preacher and he seemed like an oak tree.

"I feel like preachin' this morning!"

"Go 'head on and bring a Word, Pastor!"

"That's all right, preacher!"

"Lift Him up!"

"Come on and do the thing, then!"

The church seemed as ready for a good word as the preacher seemed prepared to bring one.

"Turn with me to the Book of John, Fifth Chapter, Verse 5:

> **5**One of the men lying there had been sick for thirty-eight years. ***6*** When Jesus saw him and knew how long he had been ill, he asked him, "Would you like to get well?" ***7*** "I can't, sir," the sick man said, "for I have no one to help me into the pool when the water is stirred up. While I am trying to get there, someone else always gets in ahead of me." ***8*** Jesus told him, "Stand up, pick up your sleeping mat, and

> walk!" **9** Instantly, the man was healed! He rolled up the mat and began walking!

"Stand up, pick up your sleeping mat, and walk! That's what the scripture says, so I would like you to consider as a word from the Lord today this title. Ready?"

The congregation gets excited and screams out "Yes!" and people are rocking and waiting, anticipating the Word. The preacher said:

"ALL YOU GOTTA DO IS SAY YES"

The church ignites, knowing that this word is going to be strong.

> "When Jesus came to the man who had been sitting the same spot for 38 years, He never asked him why he was there? He didn't ask him what set of circumstances or mistakes or missed opportunities found him, stuck by the riverside. Jesus asked a simple question:
>
> 'DO YOU WANT TO GET WELL?...'
>
> In other words, do you want to get up? Do you want to be healed? Do you want to live better? Do you want change in your life?' Jesus asked the man what he wanted. The man instantly started flapping his mouth to tell Jesus how he got stuck here. But Jesus never passed the judgment of asking how he got there. Jesus didn't care. Jesus just wanted to give the man the desires of his heart, and in this case, that was to be restored. The man was prepared to sit and moan and whine about his situations and others' betrayals and the disappointments of his past and the ones who left him and the things he messed up with and that one time, when I was close and it started raining and thus and such.
>
> But Jesus, being masterful and mindful, never asked him how he got stuck. He simply asked DO YOU WANT TO GET WELL?
>
> And when the King of Kings is in your heart, speaking in your spirit, commanding and compelling you higher, you don't have to explain why you weren't at church sooner, or how so many times

> before you have been disappointed by others or tell Him how you got in your predicament. When Jesus speaks to you, ALL YOU GOTTA DO IS SAY YES!"

Joshua liked the play on that song that he liked on the radio. He liked the way it connected to so many in the church. Something about hearing the title in another place put so many at immediate ease, but also seemed to give them a connection to The Word. But the preacher took it somewhere else completely:

> "See Grace and Mercy will give you another chance to be healed, another day to be blessed, another moment to be elevated, another heart to share love, but you have got to be willing to look beyond your faults and give him your needs.
>
> Do you want hope in your life? SAY YES!
> Do you need healing in your body? SAY YES!
> Do you need peace in your mind? SAY YES!
> Do you deserve love in your heart? SAY YES!

The preacher talked for about 10 more minutes before he seemed to just catch fire. His tone went from strong and authoritative to ignited and charged.

> You can't hold the past against the future! One has nothing to do with the other and when a new chance to do a new thing comes along, and you have belief in your heart, then ALL YOU GOTTA DO IS SAY YES!
>
> Grace and Mercy didn't come along to remind you of your mistakes or to shame you for the times you didn't do right or didn't see a good thing or realize that a bad thing was in your face and you picked it and so you got what you deserved!
>
> Grace and Mercy are A VERY PRESENT HELP IN TIMES OF TROUBLE and when you need help, when you need a hand, when you need to get up from where you were, so you can get where you are going, ALL YOU GOTTA DO IS SAY YES!
>
> Somebody is holding onto a "YES" today. Somebody wants to be healed, restored, renewed, uplifted, saved, blessed, lifted, changed,

> moved, unleashed and you are sitting in your seat, worrying and wondering about all the stuff you have to let go of for God to like you.
>
> But today, hear me when I tell you, in Jesus, ALL YOU GOTTA DO IS SAY YES!

Joshua was really moved. He didn't realize he was as moved as he was until an usher handed him a tissue. Joshua was crying the tears that he had held back, even with Eli. These tears were the tears of the young boy who thought he had to be perfect. These tears were the tears of a man who had sacrificed joy because he thought it was too much to ask. These tears were the truth of a person who realized that the weight of his fears was going to kill him and he wasn't ready to die. Joshua hated that he had become such a crybaby. He wanted so badly to fight back these tears, but that preacher just wouldn't shut up. He kept hitting all of his buttons.

> "SAY IT FROM YOUR SOUL! YES!
> SAY IT FROM YOUR PAIN! YES!
> SAY IT FROM YOUR PAST! YES!
>
> Let go of all of the stuff that's trying to hold you back.
>
> Get unshackled and say YES! Run on and see what the end will be!
>
> SAY YES! SAY YES! SAY YES!"

"YES!"

Joshua heard himself say it and almost laughed, except he was entranced. He wanted to just injoy the remainder of the service and leave quietly. But then the preacher said, "DO YOU WANT PEACE OF MIND?"

"YES!"

He did it again. Joshua couldn't believe himself. He was never a vocal person and surely not like this and definitely not in church. Joshua Arrington Knight wasn't raised to be expressive. But surely, as he wasn't the only one, it wouldn't seem too out of place.

"YES!"

Not again! Joshua was glad this time it wasn't him. He had some company because someone had screamed out "YES!" much longer than him and it was just a sign that the service and the word was affecting others, making Joshua feel ease in his own Public Display of Affliction! He wasn't in this thing alone. From where he sat, he could see an usher fanning a woman in the row in front of him, someone was running and there seemed to be one corner where all of the people who shouted like they did in "The Blues Brothers" ended up. Joshua didn't feel so bad, especially with that voice screaming out "YES!" so loudly. Joshua couldn't believe that he would dare be rude enough to have stood to see who else was screaming out, but he must have. There was no other explanation for that fact that he seemed to be standing over everyone else and he didn't remember standing. As the usher approached, this time not with tissue but reinforcements, Joshua thought that perhaps they were coming to tell him to be seated, but the looks on their faces said that wasn't it at all, but there was some kind of church emergency. Whoever screamed out must be in need of assistance.

Joshua started to look around to see who his co-reveler in God was, when the preacher took the microphone from the mantle and leapt into the congregation. It took Joshua a moment to realize that the ushers and the preacher were headed towards him. He wanted to tell them that he was fine, but when he opened his mouth, "YES!" is all that escaped.

He wanted to tell them that he would just sit down and calm down and he'd be fine, but "YES!" rang out from him, as a hand touched his hand and a voice spoke into his ear.

"Do you want to be free? Do you want to have peace? Are you tired of taking care of everybody else and feeling like you always have to fix it? Come on, Son. God wants to restore you and all you gotta do is say YES!"

"YES!"

Joshua didn't understand what was happening. He really did want to just open his eyes, wipe his tears and leave. He didn't want to be held by two ushers and that robed clergyman, while the Man of God anointed his head. He didn't want that male couple beside him to think that he was normally like this. He didn't want people who had hugged him on the way in to think that he was broken and hurting. Joshua didn't want this to happen now, while he was so troubled over what to do about Eli. Joshua didn't want this to happen, while he was still hearing Carlton's voice in his head. Joshua didn't want this to happen at all. It just wasn't like him, but there he was.

Joshua could feel people all around him, but every time he tried to move, his hands would shake and his feet would shuffle. Joshua didn't know what was happening, because surely he wasn't living out a moment from a movie, but maybe God was trying to tell him something. Whatever it was, Joshua wished it hadn't been so public, but there he was.

"It's all right, baby. Let Him have His way."

Her voice was sweet and soothing. Joshua could smell Tea Rose, that scent Miss Beulah used to wear when he was young.

Miss Beulah Sanford was the Mother of The Church and was always quick to hug you and slide you a piece of rock candy on Sunday. All she seemed to want in exchange was a hug and a smile. When Joshua left for college, she replaced that rock candy with a crisp $100 bill. Joshua tried to refuse her, but she hugged him and said, "Baby, God blesses me every day with health and strength and a sound mind. Don't insult this old lady by not taking my gift. I'm proud of you."

Joshua hugged her so tight he thought he would break her, but she was just fine.

"Don't you tell your Momma I gave you that. Spend it on somethin' nice for yo'self. You deserve it."

"It's all right baby. He's with you."

The voice wasn't Miss Beulah at all, but the comforting was exactly what Joshua needed. He couldn't tell if he was seated or standing for a moment. He realized that his head was in someone's lap and that they were wiping his forehead. Joshua wanted to sit up and tell the woman he was fine, but "YES" came out again. This time, it was softer and more controlled, but it was still the only word that would come from his mouth. He didn't even hear what the preacher was saying, but he knew he needed to sit up. He did. Then, when he finally opened his eyes, a beautifully elderly woman, with long gray hair, smiled at him and handed him her Tea Rose-scented kerchief. He looked around and people were being consoled and there were others on their knees at the altar. Joshua didn't understand what had happened. Nothing like this ever happened at St. Stephen's Episcopal Church. He had heard about it and even seen it in movies, but he never thought that it would include him in its victims, but something like…he didn't know what to call it, but it made him feel like he'd never felt before.

"Is there one more? The doors of the church are open to you today. If you want to be saved and welcomed into the House Of The Lord, just as you are, all you gotta do is say Yes."

"Yes."

There it was again. Joshua didn't know what had gotten into him today, but he stood and looked back at the sweet elder who had comforted him and she nodded. Joshua headed towards the altar. He had only expected to visit this Sunday and maybe find some peace. He didn't expect this. But when the pastor asked it he wanted the right hand of fellowship, all Joshua Knight could say was Yes.

After service, the couple that was originally seated beside Joshua approached him. Joshua didn't know what they would say. Maybe they would comment on his behavior, suggesting that it seemed out of sorts for a gentleman of his breeding. Maybe they would say something snide.

What they did say was "here's your watch."

The shorter of the two, with a warm smile, simply said "Here is your watch. We got it from under the seat." Then, as he handed it to Joshua, he hugged him. It was a hug of understanding. He held Joshua for a moment, and as Joshua looked at his partner, he knew that something unspoken had occurred with them.

"When I first saw you come into the church, I said to Calvin 'Look at him. He's troubled. There's so much pain in his eyes.' So we said a prayer for you and you sat right beside us. We know what God can do and we just felt so blessed to be so close to your breakthrough. I'm sorry. I'm Calvin and this is my partner of 8 years, Steven."

"I'm Joshua. Thank you for your prayer. Clearly, it worked."

They shared a laugh and Joshua put his watch on and hugged Steven as well. They stood conversing until a woman approached and said, "Excuse me, sir. Pastor Jeff would like to speak with you." Joshua thought that she had meant one of the members of the couple, until the woman stood by Joshua and held out her hand towards the front of the church. The pastor was still there, consoling some folks and he asked for "that young man who had his breakthrough today."

"You alright? I know that was new for you. I could see it all over you, so I just wanted to be sure you were okay before you left. The Spirit was really present today."

The pastor had a warm concern, as he shook Joshua's hand.

"I am not sure if 'fine' is the correct answer, Sir. I do know that what I came in here with is going to stay here. I got the answer that I have been praying for. I have some things to say Yes to in my life and I am going to start today."

Joshua meant it.

He was going to go home and shower and go and work this thing out with Eli. He had ignored his 11 calls yesterday and didn't call when he and Carlton returned from dinner and he found a note on the door that said:

> ***"Josh, I'm not sure what happened at the apartment. I got home this morning and found my TV busted. I started to call the police, until The Super told me that 'my friend' had been into the apt. and when I told him that you were always there, he said 'no, your other friend, your before friend.' Baby, I don't know what he's talking about, but my place is wrecked and you ain't answering the phone and now,***

> ***you're not here! What happened!? Talk to me. I'm worried about you. I'm worried about us. It's never too late. What's going on baby? Whatever it is, I'm right here!....Love, Eli."***

At the time, Joshua actually thought that it might be, too late that is. He thought that just maybe the timing was wrong or that Eli still had some oats, wild or not, to sew, or maybe they weren't the right fit.

I mean Reggie, no matter what happened or didn't happen, was still his ex and clearly nothing like Joshua. Joshua thought about just trashing the note and then he changed his mind. He would keep it and give it back to Eli when they said 'goodbye,' so that there were no loose ends.

But that was before Sunday came and Joshua went to church and got his answer. He had to talk to Eli. He had to be willing to push past his fear and deal with their relationship, in the here and now, and not all of the ones that came before. Joshua needed to see Eli.

"Yes, Sir. I am much better now. I think I also found my home." Joshua looked around, realizing that he had joined the church today and was okay with his decision.

"Someone will contact you about new membership classes and I will see you next Sunday." The pastor smiled and turned his attention to someone who was standing beside him. He knew that Joshua was going to be just fine, after he worked out whatever was troubling his heart. "As long as he wants better, he'll get better."

What was in store for him would put better to shame.

Joshua took his time going home. He just wanted to walk and get some air. He got off the train a few stops early and just strolled. He knew that he needed to see Eli and work things out, but he was feeling so revved up that he just wanted to breathe and come down. This feeling was like nothing he'd ever known and somehow Josh thought that afternoon air would calm him down. He felt high and he really didn't want to come down, so he strolled and absorbed it all.

Josh was a block away from his house when he saw someone sitting on his stoop. He thought for a minute that perhaps he was off by a house or two, but you know your own home. To be sure, he counted from the corner and, yes, someone was on his stairs. He thought that perhaps it was Carlton, but this guy was…wait, Eli?

Joshua sped up his stride and in 22 seconds, he and Eli were face to face.

"Baby, I don't know what happened, but I was so worried. I thought the place got robbed and you got hurt. I thought that maybe Reggie had come through and the two of you fought or something, then I realized that that was a crazy idea. I mean the Super said something about my 'before friend' and I don't know what the hell he's talking about because there was nobody before you. Baby, talk to me. What happened? Are you okay? Are we okay?"

Joshua had to smile at that.

"I didn't know what to think. We were fine the last time we talked and then, you don't call when I got home and don't answer the phone and then, when you weren't here when I came by yesterday, I was going crazy. What happened?"

Josh kissed Eli.

Right there, on his stoop, with neighbors walking by and cars whirling by, Josh kissed Eli and the kiss took Eli's breath away, because it was unexpected and because, somehow, it came with force this time. A force of nature, almost, that seemed to make Eli think, for just a hot second, he was going to scream.

CHAPTER 16: THE UNRAVELING

breathe&stop...

"Oh, My God!"

That's all I could think when I opened the door. Things were cool at home, Mom gave me here blessing and told me to get on a plane and get home because I wanted to surprise Joshua. I was just gonna drop by bags and head to his house like he did with me that night he got back from ATL.

I just wanted to see my baby. I just wanted to touch him and taste him and kiss him and chill with him. I'm saying my family is cool. I love them to pieces. Moms cooked everything I like and Dad and me had some good conversations, especially about love and me not always being so down on myself for being raised right and wanting something real. I'm a whole man and it's all or nothing when it comes to being with me.

I love Josh, but damn, sometimes he seems like he's never gonna get over what happened to him. But I love him to death and I know what Reggie did to me, so I gotta be patient.

Anyway, like I said, all I wanted to do was come home and grab some stuff and then go home and get with my baby. All I wanted to do was see his face light up when I rang the bell and he couldn't see me because I was ducking and then he opens the door and I stand up and grab him and kiss him.

I didn't expect to find my spot torn up like a fight had broken out.

I definitely didn't expect the super to tell me that one actually had.

"Your before friend was here and your now friend and when I came in, they were fighting and throwing things and one had a bloody nose and I did not know what was happening, Mr. Elijah." The super was beside himself because he had just left Reggie not 20 minutes before Elijah arrived. He was still trembling from Reggie's expert mouth-ejaculation. He felt bad because Mr. Elijah was a good tenant. He should have protected his space better.

Shame isn't just an American delicacy.

"So where is my 'now' friend now?!" Eli was frantic. What the hell was Reggie doing here? What had happened between them?

"Oh My God!" Reggie would pick now to try and come back and try to start something.

"Damn him!" Elijah was so sick and tired of dudes realizing he was a good thing after they were finished. Kyle called for months after that stupid night and here's Reggie up in my spot!

The first thing he did was call Josh. He needed to know what happened and to see if he could figure out what to do next.

No answer.

The second thing he did was call Josh. Eli was frozen. Cleaning up didn't matter. What the super and the neighbors thought didn't matter. Only J's whereabouts mattered now and he wasn't answering the phone.

"Okay, so he was here not that long ago and they fought. Maybe he went to the hospital. The super did say that there was blood. Oh My God, if Reggie hurt J, I swear to God, I am going to kill him."

Eli's next thought had him on the street before he realized it. He needed to get in a cab and get up to Harlem. He needed to do to Reggie what he should have done first…KICK HIS ASS TO THE CURB. But this time, Eli was thinking, he might have to do it literally and not just figuratively. Eli was on fire. He knew that Josh was a bit…shy and sometimes a bit reserved and he can't imagine what he would do when Reggie's street savvy ass starting swinging on him.

"That's alright. I'll handle this. I got something for him." Eli was talking aloud as he walked.

"Mess with me and I'm cool. I can take it, but you messin' with my baby. Naw, Reggie. You picked the wrong one." Eli was on the corner and preparing to hail a cab, when he looked down the street and saw…Reggie.

"Naw, that can't be him. He wouldn't still be around here after…" Eli knew then that it was him because Reggie was crazy enough to just go out for drinks and he definitely wouldn't waste a trip to the Village.

Eli flew towards Reggie. He wasn't the kind to have it out, in the streets, especially two Black men in the Village, but this wasn't about tact and temperament. This was about not letting anyone—especially not some trick that didn't want to be with him but now wants to act like "IF I CAN'T HAVE YOU, NOBODY WILL!"—mess with his baby.

Eli knew in his heart and soul that he loved Josh. He knew it from the first time he approached him and asked who he was. He knew it from the sexy way Josh talked about his sandals when Eli was talking about his feet. He knew it when he had to say something about his feet, when he would have never normally been that forward. He knew it when he danced that first dance. He knew it when they showered together and lay together and didn't do anything. He knew it when he didn't have to do anything with him and still felt high as a kite.

Eli felt all of that love as he flew towards Reggie and prepared to finish the fight that he was sure that Josh had not started.

"REGGIE, YOU SON OF A BITCH! WHAT THE HELL WERE YOU DOING IN MY…"

As Reggie turned, Eli noticed his lips and his eye were both swollen. He noticed that Reggie was clearly shaken and disarrayed. He knew that Josh had fought for him and that Josh didn't lose.

He almost laughed.

"Oh, so you think this is funny. Some crazy heffa attacks me up in your apartment and now you are laughing. Eli, you are wrong. That ain't hardly funny."

"I'm wrong?!" Eli couldn't believe how Reggie made everything about him. "I'm wrong because what? I didn't tell you I had moved on even though you've been gone for 2 years? I didn't come looking for you after you kicked my heart to the curb? I'm wrong because I didn't fight for you even though you are the one who told me you didn't want what I wanted? Huh, Reggie! Is that why I'm wrong?"

Reggie realized that Eli was furious. He was furious because Eli was still hurt over the way that Reggie bounced. He was furious because Reggie was so flip, so Eli flipped out for a minute.

"Damn, I'm sorry. I just didn't know how to handle you then. I know how to handle you now."

Reggie tried to place his hand on Eli's crotch.

Eli grabbed his wrist and had to stop himself from breaking it.

"We are done, man. You ain't never got to worry about handling me. But if you ever show up at my spot or even think about putting your hands on Josh again, you are done."

Reggie could tell that Eli was serious. Reggie could tell that Eli was in love.

"Whatever, man. You ain't all that. I thought maybe we could kick it again. Stupid me. I forgot you came with so many instructions."

Reggie tried to sashay away, but Eli stopped him.

"Reggie, give me my keys. I know that's how you got in. I can't believe you even kept them. But that ain't happenin' again. Give 'em up."

"Your bourgie ass boyfriend has those keys. I ain't even thinking about trying to come your way again, niggah. You were good, but you weren't that good."

Reggie bobbed his head like he had really said something.

"Oh really. If I'm not that good, what is your Harlem ass doing all the way down in the Village, in my apartment, getting whooped up on by My Boyfriend?"

Reggie had no answers.

Eli had no more questions.

"I was holding onto the way you dogged me out for a long time, Reggie. But I'm worth more than this. I'm worth more than just being somebody's sometimes dick or sometime man. Me and Joshua have something real and I swear to God, if you have messed things up with him, you will wish me and your ass had never known each other!"

Reggie knew that Eli was not playing. Again, he looked into those eyes, the eyes he was really thinking about loving and trying to commit to and be with, and realized that he had messed up the best thing that would ever happen to him.

Reggie turned to walk away from Eli. When he turned around to see him one last time, Eli was gone.

Eli's next moves were hectic and frenzied. He went back into the apartment. He called Josh.

He tried to see if there was a note anywhere, explaining where Josh was, in his being or in his thoughts. He called Josh.

He panicked and hoped that Josh wouldn't close him out, thinking that he had something to do with Reggie being in his spot. He called Josh.

He went to make up his bed, because he couldn't find anything else to do and he didn't know where his baby was and he was freaking out. He found a pair of tight bikini briefs, that he knew belong to Reggie, because nobody was more in love with Reggie's behind than Reggie and he would make sure even his underwear got a good look.

Eli called Josh.

He panicked and took a cab to his house. Nothing. He banged on the door. He called. He looked into windows and even thought about breaking in, wondering if Josh had done something dramatic. He laughed, knowing that Josh wasn't that dramatic, but he still didn't know where he was.

Eli fell asleep, seated on the ground, leaning against Josh's door.

He had no idea Josh was upstairs, asleep.

Josh had no idea that Eli was downstairs, sleeping against his door, crying.

When he got cold enough to be shaken, Eli woke up and realized that it was 4:18am. That was the same time he woke with Josh the first time he spent the night and they fell asleep. He was lost with grief.

If Reggie had destroyed his chances with Josh, Eli really thought he would just go home. Not to Manhattan and his apartment, but to Louisiana and his family. Eli had to admit it but he wasn't built for loneliness. He definitely wasn't built for all the games and foolishness that big city loving had to offer. He was done. He was willing to give everything to fix this thing with Josh.

But if Josh wasn't going to meet him halfway and talk to him and find out what happened, then he must not think much of me in the first place.

Eli wanted to convince himself that it would be easy to get Josh out of his system if they didn't fix this. He knew he couldn't. He knew it when he found himself looking up at Josh's window til 5AM. He knew it when he tried to call him one more time, at 5:07AM. He knew it when he decided to walk home just so he could think. He knew it when he realized that Joshua wasn't the only one who had been holding back tears.

Eli cried the entire expanse of the Brooklyn Bridge. With each step, he considered his life with Joshua Knight, the only man he ever met who got him, and he cried. Eli even had a moment, when traffic passed and wind blew, when he looked over the side of the bridge and let his thoughts have the best of him. He wouldn't mind dying right now. Maybe then, God could explain why he gave him this big heart and not anyone who would let him love them with it.

Eli shook that thought off and wiped his tears. He still had many rivers to cross and somebody had some questions to answer.

When Eli got home, he was exhausted and it was almost 6:30AM. He took a shower.

He called Josh.

He fell asleep. He woke up. He grabbed the phone. He realized he had gotten no calls.

He called Josh.

He spoke with his mother. He explained his hurt. He listened as she advised. He talked to his Dad. He listened as he tried to console.

He called Josh.

He went by Josh's house later that afternoon and left a note. He put his hand on the doorknob and prayed to God that he move this thing out of the way, so that they could love each other.

He called Josh.

When Eli finally got back home, he was spent. He didn't know what to do.

He thought he would just lay down and mope.

Instead, he got up and wrote.

The song finished itself in less than an hour.

Eli spent the rest of the night singing that song and trying to figure a way to convince God that he and Josh were supposed to be together and he was prepared to offer his life, his career, his success, if God would give him back Josh.

Eli thought his heart would break if he didn't see Josh again. He knew that something foul had gone down, but he prayed that Josh and he had connected in a real enough way for his heart to have been opened for real, and somewhere past the pain and the confusion, they would get back on track.

Eli was so tired that he feel asleep at the piano, banging out the melody for the song that he hoped would have a chance to see the light of day and to pierce all the dark places in Josh's heart.

Eli was writing a love song for a lover who might no longer have a song in his heart.

But Eli knew, somewhere passed all the Reggie and the ridiculous, that Josh was out there somewhere, hoping and Eli was gonna be right here, singing him home.

When morning came, Eli met it red-eyed and shaken, because he hadn't slept at all. He needed to know that Josh was okay and that they were okay and he wasn't getting any answers.

His calls went unanswered, his fears uneased.

It was Sunday and Eli realized that he didn't need to go to church to talk to God. They had been conversing all night. Eli was hurting like he never had, because he really thought that he and Eli had a rhythm and a trust that was clicking and connected. But they had lost that connection and the click and Eli was…scared. He knew that something crazy had happened with Josh and Reggie, but he didn't think that J would leave him hanging. But he didn't know where the fight left Josh and him and them.

Eli tried to find some focus. Eli tried to find some rest. But all that Eli could think about was finding Josh.

Eli just wanted to leave the house and get some air and that turned into a walk around the block and that turned into a mile away and that turned into the Brooklyn Bridge and that turned into the street around the corner from Joshua and then, there it was. Eli was again at Josh's house and he hated himself for being there. He didn't want to crowd Josh, but he needed to know. He didn't know what Reggie had done to Josh, said to Josh, or brought up in Josh. He just wanted some peace.

So Eli sat there. On the stoop. In front of Joshua's house. Praying.

Eli prayed for some resolution.

Eli prayed for some closure to this all night ambivalence.

Eli needed Josh. He needed some sleep, as morning broke and his heart was still in darkness.

It was 11:30 on a Sunday morning and instead of being at church, Eli was praying at Joshua Knight Reconciliation Holiness Temple. He was on his knees and speaking in tongues, about love and long-term relationship, hope and happy ever after. The time bled into itself and Josh was nowhere to be found as noon walked into 1pm and that became 2pm almost without pause. Eli had been praying and he had finally realized that if he was going to trust God then he had to stop asking and just give it to God. It was that simple.

Eli, as much as he was wishing and hoping and praying, had to stop all of the above and just start releasing. It is well. It is finished.

"God, I can't keep talking. I give up. I give it all to you. If you want me and Josh to be together, then you will do something. I can't do anything about it. I can't say anything else. I'm finished. I'm done. I surrender. I let it go and give it to you. Have your way and I will be sure to give you all praise and glory and honor. Amen."

With that, Eli got up off of the stairs of Josh's Brooklyn brownstone and prepared to go home. Eli was ready to just move forward, write his songs, not wait by the phone, and hope that what he and Josh had was more important than Josh getting to be right about whatever he thought about men in general and Eli specifically.

Eli was spent and just wanted to go home and sleep. He stood up to brush himself and looked around because he just felt silly now, sitting on that stoop and pondering a relationship lost or potentially so. Eli had to laugh to himself because he couldn't believe he hadn't just given this thing to God…but he was just a man, just hurt. It had only been a day, be it a full and exhausting day, since he and Josh hadn't connected. Eli just wanted to go home and sleep. He just wanted to lay in his bed and hope that soon, Josh would be back in it and back in his arms. Eli was ready to go home and sleep.

That's when Eli stood and looked around and saw him, down the street, coming his way.

It seemed like forever.

Eli braced himself. He saw Josh's speed increase, as did his own heart rate. He thought that maybe Josh would be unlike the man he loved and would go ballistic right there on the street. Eli braced himself. He thought that perhaps Josh would slap him so hard that he would have to wonder for years what Reggie had said to him and if Josh believed it.

Josh got closer.

Eli braced.

Josh started to run.

Eli braced.

Josh leapt the stairs and grabbed Eli.

Eli braced.

Josh kissed Eli so hard that Eli fell against the door and could barely caught his breath before he could kiss him back.

Eli braced and felt something shoot through his body. He opened his eyes and saw Josh kissing him so intensely that he realized that everything was washed away. Whatever Reggie had said to Josh sparked something deep in Josh and this man felt different. The kiss was unnerving and soul-stirring. The kiss made Eli hard, instantly, and he didn't want to let Josh feel it and think that sex was all he had missed. The kiss made everything not alright, but clear.

Josh and Eli would be together and they would be alright.

When they finally came apart and looked into each other's eyes, Eli tried to find words.

"Baby, what happened? All I know is that I came home and the house was wrecked. Then the super said that you and Reggie were both there and there was a fight. Then I saw Reggie last night on the street and I wanted to whoop up on him and when he turned around, it looked like you had already handled him. What happened, baby?"

Eli awaited an answer and looked at Josh, deeply, diligently waiting for his response.

Josh didn't say much. He reached into his pocket and grabbed Eli's hand and placed something into it and kissed his clasped hand.

When Eli opened his hand again, there they were.

Two. Simple. Keys. No chain.

He looked into Josh's eyes and wanted to ask another question. Josh's reply was simple.

"I simply fought for my man."

Josh led Eli into the house. They cooked dinner. They watched TV. They cuddled. They washed dishes and kept house and rubbed feet and talked about The Monroes.

They never talked about Reggie. Not that night or ever. It was finished.

Eli knew that he could take the next step in his own life because it now had Josh in it.

CHAPTER 17:
THE NEXT DAY(S)
All You Gotta Do Is Say Yes

Josh got up that Monday, for the first time in his life, whole. He wasn't worried or already thinking, even before he woke. This morning he felt clear.

He looked back, from the mirror, and watched Eli sleeping still. He couldn't believe that Elijah Monroe was still lying there, after all he had taken him through, but there he was. It had been six months since that Sunday when Joshua had finally let it all out. Joshua had thought time and again that he had released the stuff. But that Sunday, at the church where he was now not only a faithful member, but working with fundraising and the mentoring programs, Joshua found some purpose in his life that included taking himself and all that he had done, and putting it to some real use. Josh and Eli were also more in love at home that they could have ever imagined. Eli wanted Josh to consider moving in with him, but Josh wasn't about to sell his home and Eli had created a small recording studio in his place, so they were both married to their spaces. They also seemed to really like the idea of each having somewhere to go, so for now, they were cool with that.

The Coke Campaign was going through the roof, driving up sales and sounding Coca-Cola's return to form as the industry leader. The commercials had grown to feature Maroon 5, Common and John Legend, The Sugar Water Festival (Jill Scott, Erykah Badu and India.Arie; Latifah couldn't do it because of her other endorsements) and the coup, a commercial that featured Tyra Banks and Naomi Campbell fighting over the last Coke and then splitting it. It caused such a buzz that it won KNIGHT IN SHINING ARMOR PR a Cleo Award.

Joshua was on a cloud.

He had a great relationship, work was solid, his family was well, especially after he and his father took a trip to the shore and had a man-to-man conversation that included the words that Joshua Knight had wanted to hear his entire life:

> "Son, you are the man I always hoped to be and more. I am happy for you and your life. I am happy that you found somebody to love you like your Momma loves me. Anytime I don't feel like I deserve goodness in my life, your Momma's smile changes my mind. I hope that you have that with Eli, cuz he seems like a good man. He called me one day and we talked for 2 hours. I ain't never talked to anyone on the phone that long, including your Momma, but he wanted to tell me all the reasons he loves you and he meant every one of them. Now, I know you are happy and that gives me peace. Now, if I could just get you to rest a little and take better care of you."

Joshua hugged his Dad, who smacked him upside the head and said "Boy, let's walk before I get a cold out here. Why didn't you bring me to New York to have this conversation? Your Mother gets trips to New York City and fancy clothes and high-siddity restaurants. I get to come down to this damn cold lake. Thanks! Next time, I want a trip somewhere where they got good shoes. You owe me a few pairs."

"Yes, Sir!" Joshua laughed out loud. He always thought his Dad was just a simple guy, so he thought he wouldn't like the "big city." Again, and happily, he was wrong.

Things were going so well for Joshua and he didn't even want to begin to think about it too much. He just wanted to "injoy" it because if you can't do it in joy, then you shouldn't do it. So he was injoying life and love and success. Nothing bothers him, except that sometimes Eli was in his studio forever.

He wouldn't let Josh hear his music, but Josh understood that because Eli said that his "soul was in his music and music was in his soul." Things were going well and Josh just refused to go looking around for something to fail. No more "Too Good To Be True" statements for him. He had worked hard for everything that he had been blessed with and he wasn't about to curse it with his past fears and faults. Today was a new day for Joshua and he was glad about the whole thing.

When Joshua walked to in the offices, he noticed that Tasha was looking his way and abruptly hurried off the phone when she saw him coming.

"Good morning, Tasha."

"Good morning, Mr. Knight. I have several messages for you and…you need to come this way for a moment."

"Let me put down my briefcase and check my messages first."

"No, Sir. That will not be necessary. I need you to come with me."

"Tasha, what's going on here? You never act like this. What's going on?"

"Sir, I cannot share that information with you at this moment, but please, don't be antagonistic. Just come with me if you please."

"And, now I'm Mr. Knight? This must really be a big deal."

The big deal was that Tasha poured Joshua Knight a cup of coffee and asked him some banal questions about his day and his parents and his suit. Joshua was laughing, because Tasha was so clearly trying to get him occupied. He played along, filling her in on the details of his recent conversations with his Dad and telling her about Eli's time in the studio. They spoke for about 7 minutes or so, before a messenger, dressed in a tuxedo, approached him in the main lounge area.

"Pardon me, sir. Are you Joshua Knight?"

"Yes I am." Joshua said, puzzled, focusing so much energy on trying to figure out what Tasha was doing that he didn't consider the arrival of someone else.

"This is for you, Sir."

He handed Joshua a black envelope with a gold ribbon on it. He turned it over and it read "To The Love Of My Life, I Offer My Life." Joshua opened it and it read:

> "Joshua Knight. I wanted you to know, today, right now, that I have waited my entire life for this love, your love, Our Love and I pray, daily, that I never know a day without you. Love, Always and All Ways, Elijah Monroe."

Joshua didn't know what to say. He looked at Tasha, who was beaming from earring to earring. She said nothing, but nodded towards the messenger, who then handed him a brown envelope with a copper bow. It read:

> "Josh, I adore you. I wanted you to be the first one to know, in writing, that I am finally ready to move forward in my life and career. Please, if you would be so kind, accept my invitation to be my Special Guest at my first live performance as a recording artist. Please RSVP immediately, as I am waiting in your office."

With that, Joshua looked up and Tasha was grinning again. He couldn't move.

Tasha had to nudge him and say "I'm sure he's wondering when you are going to show up, so please, hurry up and take him out of his misery! He's waiting on you!"

Joshua bolted to his office and grabbed the knob. When he opened the door, Eli was leaning back against his desk, surrounded by posters of Eli and Eli in the studio and Eli writing and Eli posing. Eli was preparing to take his career to another level, but wouldn't do it without Joshua's full support.

Eli was wearing the exact same outfit he was wearing The Day They Met. He was also holding a huge arrangement of flowers that made him look like he was about to do something sexy. He was. He presented Josh the flowers and at the same time, he produced a remote control that he pointed at the stereo in Josh's office, and as he grabbed Josh and pulled their bodies together as one, Nina Simone started to sing.

In that moment, holding each other so close that air couldn't penetrate their fusion, Josh knew he was never going to spend a day without Eli in his heart. They danced until the song finished. That's when Josh remembered to ask about the pictures. Before that, all he could see or remember was Eli.

"Honey, what's all this? What's going on? A recording artist?! Is that what you have been doing all these weeks, locked in your studio?"

"Yes, baby. I have been producing for so many cats, but one day, I was working on a song and when I couldn't remember who I was doing the track for, something just told me that this one was for me. So I put it away. After a while, I would have to do that with more and more tracks. I realized that I was giving away myself, trying to fulfill a dream that was only going to happen if I stepped up and stepped out. I realized that with you. I had to step up and step out. So, you okay with this? I don't know what it's gonna become, but I know that I'm putting my career and my heart on the line. I'm not *doing* 'the sexy R&B cat who is macking on the ladies' routine, Josh. I want to be out. I want to be myself and sing love songs about the love I know. I want to sing songs about you and us and just be real. I know it's a big step, but anything else would be a lie and I'm tired of listening to dudes I know get down with dudes singing fake love songs or this R&B sex-you-up stuff. I need to come with something real and I think that if I really come, from my heart, that dudes and ladies will feel that love. So, what you think baby? You with me? You think I'm crazy?"

Josh just grabbed Eli to his side and they looked around at the pictures together. Eli was PHYNE. He was thick and broad, tall and had a smile that was just sexy. His eyes were piercing and his shoulders looked like he could bear the weight of the world. Eli in a tank top. Eli in a suit. Eli in silk lounge pants. Eli in the studio, with headset on and singing from his soul. Eli had clearly been working on this thing for a while, this journey, and this next level of his life. Josh looked at him and touched his lips.

"Eli, I want you to know that I support you 1000%. I will do whatever you need me to do. This is so sexy and so brave. I think it's time, but I haven't ever heard you sing much. You wouldn't ever let me and now, you are going public? WOW! When and where is your first performance and can I get a front row seat?"

They hugged and Eli filled Josh in on the details. The performance was Friday night at SOBs. Eli had secured one of the hottest spots in New York City. He had big plans for the night and told Josh that he just wanted him to show up.

"No looking around for clues. No calls asking people, including Carlton OR Tasha! You have to just let the night happen. Agreed, baby?"

"Agreed, but you told Carlton and you didn't tell me?!…That's cold. Using my best friend as a part of your ruse! Curses! And you KNOW I am going to grill Tasha all week! Wait, who am I kidding? She's a rock. She'll never break."

"You better believe THAT!" Tasha said as she stuck her head in the door to make her statement and POOF, she was gone as quickly as she appeared.

Josh and Eli cracked up. That Tasha really was always on point. Joshua knew that not only would she never tell him, she would make sure that no one who spoke to Joshua all week would give him a slightest clue. If Tasha perceived, at every level, that the caller would not keep the secret, they would not speak to Joshua Knight directly. She was a Rock, indeed.

⌘

It seemed like the shortest week of Joshua's life. Time flew by and that was a good thing, because all he could think about was Friday night and seeing his baby, singing in front of a live audience.

Joshua had hired a car for the night, because he wanted to be able to celebrate in high style with Eli and champagne would surely make his head too light to travel back home without assistance. Joshua knew that Tasha was coming, but she had asked for the afternoon off. He thought it was to do something girlish, like get her hair done. He had no idea.

⌘

6:13pm.

It was 6:13pm when Joshua started to get dress. He had a small bathroom in his office and changed into a caramel suede jacket and a striped shirt, with shades of green and blue. Josh looked amazing and he knew that Eli would love the colors against Josh's hazel eyes. He completed the look with some cool jeans and a pair of brown ostrich cowboy boots that Eli had brought home for him after a recent trip to see his family. Josh would proud to wear them, especially since they were from Eli's Dad. Josh was more nervous than he was sure Eli was that night. Eli kept texting him and leaving him messages that went directly to his voicemail, but he would never speak to him directly. It made the evening all the more titillating and exciting. Josh was about to see Eli change before his eyes and he was trembling at the transformation. Eli couldn't get any sexier, but singing could make him unbearable. Josh didn't want to bumrush the stage, but if Eli sang as sexy as he looked, there might be trouble.

Josh's car got there at 7:15pm and he was on his way. He couldn't believe the crowd. There were throngs of people outside and Joshua thought that perhaps something else was happening. But they were all there to see ELI MONROE, LIVE! Unbeknownst to Josh, Tasha had been busy sending out press kits and music samples to The Village Voice, NEXT, HX, GAY CITY NEWS, ROD 2.0 and other websites around the world. The show sold out in a week. With pictures of Eli accompanying the featurettes in the gay press, and Yahoo internet groups being flooded with "unauthorized" pics of Eli shirtless and singing, the anticipation was audible.

As Josh exited his car, a young man who said, "Please come this way, Mr. Knight", greeted him. Joshua almost didn't notice that it was the messenger from the office who had delivered the original news and was now, once again, delivering Josh to Eli. He'd have to ask Eli who this young man was, as he seemed like such a professional young worker. Maybe he could be of better use around the office.

As Josh made his way into the club, he was overwhelmed. There was a piano, with the same arrangement of flowers on the top as Josh received from Eli directly. A saxophone, a keyboard, 2 guitars and a serious set of drums told the crowd that live music was the order of the night. Josh took his seat and looked around. He was a little uncomfortable sitting by himself. He thought that perhaps Eli would have him at this table for 6 all by himself, for effect or something. He wasn't comfortable sitting alone.

He prayed he wouldn't be and after his quick conversation with God, God answered.

"Do you mind if we sit here?"

Josh looked up and there were Mr. and Mrs. Monroe. They were holding hands, and let go of each other only to open their arms for a group hug.

"When did you two get into town? Has Eli been hiding you from me?"

"Hiding is so suspicious, Joshua," said Mrs. Monroe, looking so resplendent in a burnt orange pantsuit and brown pumps that told you she IS fly, WAS fly and WOULD DIE fly. She was such a lovely woman and must have made women of many ages wish for her gene pool. Mr. Monroe was in a nice sweater and slacks, looking completely the Bill Cosby as Loving Husband, But Still Cool role. They were seated and Josh knew that this was now officially A Big Deal. They laughed and bantered for a bit, before they were interrupted.

"Anybody mind if we join this little soiree?"

Joshua couldn't believe his eyes or ears. He knew that that was his father's voice, but they couldn't be here. Dad didn't like to travel and Mom would have told him. But, lo and behold, as Joshua stood and turned, there were his parents. His Mom and Mrs. Monroe could have been old running buddies, because they clearly shared the same style, the same panache. Joshua didn't notice that they were exchanging niceties as he was hugging his father. The Knights and The Monroes were sharing the same space tonight, here at the debut performance of Eli Monroe. That's what Joshua thought and that's what he would think until he was told otherwise.

His parents joined the table and a bottle of champagne was instantly produced, with glasses. The wait staff was on point and it was like they had pictures of the attendees at this table on a board backstage, but they knew names, likes and needs. Things were going great. Josh thought he would slip backstage to see Eli, but all of the parents shut that idea down quickly.

"But I need him to know that I am…"

"What? Here? Proud? In Love With Him? He knows all that. Now sit your happy ass down and let him get ready."

Joshua knew that his mother meant business. She never said "happy ass" unless she meant business.

As the MC came onstage to silence the audience and prepare them for the show, Josh swore he saw Tasha slip from the curtain backstage. It was close the Ladies' Room, so maybe he was mistaken. But anyway, there she was, in the 6th seat at the table, kissing all of the parents, asking how each was doing and ordering from the wait staff, who all seemed to know her. The MC silenced them all.

> "Ladies and Gentlemen. Welcome to SOBs! How you doing tonight?" The crowd roars. "You ready for a great time tonight?!"

The MC wasn't a comedian and wasn't about to waste a bunch of time bantering with a crowd that came for singing.

> "Before we bring the star of the show to the stage, he wanted you to hear his band. So, give it up for *SOUNDSCAN*."

The musicians hit the stage to hoots and hollers. Maybe some of the crowd included their friends. Maybe they were just reacting to the sight of 6 brothers in winter-white wool tailored suits and open, stylish shirts that were each a primary color: RED, BLUE, PURPLE, YELLOW, GREEN, and ORANGE. They were a sexy bunch of guys; the drummer seemingly the youngest, the sax player with gray in his temples and goatee, the oldest. But they played this groove that wore the crowd out. The sax player gyrated, while the guitar player ripped a sexy solo that could make any church lady scream. They were a tight ensemble. It was so smart of Eli to let them have a spotlight moment.

"That's my baby. Always doing right by people." Joshua smiled while they were jamming and Eli's Momma noticed him and leaned in and said "I know baby. He wasn't going to take the whole spotlight. He had to share. He was raised like that." She tapped his leg and smiled. She understood. The band features solos by each of the musicians and then, BAM! They were finished and the MC returned to introduce Eli Monroe.

Josh couldn't breathe. He was so excited for Eli and for himself. He was so proud of him and just wanted him to fulfill his dream in a big way. He didn't know what to expect because he and Eli hadn't discussed a single detail. For once, Josh felt completely oblivious and for once, not having control was not only fine with Josh, it was exhilarating. He was shaking and The Knights and The Monroes could tell it. Tasha seemed at ease. She was watching like a hawk. She seemed to be surveying the musicians, the lights, and the backstage. It was as though she was in on the details and was watching to insure that all were properly executing.

Maybe Josh was just projecting. He didn't really care right now. He just wanted to see his baby sing.

The MC spoke:

> "Ladies and Gentlemen. This is quite an exciting night. Many of you industry cats know Eli Monroe as a skilled producer and songwriter. He's prolific and has displayed that by having hits with both multiplatinum rapper Slim Ice and the biggest selling female artist of the last 3 years, Symone Devereaux. But tonight, you are

going to see him in a different light. Making his singing debut right here at SOBs, I give you Mr. Eli Monroe."

The band rumbles. Two female singers take the stage and each is wearing a sexy version of the same rainbow striped fabric. One is flowing with an empire waist and spaghetti straps. The other is tight at the hips, but with full billowing sleeves. They are both very busty and leggy and you can tell they can sing. They wear their air of confidence likes the garments—well. The introduction is big and soulful. The guitar player gets it started and the crowd reacts instantly. Josh didn't recognize the song, but that isn't saying much since he and music don't have the best relationship, especially contemporary stuff. But the crowd is on their feet and WOW. There he is. Eli Monroe is a vision.

Eli takes the stage with great aplomb and to thunderous applause. He looks amazing. Josh's mouth fell open as Eli hit the stage in the same winter white as the band, just cut differently, more tailored, and a rainbow-striped shirt that included each of the band's colors. That's when Josh realized that Eli was going to do this thing and do it well and with some style. No need for flags, when a shirt will tell the same truth.

Eli grabbed the mike, did a sexy spin and ripped into Luther Vandross' "NEVER TOO MUCH." His voice had tones of Peabo Bryson and Donnie Hathaway, with some unexpected gravel a la David Ruffin. But when he smiled, it was exclusively and electrically Eli! He worked the stage and the crowd with a sexy tenor that had everybody screaming, including Mrs. Knight.

Eli stopped at their table, which was directly in front of the stage and bowed and blew a kiss. The entire table was aglow. He danced and gyrated a little, but never took the emphasis off of his voice. He grooved and played vocally with his background divas and BAM. Song number one had finished.

He talked to the crowd about how important the night was to him.

"So many of the songs you will hear tonight are the fabric of my life. They helped me. They healed me. They hoisted me when I was down. Most of them I love because they are American treasures. The others of them I love because I wrote them and they are special to me. So injoy the night and injoy the music."

Eli went back into "NEVER TOO MUCH" for a quick vamp and then, right into "STOP THE LOVE" by the Jackson 5. His material included:

NEVER TOO MUCH—Luther Vandross
STOP THE LOVE—The Jackson 5
JUST TO BE CLOSE TO YOU—Commodores
LOVE SONG
AFTER THE LOVE IS GONE—EWF
SOMEWHERE IN MY LIFETIME—Phyllis H.
WHERE ARE YOU TONIGHT
THE FACT IS
WATCH YOUR STEP—Anita Baker
SOMEONE TO LOVE—Mint Condition
THIS MASQUERADE—George Benson
LA COSTA—Natalie Cole

Eli was on fire. He seemed to smile in all right places, sweat in all the right moments and he was so visibly overwhelmed when he dedicated "LOVE SONG" to his parents and Josh's that Josh almost took the stage to comfort him. It was a pure and sweet moment and when Josh looked over at The Monroes, he realized that Eli was so choked up because The Monroes were bawling in each other's arms. It was a beautiful sight that would bring anyone to tears. The Knights just held each other and Josh prayed that they didn't get up to slow dance in the middle of the song. That prayer went unanswered. They danced like no one else was in the room. Luckily, Eli had a few friends who were in a different production business and the entire night was being videotaped. His parents would deny it when he brought it up again, so he was glad to have proof.

The night was perfect. Josh was so proud and happy and full and, in love. He couldn't believe it but watching Eli singing from his soul, and doing it well, and so passionately, made Josh fall even deeper.

It's like another part of Eli was born that night and Josh saw so much power and fire in Eli that he couldn't contain himself at times. Once or twice, Joshua was the first to instigate applause in the middle of the right note or at the end of a song. Josh was so honored to be in the room that night and the thought that he would have this man in his life for the rest of his life was almost overwhelming. Almost. But that was about to come.

Eli was bathed in warm, soft lights as he finished "LA COSTA." Josh assumed that it was Eli's special, but private dedication to him. That was their song and they shared it so often that it had to be Eli's way of being tactful (to his parents and just the night) and still showing and sharing love with Josh. Josh wanted to kiss him for that moment. When Eli finished, he blew a kiss to Josh and Josh caught it. He didn't care what it looked like. He wasn't about let his baby's kiss hit the floor. Josh was content. That public moment was a declaration to him and that's all he needed. He wasn't the muse to Eli's music. Eli clearly had music in his soul. Josh was just glad to be sharing the same place.

The lights went dim.

The crowd yelped. Then, something in the night told them to be chill. The room wanted silence and she was willing to wait.

In haunting stillness, Eli took the microphone to his mouth. You could hear him breathe as he sang out, a cappella:

BIRDS FLYING HIGH
...YOU KNOW HOW I FEEL.

Josh burst into tears. That song was something so sacred and so dear to his heart and his love for Elijah Monroe that he rarely played it. He couldn't hear it often because he always had the same response. He covered his face and wept. He couldn't believe this moment.

It was Beyond Dreaming.

SUN IN THE SKY
...YOU KNOW HOW I FEEEEEL.

Mrs. Monroe took his hands from his face. "Baby, don't miss all that love coming at you." Eli played with each word vocally.

The lights came up.

Eli looked right at Josh.

A spotlight hit Josh.

The rest of the room went dark. There was no one else.

Eli sang that song like it was Christmas and he had a house with a bow on it in his back pocket. He sang that song like a salve that he knew would mend every broken everything. He sang that song like a testimony of his own State of Grace.

He sang that song for Josh.

As the band kicked in full and free at the right moment, the crowd went berserk. The High Priestess of Soul had recently died and many of these industry- and music-savvy people were at the musical tribute to Nina Simone. They knew her work long before Mary J. Blige got signed to play her in a movie. They had cried with Nina. They had celebrated with Nina. They remained pissed off at the state of music because of Nina. This song meant something to the entire room. But the entire room had no idea what it meant to Joshua Arrington Knight.

Eli sang that song directly to Josh and the room was frantic with affirmation. Forget about tolerance or acceptance. This place was electric with praise, as if to say "IF LOVE MAKES YOU SING LIKE THAT, THEN SANG!"

As he approached the close of the song, Eli leaned back and ripped into it. He wanted his Dad, his Mom, Josh's father and Momma, Tasha, the band, the singers, the wait staff…he wanted the camera to record this tangible and tactile moment. He wanted the future to remember this moment and the past to disappear in it.

"I'M FEEEEEEELING
GOOOOOOOOOOD!"

The band grooved out so hard that the drummer lost a stick, but recovered so dramatically that the crowd thought it was staged. This night was masterful and magical. Eli massaged those final 3 words like they were the last bite of Momma's best dish. He caressed and accentuated them and the crowd went bananas.

The ovation was so uproarious that it could have shaken loose any pain that Josh still had from his past. But it would have another purpose this night, because pain and Joshua had separated and Josh had filed for divorce.

Eli Monroe was vibrating that night. He had finally stepped up and stepped into his purpose. He was made to sing. He was born to sing. His parents screamed so loud that the spotlight found them and Eli introduced them to the room. The crowd screamed so more. It was a perfect night. That moment was also a perfect segue way.

"Ladies and Gentlemen! Thank You! Thank you so much for being here tonight to experience my life in song and my love of song. I want to introduce a few really special people, if you don't mind."

With that, Eli introduced the band:

Skip Stevens, drummer
Ralph Johnson, bass
Butch Matterson, sax
Sissy Anderson, vocals
Paul Clemmons, guitar
Fernando Clemes, keyboards
Scott Wainwright, piano
Katrina Simmons, vocals

Then, lovingly, Eli spoke about his parents and introduced them to the crowd. They bowed and beamed accordingly and appropriately.

"That's my boy!" His Dad screamed out, while his mom waved and blew kisses. They were in their element.

After that, and this evening, Josh was sure he couldn't be more elated. He was wrong. The next trio of occurrences would see to that.

First, Eli stays to the spotlight specialist:

"Do me a favor and put the spotlight on that young lady right there."

He was talking about Tasha Holloway, Joshua's trusted assistant. Apparently, that's not all she does.

"She is a dynamic woman, who I know God gave me, because I could never have found her on my own. I made a phone call one day to a prestigious Advertising firm. I wanted to speak with someone else, but this young lady and I struck up a conversation. Months later, she had introduced me to, let me get this right, my tailor, my background singers, my piano player, and the owner of this very establishment. She's become part manager, part publicist, but all friend. Ladies and Gentlemen, please say hello to Tasha Holloway."

Joshua almost fainted. So Tasha wasn't hiding the past few days from him, but months? WHAT?! Joshua was beside himself, but he wouldn't be there long.

Secondly, Eli looked at the specialist and this time he pointed his ray of light upon Mr. and Mrs. Knight, who were beaming as though they shared a secret.

"These two people are the parents of a dear man. They have become such a treasured part of my life and I am praying that, if things go my way, they will be my future mother and father-in-law. Ladies and Gentlemen, meet Mr. and Mrs. Sterling Knight."

Josh was beaming, because now he knew that his parents and Eli would always be…WAIT? Did he say "in laws?" What does that mean? Was he being symbolic or was…. Josh didn't have long to consider that thought before Eli put the spotlight on him. Both sets of parents stood on either side of Josh and Eli said:

"I know it might not be legal on the state books, baby, but I know my heart. I also know my heritage. My great great grandparents couldn't get married in the eyes of the law, but they went back in the woods and jumped the broom, because of love.

My great uncle Riley and my great aunt Paula couldn't get married because he was blue-black and she was a Jew, but they moved to Paris and got married there, because of love.

So Ladies and Gentlemen, tonight, before you all, and with my parents' blessing and his parents, too, I would be so honored if you…"

THE SPOTLIGHT AND WHAT WAS HAPPENING BOTH HIT JOSH AT THE SAME TIME!

"Joshua Arrington Knight would do me the honor of being my husband and marrying me, because I love you and because of that love, I would die if I had to live another life without you being mine for the rest of this life."

With that, Eli bent onto one knee and his father pulled a black velvet box from his breast pocket and Josh's father produced a stunning platinum and diamond band from it and both fathers handed it to Eli.

"Josh, I love you and this night, this music, this magic is all because of you. Come here baby. I have something special to say just to you."

Joshua was stunned into silence. He didn't know what to say or do and the fathers had to help him come back to consciousness.

"Boy, get up there and let him do his thing." Mr. Monroe was right.

"Son, breathe and pay attention. Don't miss this." That was his own father.

Josh was brought back to life by his father's words. He had to stop living in the past or the future and injoy the Right Now. Josh took the stage and took a seat that seemed to appear from nowhere.

He sat down.

"Josh, baby, I have been trying to figure out for weeks now how I wanted to say these words. I kept thinking and writing and nothing seemed right. Then, one day, in the middle of the day, you called me to say 'I can hear you thinking too much baby, just relax and let it flow.' The moment you said that I realized that I was made to love you. I wrote this song on the saddest day of my life. The day I thought I'd never kiss you again. I wrote this song, and it told me that you would be mine because if this came from our pain, then imagine what's going to come from this love. This song is for you. So I hope you don't mind if I give it to you now, with a few people watching."

The pianist plays a dazzling intro, as the stage goes dark, except for a single spotlight on Josh. Then silence.... and then,

I Was Made To You

A CAPELLA

When I was young
I dreamed of planets far away
And flying high in the sky
I thought that I could cure a pain
Or maybe save somebody who
Had lost their way,
Maybe I could change the world
Maybe I could change the world

PIANO PLAYS SOFTLY AND THEN
SAXOPHONE,
AS THE ENTIRE BAND ENTERS THE SONG

When I grew up
I hoped for things to make me happy
And riches that bling and gleam and
Hopefully one day I'd find a love
Somebody who could share my dreams
Then I found you and now it seems,

I was made to love you
I was born to adore you

And baby I implore you
Let me take your hand and together
We just might change the world
Together, we
Just might change the world

I thought I found you in other eyes
In other places around the world
I searched all over
For a love that understood my ways
And arms to hold me when I was weak
And lips to kiss me when I was blue
And hands to applaud me when I was soaring
Baby, I found that all right here in you

I was made to love you
I was born to adore you
And baby I implore you
Let me take your hand and together
We just might change the world
Together, we
Just might change the world

All you have to do is (say yes), to right now, (say yes), to tomorrow, (say yes) to my heart and my words and my wishes and my vow
and we'll become One
BABY, JUST SAY YES______!

(Eli drops to his knees in front of Josh, bows his head and extends the ring, and holds the YES until Josh screams "YES," takes the ring, and pulls Eli to his feet and hugs him, while he finishes singing…)

Because
I was made to love you
I was born to adore you
And baby I implore you
Let me take your hand and together
We just might change the world
Together, we
Just might change the world

THIS LOVE CAN CHANGE THE WORLD!
OUR LOVE CAN CHANGE THE WORLD!
REAL LOVE CAN CHANGE THE WORLD!
SWEET LOVE CAN CHANGE THE WORLD!
WITH LOVE, WE CAN CHANGE.... THE WORLD!

The song ends.

The crowd is roaring.

Joshua looks down and sees all the parents are crying. They are each happy and proud, each for their own reasons.

Joshua feels powerful in this moment; all that love and energy rushing at him and he understands the power of the stage and why Eli needs to be on it and express himself.

As the crowds applauds and Eli holds him, Josh looks around and "OH MY GOD" leaps from his mouth as he realizes that Carlton was there, too, just a few tables away, with Donny (his new "nickname" for Donovan). They must have slipped in late.

But the moment that almost made Josh lose it was when he looked towards the back of the crowd, and basking in the expression of their own public love, he saw Mr. and Mr. Henderson, at a quaint little table, holding hands and staring into each other eyes. It was as though Joshua could see into the future. They never even looked up or came over later. The Hendersons were just injoying the night, out.

He and Eli had a future and it would be filled with music and moments and a magic that could never have shown itself if Josh hadn't let himself be vulnerable to music and moments and the things that happen when we least expect them.

Josh smiled and said, just loud enough for Eli to hear it, but he was talking to God when he said *"Thank You, for this and for everything."* Elijah Monroe leaned into him and it seemed as though the room stopped and all else disappeared. He had said everything he wanted to in that song, so he simply took Josh's hand and said, as he stared into his eyes "You Are Welcome, My Love. And Thank You for waiting for me to arrive. You could have been married to somebody else, doing something else, somewhere else, but I love you and I thank you that you waited for me to get here. I will never leave you side again."

They kissed. The room swirled. They were ready to spend the rest of their lives in this moment, until..

"Move boy. Y'all got forever to do this thing. We got people's here and a kick-ass band. Let's sing something."

Joshua realized that Eli's father had gotten onstage and brought Sterling Knight with him. Mr. Monroe was in full conversation with the band, and then BAM…The guitar riff started and the room went wild and Ezekiel "Zeke" Monroe took on the lead mike and pushed his son and Sterling to the other. The groove was classic and everybody knew they were about to get down as Daddy Monroe sang…

"Every time I move I lose,
When I look I'm in.
Every time I turn around,
I'm back in love again!"

It was evident where Eli took his voice. His Dad tore that LTD song up, as Joshua grabbed the Mothers and they all joined the background singers and sang the night away.

There they were, The Monroes and The Knights, and they weren't simply back in love. They had forged a brand new love indeed.

THE EPILOGUE: ONE YEAR LATER

<u>THE RIVERSIDE CHURCH</u>
Upper West Side, NYC

Joshua Arrington Knight

&

Elijah Cleophus Monroe

Invite You To Bear Witness To Love

⌘ ⌘ ⌘ ⌘

"You okay? I didn't fly in from Paris just for you to freak out at the last minute, man!?"

Carlton was only half-playing with Joshua. He had indeed moved to Paris though. He loved the energy and the artistry and decided he wanted to live out his fantasy of writing by the Eiffel Tower and walking The Arc d'Triumphe on his way home. Carlton came home to the States a few times a year, but really seemed happier than ever. He and Donovan shared so much in common and "Donny" was down for the move, too. He had never traveled and was game for expanding his Universe. But they had to be here for the wedding, so Carlton wasn't having any part of this angst he was seeing all over Joshua.

"What's going on Joshua? Where are you?"

"For real, Carlton, I'm fine. I'm right here. I am just a little overwhelmed. My parents are here and so are his. You are here and Donny is so in love with you that it's palpable. Tasha is coordinating the entire day. Come on, this is a BIG piece of Heaven and I just never thought it could be this good."

"But it is, and you better not miss a moment of it. So, finish getting dressed so we can get to this reception. Tasha tells me that the party is going to be GANGSTA and you know she doesn't play around like that."

Joshua and Elijah had thought long and hard about how the service would look and they decided that they wanted to let their love ceremony be a symbol of love to everyone who witnessed it.

Every little detail mattered.

That's why Elijah recorded a song with Carlton ("I Vow To Love You") that was very Floetry—part vocal styling and part spoken word—that was two male voices, so that they didn't have to try to squeeze affirmation from a wedding song that didn't fully speak to their life and their love.

That's why The Monroes walked Joshua down the aisle and the Knights walked Elijah. Their parents wanted to say that we support this love and we freely give you to each other, to share love like we do.

That's why they asked the lesbian couple that they had grown so fond of at church to stand with them, because they had been together almost 45 years and they wanted everyone to see that love, and they wanted to be reminded of it as they took this great step together.

That's why they were so tearful that the Mr. Hendersons said yes to being in their wedding party. They spent lots of time with them in the last year, listening to music, going to concerts and a wonderful trip to the Hamptons that was spotlighted by a Soul Train line at a neighboring house party that went crazy when the quieter Mr. Henderson did a spin and split that turned the party OUT!

This wedding was almost too much for the eyes.

Elijah's performance had garnered so much notice that he was asked back twice and he opened for Patti Labelle at Westbury Music Fair, after she heard he was the talent to watch in NY. Later shows with Stephanie Mills, Rachelle Ferrell and even a headlining gig at The Beacon Theatre were making a real celebrity of Eli, who couldn't be happier.

He had lots of offers on the table, but the major labels just weren't really ready for an out R&B singer/songwriter.

"With your looks and talents, you can be HUGE. Why would you want to isolate your female base?"

"I don't want to alienate them, man. But I don't want to lie to them either. I just want to sing love songs and tell stories and not have to lie about the pronouns!"

So Elijah just decided to give birth to SleepyOwl Music, which was a play on his and Josh's nicknames for each other. Elijah was hoping to have a cd out by the following spring and be on the road for Pride Season and beyond. He was also talking to MeShell N'DegeOcello about being his musical director.

Joshua, in the meantime, was busy building up the KNIGHT IN SHINING ARMOR family. He had promoted Tasha to VP of Strategic Development and Expanding Markets. Tasha had this great knack for meeting people and being on top of the happening things of NYC, so Joshua decided to put that talent to use.

Not only was KNIGHT IN SHINING ARMOR able to work with the new hotspot around town—SHALIMAR—and the new, hot, young designer from F.I.T., but they had also taken on HP and BET as clients.

⌘

Things were looking up, up and away for Joshua. It took a minute for him and Eli to decide what they were doing about living arrangements, but Eli didn't want Josh to sell his great brownstone, especially since they had so many great memories in this house, so Eli decided he would move in, but not without major changes. Josh built Eli a studio on the ground floor and that was Eli's separate sanctuary. That way, Eli could conduct business from home, without disturbing home.

He and Gordon Chambers were working extensively on material for his new cd and Eli is still trying to get Gordon to sing a duet with him on 'OUR LOVE,' the title cut, which was a remake of the Natalie Cole classic.

The studio wasn't the only change to the house. The space had so much of Josh in it, as it should, but now, with I becoming We, Josh wanted Eli to feel welcome and at home. So Josh asked Eli what he wanted to change. Josh thought that colors were about to change or furniture and he was bracing himself. Eli, however, only wanted to change one thing. In the entire house, he only wanted to make one modification and he didn't share that with Josh. He just met him at the door one Wednesday evening and took his briefcase.

"I got something to show you, baby."

Josh was looking around as they walked hurriedly through the house.

Living Room, the same.

Kitchen, the same.

Walls, windows, Momma's picture and nameplate…the same, the same and the same.

Every picture, every chair was still in place, so Josh didn't know what to think.

Even as Eli opened the bedroom door, Josh noted that the sheets and the paintings were all the same. He thought that maybe Eli had decided to let him see that he loved him so much that everything would stay exactly as it….

Then Eli opened the bathroom door. The shower, which had been their sexy morning meeting place, was gone. Now, in its place, was a tub, white and brass, surrounded by candles and incense. A smaller shower had also been installed.

"I wanted us to have someplace where we could always go to just be alone, and us, and together. I loved that shower, but we also rushed in there. Here, we can slow down and chill, baby. I hope you like it."

"I love it, baby. It's perfect. Man, you really are something special. Who Are You?"

"I am the Man who was created to love you and sing you love songs for the rest of your life. I'm the man who knows your every spot and your every weakness and I will keep them secret for only me. I am the man who is proud of you and who would be glad to know you, even if you weren't the Life Of My Love. I am the man who thanks God for you every day."

Josh grabbed Eli and kissed him deeply, preparing to get him naked and thank him.

"Baby, don't start nothing," Eli said as he smacked Josh on the butt. "You know that Carlton and Donny are on their way here for dinner and to help us lay out this ceremony and you trying to start something?"

"Oh, that's tonight?! I had completely forgotten."

"Forgotten? You called me about it at 11:30AM, 2:45pm and on the way home?!"

"I know, but this tub made me forget all about it."

"Yeah, well you better remember with some quickness, because…" and with that Eli kissed Josh back and backed him against the wall, as he peeled off Josh's shirt and kissed his collarbone…"it wouldn't take much for me to forget, too."

They loved each other so tenderly and so clearly that they had to get married.

⌘

The funny thing was that each of them had friends question "WHY?" they needed to get married, when it wasn't legal anywhere except…"In The Eyes Of the Lord," said Delores Knight, who had raised her child to believe certain things and she wasn't about to have Josh and Eli living together without a wedding. She was marrying off her third child and Delores loved herself a wedding.

Her dress was so stunning that you knew she had decided to take the spotlight for herself that would have been reserved for the bride. Without one, she and Lois Monroe would be the focal point and they both LOVED it! Ms. Delores would wear apricot, with a long silk skirt and jacket, with rhinestone button shaped like flowers. The color was breathtaking against her honey-caramel skin. She rocked an ol' school "snatchback" style that was her "signature 'do since '72" and it still worked, well. Lois was cocoa-colored woman with the same warm brown eyes as her Eli and she chose a rich mauve that really made her skin glow. She decided to have more flow and her outfit was a lovely cocktail dress with enough chiffon to make you think she was hiding something. Her hair was sable with highlights of auburn throughout and you can tell that the Hair Up In Harlem, got tossed when she and Lois came through.

Both mothers looked amazing.

Over the three weeks that they had moved themselves to NYC to help with arrangements, they had become great friends. Both sons' offers for beds in their homes were soundly rejected, as the ladies told their sons to "put us up in a suite in the Times Square and let us be grown. We don't want to see y'all and our husbands ain't coming for 2 weeks." Luckily they had some connections and didn't break the bank with their mothers' request. "Dee" and "Lo" had become so close that sometimes they would rush the "boys" off of the phone, so they could injoy "New York Ci-Tay!" But they weren't just girlfriends. "We are family and we got catchin' up to do," Delores Monroe said, as Lois Knight co-signed in the background, while screaming 'HANG UP.'

They were family.

As Joshua Arrington Knight and Elijah Cleophus Monroe stood before the preacher and some 450 friends and associates, including NYC press who considered this "power pairing" newsworthy, Tasha stood off to the right of the amazing Sanctuary of Riverside Church, looking at her mastery come together. No one in the church knew what final gift that she was had left to present.

As the grooms prepared to light a Unity Candle, with their parents standing with them, Josh lit his candle from his parents and Eli from his and they walked towards the center candle, lighting it and merging their lives into One. At that very moment, all eyes seemed to shift to the upper left lectern, where a strikingly gorgeous woman stood before a microphone. She was wearing a beautiful ivory suit, cut to her shape and holding onto every curve. She was gossamer in her presence, as she stood before Joshua and Elijah and started to sing that song that they vowed to never listen to again until they were married.

"Innnnnseparable."

It was her.

Eli's mouth fell open and he squeezed Josh's hand and pulled him to his side, as they looked up and the stunning woman, with the beautiful suit and angelic voice was Natalie Cole.

There she was, singing her song to Josh and Eli and there wasn't a person in the building who didn't feel the impact of it. Couples cleaved to each other and dates became just a little closer as she sang about flowers and trees and words and melodies of love. The Monroes couldn't help themselves and stood and began to slow-dance. The moment was so ethereal, so Oh My God. Josh wanted to hug Tasha, who was glowing in the light of her coup, but he couldn't move. Eli had him in his arms and he couldn't move, also because he knew that his legs wouldn't have moved from that moment.

There she was, Natalie Cole. Looking resplendent and sounding like she was still 25 and in a studio in Chicago, singing to her own Mr. Melody.

As she finished and moaned that last MMMM, she was gone. She didn't return to a seat, because no one besides Tasha knew she was in the building.

There was a service to complete.

"By the power vested in me, by God, your parents and the city New York, I pronounce you..."

Everyone in the room had wondered what Elijah and Joshua would say in this part.

Partners For Life?
Husband and Husband?
Spouses In Love?

The Gay City News was already prepared to make it the headline for the following week.

"Elijah and Joshua Knight-Monroe, married."

The headline was so simple and perfect that you would have thought that they planned it. But it wasn't that strategic. After dinner with Carlton and Donny, they had debated and argued and considered and realized that they just wanted to be married. Not a political statement. Not the poster children for Holy Unions or Domestic Partnership. Eli and Josh were just two pretty regular guys who searched their entire lives for each other and finally, by the Grace of God and good parenting, decided that marriage was the next level of their love. So when the preacher said it, it was poignant and simple and sweet. Married. Just, Married. That's what the newspaper would look like when it came off of the presses the following week. A beautiful picture of Josh and Eli, holding hands, leaving the church, and the headline said:

"Just...Married."

They jumped the broom and walked down the aisle beaming, both of them. Then came the parents and then the Hendersons and ladies from church, then Carlton and Donny.

They went right out the door and into the waiting limousine, which took them The New York Public Library, which was a wonderful piece of architecture that was also utilized to host major events. Its reception and main halls were epic and the perfect place to welcome the newly merged Knight-Monroe Families.

The Mothers Knight-Monroe had gotten on the phone and said, "Anybody that has any problems with my son and his new husband, y'all can just stay at home. This is a day for love, so come in love or keep your hell at home!"

That was that.

Those on either side who had their "problems" with the wedding simply stayed at home. The blessing was that that wasn't many. Senior aunts and play cousins all showed up, awed by New York City, the church, the library and Natalie Cole. One elderly matriarch in the family said, as she descended the stairs of the library, "Lord, these boys ain't never gonna be able to read all these books. They don't need this much space for no library!" Her young escort laughed.

The guests gathered and injoyed hors' d'oeuvres and champagne, crudités and fresh fruit and good company. They took pictures and posed for photographs. Young children were on their best behavior, while mesmerized adults carried on like teenagers, two-stepping and twirling, like they had rediscovered The Joy of Life.

Everything came to a halt when Mr. and Mr. Knight-Monroe entered.

They were a vision. Eli had gone to a shop in Brooklyn to get his locs tightened and he really didn't know that The Locticians in BK put it down. His long locs were now at the nape of his neck, and they had been twisted and choreographed on his head with such expertise that black women were awestruck, and you KNOW that is saying something.

These two handsome Black men descended to the stairs, as a harpist played "Inseparable" again and they held hands and smiled. Their matching brilliantly white linen Courtney Washington custom suits and matching crisp white shirts, with bejeweled rainbow cufflinks that a jeweler at 4W crafted for them made them look unbelievably perfect. But, as they looked into each other's eyes, they knew that this was believable and not always perfect.

They had cried tears and faced fears to be in this moment and although the end result appeared photo-ready, they knew that there were subjects that had to be touched upon and retouched in order to be sure that this relationship would weather any storm.

As they walked down the stairs, Eli clenched Josh's hand tighter and whispered "couldn't we have just gone to the Justice of the Peace."

"Um, no baby, we couldn't. Remember?"

"Oh, yeah, that's right."

Josh shook his head and knew that Eli would have him smiling for the rest of his natural life.

As they took their place at the head table, the crowd began to part.

There she was again. Stunning. Natalie Cole was such a stunning woman, but her smile was disarming and made her approachable. It also most her green eyes dance.

"I just wanted to congratulate you both. I've been here a few times and I know I'm no expert, but I hope that you always look at each other and see the You you see right now. That will keep you together. I have to go. I have a benefit to rehearse for at Radio City. Tasha would hurt me if I didn't say hello, though. Best of Love!" Natalie said as she received kisses from Eli and Josh on each cheek as she scurried away.

As she made her way through the crowd, she saw Tasha and said "I'll call you later, girl." They flashed Delta Triangle to each other.

Poof.

The Sophisticated Lady was gone.

Tasha almost instantly appeared at their table.

"You guys okay? I hope that you know that I love you, Joshua. Eli, you are under that same umbrella of love. I hope you like everything."

Tasha smiled, knowingly. She knew that she had wrecked them with Natalie, but not just that. The flowers, the church, the library, everything was just amazing.

"Who **ARE** you?"

Josh said it aloud, because he knew that Tasha could work a miracle or two on deadline or creatively make a dollar out of 15 cents, but this was crazy.

"Tasha Holloway, have you been keeping secrets from me? How did you get all of this together? How do you know Natalie Cole? How did you secure this library, which I didn't even know was accessible for events? How did you…?"

Tasha covered Josh's mouth and looked at Eli, who has already experienced the Holloway Hand on his career. Eli knew better than to ask. You just give it to Tasha and let her do her thing. But Josh was just lost. He didn't doubt that Tasha could get the thing done, but this was something else.

Her reply was simple.

"I'm a Black woman who knows how to get the job done. If you don't believe me, ask your Mother."

As Eli and Josh look over, it was as if their mothers and Tasha belonged to some secret club and they could speak without talking. Tasha looked over at Delores Knight and Lois Monroe, who just happened to be engrossed in conversation, stopped, raised their glasses and smiled.

Eli and Josh looked at each other, as their mothers grabbed their fathers and brought them to the dance floor. The Knight-Monroes had already danced to "La Costa," their special dance, and then they lead everyone onto the dancefloor with them, as they cut up to "Whatta Man" and Salt, Pepa, Spinderella, Cindy, Terry, Maxine and Dawn sang to the highest heavens about the virtues of a Good Man.

Now, they finally got back to their seats and were sitting still to receive guests who were coming to offer congratulations. Josh and Eli thought that they would be seated for a while, after working the entire room and greeting almost every single guest. That was until their mothers cued the DJ and BAM!

The angelic voices of Sheila, Wanda and Jeannette Hutchinson, sometimes filled in by sister Pamela, filled the air and they chirped about it not taking much to make me happy and demonstrating sweet love and affection and such.

Lois and Zeke Monroe danced side by side with Sterling and Delores Knight and turned the New York City Public Library into Girls' Night Out! This time the women got to take over and Lo and Dee took over the center of the dance floor. The Mother Revue looked as though they had choreographed their entire routine, while they pointed and mimicked, cooed and sashayed around their happy husbands.

Josh and Eli wanted to be embarrassed but how could they be. Two still attractive older Black women, dressed to the nines, dancing around their husbands, declaring publicly after 34 and 42 years respectively, that they still get the best of their love.

"Should we stop them?" Josh leaned in and asked Eli, as they stood by and watched their Moms dip it low, drop it like it's hot and two-step like teenagers.

"Stop 'em?!" Eli said. "Baby, we're about to join 'em!"

Eli grabbed Josh's hand and before he knew it, Josh was right up in the midst of it, just in time to hit the

"DO DO DO DO DO DO DO DO! OWWWW! OH OH OH OH OH! YOU GET THE BEST OF MY LOVE!"

The members of the Knight-Monroe Family all sang it so loud that you had to believe it was true.

The Beginning

ABOUT THE AUTHOR

Kevin E. Taylor (www.KEVINETAYLOR.com) is an acclaimed TV producer (Testimony, Access Granted, Lyrically Speaking, Notarized, BET specials) and writer (Anita Baker, Sister2Sister/Tina Turner, Rachelle Ferrell). Taylor has authored *UNCLUTTER: CLEANSE YOUR SPIRIT AND CLAIM YOUR STUFF* (2003), which he published independently and did research and wrote the discography for Natalie Cole's best-selling autobiography *ANGEL ON MY SHOULDER* (Warner Books/NBC "Livin' For Love: The Natalie Cole Story"). Taylor pastors Unity Fellowship Church New Brunswick, NJ and is raising his son, Ga'Vel.

If you are interested in having me speak to your book group by personal visit or even by phone, I am more than happy to talk about love, life and the journey to Jaded. I am available directly at kevin@jaded-thenovel.com.

Thanks for your love and support,

Kevin.

978-0-595-40787-3
0-595-40787-0

Printed in the United States
74143LV00005B/43

9 780595 407873